Be Frank
With Me

Be Frank With Me

Julia Claiborne Johnson

HARPER **LUXE**

An Imprint of HarperCollins Publishers

BE FRANK WITH ME. Copyright © 2016 by Julia Claiborne Johnson. All rights reserved. Printed in the United States of America. No part of this book may be used or reproduced in any manner whatsoever without written permission except in the case of brief quotations embodied in critical articles and reviews. For information address HarperCollins Publishers, 195 Broadway, New York, NY 10007.

HarperCollins books may be purchased for educational, business, or sales promotional use. For information please e-mail the Special Markets Department at SPsales@harpercollins.com.

FIRST HARPERLUXE EDITION

HarperLuxe™ is a trademark of HarperCollins Publishers

Library of Congress Cataloging-in-Publication Data is available upon request.

ISBN: 978-0-06-244031-0

16 ID/RRD 10 9 8 7 6 5 4 3 2 1

For
CHRIS, WILL, AND COCO,
who make me laugh every day

and
EILEEN SCHNURR,
who would have loved to see this

Be Frank
With Me

Prologue

February 2010

Because the station wagon blew up in the fire, Frank and I took the bus to the hospital. When I told him we'd get there in less than half the time in a taxi, Frank said, "I only ride in taxis with my mother. You are not my mother, Alice."

This was a fact. Once the kid latched onto a fact there was no point in trying to talk him around to practicalities. "Fine," I said. "We'll take the bus."

We hadn't been on the bus very long when Frank said, "People are staring at me."

"So? You're fun to look at." This was also a fact. Frank was pretty in the angelic way ten-year-old boys are sometimes: skin all pink and white and smooth, outsized dark eyes with ridiculously long lashes, freckles spilled across his nose. He had red hair, but not the crazy, curly orange kind that gets kids cast in television commercials when they're four and ostracized on the playground when they've grown to a pasty, lumpy eleven. Frank's was the Irish setter auburn you almost never see in real life, shiny-smooth and heavy, with a way of falling across his forehead that made you think there was always a stylist standing just outside the frame, keeping it perfect. Casting agents would have gone nuts for him in the early days of Technicolor.

But his looks weren't what had our fellow travelers transfixed, certainly not in a place like Hollywood where gorgeous kids are so common that you even see them on city buses. No, what got people staring was Frank's *look*. Before we left the house that morning he'd shellacked his hair like a mini Rudolph Valentino, put on a wing-collared shirt, white tie and vest, a cutaway coat, morning pants, and spats. Also a top hat, which he balanced on his knees while we rode to the hospital because, as he'd explained to our bus driver when the man admired it, "A gentleman never wears his hat indoors."

I was the only person on that bus who understood what a sacrifice it was for him not to wear the hat. Out in the world, Frank needed to be 100 percent buttoned up, buckled down and helmeted, even if it were a hundred degrees outside. *Seasonally inappropriate* is what mental health factotums call his way of dressing, while people into fashion call it *style*.

"Alice, can you make the people staring at me stop staring at me?" he asked.

"I can't," I said. "Close your eyes so you can't see them."

He did, and put his head on my shoulder. I almost put my arm around him, but stopped myself in time. When he leaned against me I caught a whiff of fire and maybe a little brimstone. Frank usually smelled like a mix of lavender and rosemary and little boy sweat so I guessed the smoke had gotten its fingers into his wardrobe, even if the fire hadn't. I'd have to take all his outfits to the cleaners. I'd have to rent a U-Haul.

"They're just staring because you're the only kid on the bus dressed in a morning suit," I added.

"I chose this ensemble because I am in mourning," he said. He sat up and turned his face toward me, but kept his eyes squeezed shut.

"Your mother is going to be fine," I said. I hoped I wasn't lying. "For the record, that kind of mourning, the feeling sad kind, is spelled *m-o-u-r-n-i-n-g*. *Morning* like a morning suit is spelled *m-o-r-n-i-n-g*."

"I am not a good speller."

"We all have our strengths and weaknesses."

"I imagine Albert Einstein was a bad speller," Frank said, settling against me again. "A bad speller, with terrible penmanship. Despite these shortcomings, Albert Einstein won the Nobel Prize for Physics in 1921. Do you think Einstein's mom cared about his spelling and penmanship?"

"Probably," I said. "Mothers are like that. It's their job to sweat the details, don't you think?"

When Frank didn't respond I realized he'd fallen asleep. I was glad to see it. The ride would be long and he hardly slept, ever. He had to be exhausted. I know I was. Which wasn't going to make it easier to handle whatever we found once we got to the hospital. Frank's mother had been held there for three days of psychiatric observation after the fire.

Frank's mother was M. M. Banning, the famous literary recluse.

Long before she'd become famous or a recluse, Frank's mother or my boss, the nineteen-year-old version of M. M. Banning, a college dropout from Nowheresville, Alabama, wrote *Pitched,* a novel that won her a Pulitzer and a National Book Award by the time she turned twenty. It became the rare book—there must be only a handful—that still sells about a million copies a year, thirty years after its publication. *Pitched* revolved around a handsome, enigmatic, and unnamed baseball player who dazzled the world before going off his nut. It was short, simply written, and ended with someone dying, a magic combination that made it a fixture on every junior high school reading list in America. Over time the book became a touchstone for disaster, too, a handy symbol for anyone with a story about a failed athlete or other cursed soul. Toss a copy of *Pitched* on that character's bedside table and the audience knows to think *uh-oh*.

After *Pitched*, M. M. Banning never wrote another word as far as anybody knew.

PART I

Who Is Frank?

June 2009

1

M imi's prickly," Isaac Vargas told me when he asked if I'd go to California to work for M. M. Banning while she wrote her long-awaited second novel. I'd been his assistant for the past year at the publishing house in New York City that had brought out her literary blockbuster back in the late 1970s. As a junior editor, Mr. Vargas had pulled *Pitched* from a pile of unsolicited manuscripts and had been M. M. Banning's editor ever since. In theory, anyway, since there had been no more manuscripts to edit after that first one. Or even much communication between the two of them. When she'd called, Mr. Vargas hadn't talked to M. M. Banning since before I was born.

"Mimi's in a tight spot. She has to get this novel written, and she has to do it fast," he explained. She wanted an assistant to help her navigate computers and keep her household running until the book was finished. "She needs somebody smart and capable, someone we can trust. I thought of you, Alice."

It was a lot to take in. *Pitched* had been my mother's favorite book in the world. If I closed my eyes I could still see her girlhood copy of it. She'd handled that paperback so much its covers felt like they were made of cloth. Its yellowed pages had stiffened and were missing little triangles of paper that had gone brittle and broken off where she'd turned down corners. The blurb on the back cover read: *A sensitive work of incredible insight, a writer of startling gifts. One of the premiere voices of this or any generation. An instant classic!*

Underneath that was a photo of young M. M. Banning. Cropped carrot-red hair, big chocolate eyes behind heavy masculine glasses, wearing a cardigan sweater that engulfed her, looking more like a scrawny preteen boy in Dad's clothes than a young woman on the cusp of her twenties. My mother was such a fan that she stole her father's cardigans and glasses every Halloween in junior high so she could trick-or-treat as M. M. Banning. I think she would have dressed me in my father's sweaters and eyeglasses, too, except by junior high my father wasn't around for us to steal from.

"Ha!" Mr. Vargas said when I told him about my mother. "What's funny is that Mimi borrowed my glasses and sweater for that photo shoot because she didn't like anything the stylist brought for her to wear. She told the hair and makeup person to give her a crew cut. 'What you want is a pixie,' the woman told her. 'No. What I want is to look like a writer,' Mimi said. 'Not like some girl who got elected to homecoming court to make the prom queen look prettier.' When I told her I loved the photograph, Mimi said, 'You know who'll hate it? My mother. That's what I like best about it.'"

"Did her mother hate it?"

"I don't think her mother ever saw it," Mr. Vargas said. He stroked the stubble on his chin and looked out the window. "Listen, don't tell Mimi any of that business about your mother. She has a complicated relationship with her fans. And her mom. I think there are times when she wishes she'd never written that novel. Which reminds me. Did I tell you Mimi has a kid now? Named Frank. First I've heard of him. Imagine that."

In the foreword of the latest edition of *Pitched* that I bought at the airport bookstore to reread on the plane to California, scholars floated many theories about what had silenced one of the premiere voices of this or any generation. M. M. Banning hated writing. Loved writing, but hated critics. Felt suffocated by her sudden, outsized fame and wanted no more of it. Had stored up a trove of manuscripts to be published after her death, when she'd be past caring what anybody else thought about her. Hadn't written the book in the first place—that it had been a sort of long-form suicide note penned by her brilliant, dead brother.

A mystery kid she was raising on her own? Not a one had volunteered that.

I bought a notebook at the airport bookstore, too. There wasn't much of a selection there, so I'd been stuck with a pink one with a unicorn on its cover and a pack of crayons Velcroed to its side. I left the crayons on the seat beside me in the airport departure lounge for some kid to find. "Who is Frank?" I inked across the top of its first page while I waited for my plane.

For that matter, who was M. M. Banning? Her name was as much a fiction as her book, Mr. Vargas told me. The publisher had decided the name she came equipped with, Mimi Gillespie, lacked gravitas. So she invented "M. M. Banning," a name of indeterminate gender better suited to a bank president than a college dropout. Once the book was published and became a hit, Mimi Gillespie was as good as dead. Except to Mr. Vargas, who remembered how she was before she was famous.

M. M. Banning lived in Bel Air, in the kind of place I'd only seen before in magazines—stone facade framed by palm trees to the street, all glass everywhere else. It wasn't the kind of house I'd think of buying if I happened to be a celebrity obsessed with privacy. I wondered if M. M. Banning woke up some mornings wondering how on earth she'd ended up there.

According to Mr. Vargas, ending up in Los Angeles had never been part of the plan. When she was twenty-two, he told me, Mimi had left New York to oversee her book's adaptation into a movie. "I'll just be gone a few months," she said.

Everything had gone well at first. The film version of *Pitched* won an armload of Academy Awards, one of them for the screenplay she'd worked on as a consultant. Mimi attended the ceremony on the arm of the up-and-coming actor who played The Pitcher, an exquisite cipher named Hanes Fuller, who appeared on-screen shirtless more often than not. The press called them "today's alternate-universe Arthur Miller and Marilyn Monroe" because she wore glasses and cardigans and was stunningly average-looking, while he always seemed to have his chest hanging out.

At twenty-three, she'd married the movie star. By

twenty-five, they'd divorced. Instead of coming back to New York, she'd moved to the glass house and disappeared inside. Or tried to. Before she'd unpacked her boxes, M. M. Banning's more fanatical devotees had tracked her down and pressed their faces against the glass to peer inside. *I've read your book. I feel your pain. Come out and play.*

M. M. Banning put up a stucco wall iced with razor wire to keep her public at bay. Fans and the occasional photographer still lurked outside its perimeter hoping—what? That the reclusive novelist would come out to pose for the literary equivalent of a photograph of a yeti? That one day she'd be lonely enough to invite a lurker inside and they'd become best friends forever?

When the airport cab dropped me at the gate I was relieved nobody was around watching with binoculars as I punched in the entry code in the keypad. 21 22 00 0. The gate swung open and I scuttled through, then huffed up the steep driveway with my bags. I stood at the door for a minute enjoying the irony of the word "welcome" worked into the rush doormat at my feet. My mother would have died from the excitement of knowing I was there if it weren't for the inconvenient fact that she was already dead.

"Los Angeles is paradise on earth, Alice," Mr. Vargas had said as he'd scrawled the keypad's code on a Post-it for me back in New York. "You can't blame people for being seduced by it. Have you ever been?"

"Never," I said.

"Everybody should go once."

"How many times have you been?" I asked.

"Once," he said. "Listen, I know Mimi has a reputation for being difficult, but if I weren't fond of her I wouldn't send you. She'll love you if she'll let herself. In the meantime, don't let her scare you off."

I wiped my feet on the mat and squared my shoulders. Don't let her scare you off. I practiced my smile. Businesslike, but with enough warmth to keep me from coming off as too Nurse Ratched. I mumbled lines I'd worked on during my flight. Nobody knows single motherhood better than I do. It was just me and my mom growing up. . . . No, I'm good, I ate on the plane, thanks. Just a glass of water, I'll get it myself, tell me where. . . . So this must be Frank! Only nine years old? You seem much older.

Little did I know.

I probably stood there longer than I should have, because the recluse herself opened the door before I could ring the bell and demanded, "Who are you? I've been watching you on the security cameras since you came through the gate."

I was so surprised I gasped "M. M. Banning!" like

a toddler might squeal "Santa!" if she stumbled on the guy in the red suit and fake beard sneaking a cigarette out back of the mall during his break. To be honest, I'm not sure I would have recognized her if I'd passed her on the street. In the years since that book jacket photo had been taken, her hair had grown out into a grayish-brown ponytail, she'd developed a big furrow between her eyebrows, and her jawline had gone soft. But her eyes were the same fathomless brown, so dark that the iris and pupil seemed one. She still wore glasses and a cardigan, too, except now the cardigan made her look less like a writer than a middle-aged librarian. A vengeful middle-aged librarian brandishing a portable phone.

"You'd better be the girl Isaac Vargas sent," she said, "because I have the police on speed dial."

I wasn't always an M. M. Banning fan.

When I read my mother's battered copy of *Pitched* for eighth grade English, I confess I didn't see what the fuss was about. "I hate how the guy is just called 'The Pitcher,'" I complained to her. "Why doesn't he have a name?" My mother said she guessed the author did that to make the story feel universal, to help readers imagine the character as their own brother or son. "I don't have a brother or son," I said. "It just makes it easier for me to imagine him as a water jug with a handle." My poor mother. Her favorite book, trashed by her only child. What can I say? Junior High Alice preferred Jay Gatsby, with his million-dollar smile and mansion and all those beautiful shirts.

I reread *Pitched* as coursework in Twentieth-Century Lit when I was a junior in college, soon after my mother died unexpectedly of undiagnosed heart disease. It was a different book to me then. That time it tore me apart. I confessed in class that I'd cried my eyes out when I finished.

"You realize now," my professor commented drily, "that youth isn't wasted on the young. Literature is."

When M. M. Banning called Mr. Vargas, I was sitting at my desk just outside his open office door. They talked for almost an hour. He said very little other than "uh-huh, uh-huh," "Oh, no," and "I'm so sorry, Mimi." The gist of it was that she'd been swindled of her fortune by a crooked investment adviser who'd just been thrown in jail for life that March for bilking the rich and super-rich across America. By June, she was on the brink of losing not just her house but also the copyright to her book, collateral she'd given high-end loan sharks who marketed themselves as money managers to the rich and clueless.

"They had an office on Rodeo Drive in Beverly Hills," she told Mr. Vargas. "They sent a car for me. They had nice office furniture. I wanted to believe they could save me." That was the thing she said that really broke his heart. "My wife's oncologist had nice office furniture, too," he told me. A few months after I came to work for him, Mr. Vargas's wife had died of pancreatic cancer. That fall, his daughter Carolyn shipped out to an expensive private university on the West Coast. On top of all that, the publishing company he'd worked for his whole career had been acquired by a media conglomerate. When he answered M. M. Banning's call Mr. Vargas said he'd half-expected Personnel, phoning to tell him he'd been downsized. Instead, a second book from M. M. Banning. Good, bad, or indifferent, it would be a best seller. His career was saved, at least for now. And to think she'd called him looking for salvation! Mimi didn't know it yet, but she'd thrown all of us a lifeline.

"So, how far along are you?" he asked. I thought Mr. Vargas was talking to somebody newly pregnant.

"I don't have a word on paper yet," he told me she answered. "But I have the beginning and the middle in my head."

M. M. Banning did have two very specific demands: a huge advance and an assistant, bankrolled by the publisher and hand-selected by Mr. Vargas because, she told him, "I'm a lousy judge of character. As you so delicately put it once."

"What happened to her could have happened to anybody," Mr. Vargas told me.

Not to me, I couldn't help thinking. Never to me. I'm too careful. Some people in my college dorm might have said boring, but they were glad to call me to come bail them out of jail so their parents wouldn't know where a night of carousing had landed them. The careless ones knew I'd be awake, sober, and studying. Boring saved their bacon more times than I could count.

Mr. Vargas scribbled out the qualifications Mimi listed for the ideal assistant:

- No Ivy Leaguers or English majors.

- Drives. Cooks. Tidies.

- Computer whiz.

- Good with kids.

- Quiet. Discreet. Sane.

Before I worked for him I'd had a string of fresh-off-the-Greyhound jobs, the kind people my age go for when they're not quite ready to settle into the practical careers they may have been wise enough to train for while they were in college. I had an accounting degree but hadn't quite been able to bring myself to use it yet. I'd worked as a pet groomer, leaflet distributor, barista, sketcher of tourists in Central Park, black-shirted-to-blend-in catering staff, kindergarten assistant. When we met, I was working weekends at a computer store because my salary as a private school math teacher wouldn't cover rent and food and insurance. At the store I had to wear a piece of plastic over my heart that read HI! I'M A GENIUS! ASK ME ANYTHING! After an hour of demonstrating shortcuts for managing his flow of information, Mr. Vargas told me I deserved every exclamation point on my name tag and asked me if I'd like to come work for him. "Does this job you're offering me provide insurance and sick days?" I asked, though I had never missed a day of work in my life. It did. In those days when acquiring your own insurance was both astronomically expensive and hard to come by, a paying job that sounded glamorous and provided benefits sounded like a dream come true. The job came with insurance, sick days, and two weeks of vacation annually. Mr. Vargas didn't have to ask me twice. I took it.

Which is how I'd landed on M. M. Banning's welcome mat being chewed out by one of the premiere voices of this or any generation. I pulled myself together before she called the cops and said, "I am the girl Mr. Vargas sent."

She put the phone in her cardigan pocket. "Well then," she said. "If you're done staring at me, I guess you can come inside."

2

"H is name is Frank."

M. M. Banning and I were seated on the living room couch, watching her son playing outside in the hot, bright sun. The kid, dressed in a tattered tailcoat and morning pants accessorized with bare feet and a grubby face, looked like some fictional refugee from the pages of *Oliver Twist,* one who'd walked all the way to Los Angeles from Dickens's London and had slept in ditches at night along the way.

When I say Frank was "playing" what I mean is that he was assaulting a peach tree with a yellow plastic baseball bat, scattering the green midsummer fruit as if the future of the human race depended on it.

"Does he always dress like that?" I asked.

"Some version of it."

"That's fantastic. Most kids don't care about their clothes that much. They're just as happy wearing T-shirts and a pair of shorts." My mother always said that the best way to connect with anybody who was a mother was to find a way to compliment her child. An approach that served me well when I taught at the private school, even the times when it had been a stretch to come up with something nicer to say than "Your child is such a good little mouth-breather."

"I know." She sounded more irritated with me than pleased.

Strike one. I tried again. "Frank looks pretty energetic."

"I go to sleep exhausted," she said. "I wake up tired."

Yes. I had a nice flight. Thank you so much for asking.

Frank went at the tree again, but in a slo-mo, Kabuki kind of way—his swing stylized, his face a mask. I decided to give it one more go. "Hey, is that a T-ball bat?" I asked. "I used to coach the T-ball team at the private school where I worked."

"Then you should know a T-ball bat when you see one."

She's not one for small talk, Mr. Vargas had warned me. No kidding. I gave up and settled in to watch the kid strip the tree of the last of its unripe fruit. It was awkward sitting so close to M. M. Banning when we'd just met, but there wasn't much furniture in the living room to choose from. Just the white slipcovered couch we occupied and a black baby grand player piano that had been working through a selection of jaunty Scott Joplin rags since my arrival. There was a piano bench, but I thought it would be weird to go to sit on that. No rugs, but wall-to-wall carpet in the hallway. My mother would have been interested to hear that, since she found nothing in the world tackier than wall-to-wall carpet, even though we'd lived in more apartments with it than without. There were no photos on the piano, no art on the walls. Unfaded squares of paint, though, where pictures must have hung until recently. Looking around the room, you got the sense M. M. Banning and her son were just moving into their house, or just moving out.

"Frank seems like an interesting kid," I ventured finally.

She took her glasses off and rubbed her nose. "He's a character."

Outside, Frank dropped the T-ball bat and wandered over to have a word with the battered black Mercedes station wagon parked in the driveway. He and the wagon's luggage rack came to some kind of understanding and Frank took off his belt, looped the buckle end, and opened the car door. He stood on its sill while he tied the notched end to the rack.

M. M. Banning jumped up and went to the sliding glass door. She struggled with it, but the door was stuck.

"Here, let me help you with that," I said.

"I've been meaning to get somebody to come out and fix this," she said, "but the man I have do things is out of town and I don't like having strange people in my house. What's Frank doing out there?"

The kid went about his business, slipping his wrist through the loop in his belt, then hopping down and closing the door, being careful to raise his arm to keep the belt from getting caught. Then he kicked a leg back, fell against the door, kicked and fell again, using his free hand to alternately mimic a pistol firing at the luggage rack and make his coattails flap behind himself. I was reminded of the black-and-white westerns I watched on TV in the afternoons after school. "I think he's robbing a stagecoach," I said.

M. M. Banning put a hand on her chest and stepped back from the glass. "Yes. He's playing. He's all right. The door can wait. He's fine. Calm down." She didn't seem to be talking to me.

"No worries," I said. I'm not a person who says slacker things like "no worries" or "enjoy," but I've found the best way to handle anyone difficult—rich worrywart moms, the famished Manhattan vegan ordering a late lunch—is to exude the bland calm of the heavily medicated and go about my business. I kept fiddling with the door. "It jumped the track, that's all." I gave the door a fierce jiggle that popped it back in its groove. "When it's stuck, you do this." I showed her the lift-and-bounce maneuver. "Listen, when your guy comes back, tell him to replace this glass," I said, tracing a long jagged line that split one of the giant panes. "That's an accident waiting to happen. What cracked it? An earthquake?" I didn't like thinking about earthquakes, but in Los Angeles, how could I not? Still, every place I'd ever lived in had come with its own brand of potential disaster—tornadoes in Nebraska, muggings in New York. I guess beneath my thick veneer of boring beat a heart primed to fall in love with danger.

"Frank's head cracked it," M. M. Banning said.

"Ouch. That kind of thing happens more than you might think. The glass is really clean, the kid isn't paying attention. You should put stickers on the glass at his eye level so he'll see the doors are closed when he's running outside to play."

"Since you know so much about what I ought to be doing, will these stickers of yours keep Frank from pounding his head against the glass when the door has jumped the track and he's frustrated because it's hard to open?"

"Oh," I said. "Well in that case, forget the stickers. I'll have to show him how to get the door back on track."

"You do that," she said, sliding the door closed again. Open. Closed. "Stickers. Ha. You're not from New York, are you?"

"I'm from Nebraska."

"Of course you're from Nebraska. The Show-Me State."

"I think that's Missouri."

"Those states in the middle are all the same," she said, and opened the door to call, "Come here, Frank. Be quick." She closed the door, using just her pinkie to move it as she squinted through the glass. "This could take a while," she said, and checked her watch.

"Coming, Ma," Frank shouted. He freed himself of his shackles, put his belt back on, and holstered his imaginary six-shooter. Took a turn around the yard and stopped to snap a rose from its stem just below the blossom, stroking its petals intently and giving it some clinical sniffs before stuffing it in his breast pocket and then arranging the petal tips to form a sort of pocket square. Plunged through a border of lemon trees interspersed with huge lavender bushes. Ran back and forth alongside a big evergreen hedge, brushing his finger-tips along its top. Clasped his hands behind his back and tilted toward the denuded peach tree until the tilt turned into a spectacular pratfall, set to a symphony of Looney Tunes whistles, explosions, shrieks and groans, all loud enough for us to hear through the glass. After that, Frank lay there for a while, first pretending to be dead, then scratching patterns into the dust with his fingers.

M. M. Banning looked at her watch again. "Five minutes." She opened the door and called, "Frank! While we're young." Then she looked at me and said, "While you're young, anyway. How old are you?"

"Twenty-four. Almost twenty-five."

"You look twelve." She said it in a way that didn't sound entirely complimentary. "I always looked young. Until I didn't. I bought this house when I was about your age. It was the most expensive place on the market at the time. I've forgotten your name."

"My fault. I should have introduced myself. Alice Whitley."

"Alice Whitley. I guess you don't look like 'Alice' to me. You look like 'Penny.'" She pronounced it *Pinny*.

"Why Penny?"

"I don't know. I don't even like pennies. When I was a kid they turned green if you buried them in the yard and tasted terrible when you hid them in your mouth. Ugh. That's a bad taste you can't forget. Alice. Alice, Alice. I'll do my best to remember it. I'm no good with names."

"I could write 'Alice' on my forehead with a Sharpie if that would help," I said.

She laughed then, a short, joyless bark. "You need to meet Frank. He may like you. He likes young women with blond hair. He doesn't care if they aren't pretty."

That sounds cutting, but she was right. I'm not pretty. What I am is organized and diligent. I don't complain much. I've worked since I was sixteen years old, mostly lousy jobs whose chief benefit lay in teaching me that procrastination is a loser's game and that you're better off ignoring insults from the public you serve doughnuts. My hair is pretty, I'll give you that. It's thick, blond, and shiny, and grows straight to my waist without petering out. Two of my great-grandfathers were named Vard and Thorsson, so go figure. I'll let you in on a secret, though. Hair like mine is a burden. I'm always worried my face will be a disappointment when I turn around. Still, I'm not dumb enough to cut it off to punish it for being the best thing about me.

Outside, Frank found one of the green peaches on the ground, rubbed its early velvet against his cheek and tossed it back and forth between his hands before hefting it onto the roof, following its trajectory with his eyes, as if he wished he could follow it there. After that he spun around a few times, staring up at the sky, before sauntering to the driveway, where he stepped onto a skateboard and sailed to the porch, arms extended for balance and swallowtails flapping behind him. He hopped off with a certain rubber-kneed grace and waltzed past both of us as if we weren't there.

"What were you doing out there with the station wagon?" M. M. Banning asked him.

"Oh, you mean the stagecoach. I was robbing it. That's why I called you 'Ma.' For historical verisimilitude. That's what people called their mothers in stagecoach days. Ma."

"I'd rather not be 'Ma' if you don't mind. I don't see a 'Ma' as a woman with all her teeth." Frank edged around his mother but she caught him by the shoulder and turned him to face me. "Hold on, cowboy. Notice anything?"

"The door's working again."

"What about her?"

"That her?" He pointed an accusatory finger in my direction but couldn't seem to focus on me exactly. I wondered if he needed glasses. "Who's her?"

"Who's she. She's Penny."

"Alice," I said. "My name is Alice."

"Who's Alice?" Frank asked. He fixed his eyes on the grand piano, maybe thinking "Alice" might be the invisible presence manipulating its keys.

"I'm Alice," I said.

"What's she doing here?"

"She's doing everything around here that I don't have time to do anymore."

"Staff? Splendid. It's so hard to get good help these days." Frank shot his grimy cuffs and I saw he had silver links in them shaped like the masks of Comedy and Tragedy. He extended his hand palm up, as if he meant to take mine in his and kiss it.

"Frank. Look how dirty your hands are. Go clean up. Use soap. Scrub your filthy nails. And come straight back when you're done. What did I just say?"

"Frank. Look how dirty your hands are. Go clean up. Use soap. Scrub your filthy nails. And come straight back when you're done. What did I just say?" Frank hustled down the hall.

"If you can believe it, he took a bath this morning," M. M. Banning said.

I shrugged. "He's a kid."

"Young Noël Coward in there was never a kid. Wait till he starts telling jokes. F.D.R. is in a lot of them."

"You're kidding."

"I wish. Once I took Frank to Disneyland with a boy from his class. We passed through a rough part of town down by the freeway, and the kid pointed to some guy on the street who looked like a drug dealer and said, 'Look, a gangsta!' Frank said, 'Where? Is it Jimmy Cagney?' *White Heat* was Frank's favorite movie back then. For a while his idea of fun was sneaking up on me and yelling 'Made it, Ma! Top of the world!'" Off my blank look she added, "That's what Jimmy Cagney's character shouts right before the cops blow him to kingdom come. It took Frank a couple of years to get tired of *White Heat*. I was glad when he moved on to *Broadway Melody of* 1940. Fred Astaire's in that one. Eleanor Powell. That led him to *My Man Godfrey* with William Powell, who Frank likes to imagine is Eleanor Powell's brother. After that, the Park Avenue accent started."

"The kids at the private school where I taught in New York lived on Park Avenue but tried to talk like they were dealing crack on a corner in Bed-Stuy," I said.

"I guess you're trying to tell me to count my blessings. Where has Frank gotten off to? I'd better find him." She hurried down the hall, leaving me to fend for myself.

I was glad to have a break. By then the piano had abandoned Scott Joplin for *Rhapsody in Blue*. I sat on the bench and became so entranced by the ghostly fingers working the keyboard that I was startled when Frank appeared at my elbow, smelling of soap and hair tonic, a combination I hadn't smelled since I was a kid visiting my grandfather at an old folks home.

Frank's face was shining and he wore a cravat and smoking jacket over a pair of flannel pajama pants with rockets on them. "My piano instructor is on vacation," he said. He addressed this to my left eyebrow.

"I see," I said. "So, Frank, you looked like you were having fun out there in the yard."

"I like playing by myself. This piano plays by itself, too, did you notice? There's nothing wrong with that."

"I think people pay extra for pianos that play by themselves," I said. "Can I offer you a seat?" I patted the bench. Frank climbed aboard and sat so close that you couldn't have slipped dental floss between us. I scooted over a little to make more room for him and he scooted after me.

After an awkward silence I said, "I like this song."

"It's one of my favorites."

"Do you play the piano?"

"I do," he said. "Not like he does, of course."

"Your teacher?"

"Gershwin. This computer program is based on a piano roll Gershwin cut. He made dozens of piano rolls but very few actual recordings."

"Is that a fact?"

"It is a fact. I'm very good with facts. I refer, of course, to George Gershwin, not Ira. Ira was his older brother, born in 1896. George was born in 1898. Ira was the lyricist, which means he wrote the words. George composed the music. Friends thought George a hypochondriac until he suddenly died of a brain tumor here in Los Angeles in 1937 in the old Cedars Sinai hospital building, now owned by the Scientologists, who believe themselves to be more advanced humanoids from another planet come to rescue mankind from itself. Ira lived until 1983. Are you familiar with Fred Astaire?"

"I'm from Omaha," I said.

Frank actually gasped. "Fred's from Omaha," he said.

"I know. That's why I mentioned it."

"When I was young I thought Fred was from England but my mother explained that actors in the talkies were trained to speak that way. Fred wrote in his memoirs that the last words George Gershwin spoke were his name, 'Fred Astaire.' Like Charles Foster Kane saying 'Rosebud' as he died in *Citizen Kane*. I am a devotee of film. Of mathematics, not so much." Frank had a funny way of talking, as if he were reading off a teleprompter in the middle distance. He slipped his hand into mine then and gave me one of those luminously-trusting little kid smiles that melts the hearts of cynics in Hallmark commercials and makes us believe that, yes, a greeting card can bring the world together again, one family at a time.

He pressed his face against my shoulder and we held hands for a long time before I spoke again. "That's some wingspan George had," I said when the composer's spectral fingers completed an Astaire-worthy tap dance from one end of the keyboard to the other. Then I got the bright idea of following Gershwin's lead, took my hand from Frank's, and arched my fingers over the keys.

"No!" M. M. Banning shouted from the hallway.

I snatched my hands away just in time to keep Frank from slamming the lacquered keyboard cover on them. M. M. Banning scuttled to the bench and wrapped herself around Frank, straitjacketing his arms to his sides. "There you are, Monkey," she said.

"She was going to touch my piano," Frank said. "We hardly know each other."

"She doesn't know the rules yet, Frank."

"You and I know each other a little already, though, don't we, Frank?" I said once I got my heart out of my larynx. "I'm from Omaha, like Fred. You know my first name, Alice. I haven't told you my last name yet. It's Whitley." I offered him my hand again, a little shaky and feeling fresh appreciation for the fingers still attached to it. "I hope you'll let me in on all the rules around here."

Frank twisted away and buried his face in his mother's shoulder. "Mama," he said. "Who is she?"

"Her name is Penny."

"Alice," I insisted. "My name is Alice."

"When is she leaving?" he asked.

"As soon as your mother finishes writing her book, I'll go," I said. "I promise."

"How long does writing a book take?" he asked his mother. Funny, I'd just been wondering that myself. "It doesn't take long to read one," he added.

M. M. Banning met my eyes over Frank's head. It was the first time she'd really looked at me. "There are two things you need to know if you're going to be of any use to us," she said. "Rule One: No touching Frank's things. Rule Two: No touching Frank."

"No touching Frank? But he was holding my hand just a minute ago."

"He can take your hand but you can't take his," she explained.

"Then how do you cross the street?" I asked, feeling uncomfortably like I was setting up a joke about a punk rocker with a chicken stapled to his cheek.

"I hold his hand, of course. I'm his mother. I don't have to ask." She said that with a tenderness that surprised me. Here was the Mimi Mr. Vargas was so fond of.

He was right. I had this. "So, Frank," I said, "are you familiar with Jimmy Cagney?" No answer. "*White Heat?*"

Frank turned his head a little so he could see me out of one eye. "Cagney won the Oscar for *Yankee Doodle Dandy*. His gangsters were tip-top, but those weren't his favorite roles. He got his start as a song-and-dance man in vaudeville, and was always happiest when hoofing." Frank pronounced it "vau-de-ville."

"Can we watch it sometime?" I asked. "I've never seen *Yankee Doodle Dandy.*"

"Well," Frank said, untangling himself from his mother and reclaiming my hand. "You are in for a treat then. I have seen it many, many times. I'm Julian Francis Banning, by the way. You may call me Frank. You've met my mother. I call her Mother sometimes, Mama mostly, Mom or Mommie occasionally. None of those will do for you, of course. Her brother called her Mimi because he found Mary Margaret to be a mouthful as a toddler."

"Oh," I said, "that's right. Mr. Vargas calls your mother Mimi."

"That doesn't mean you get to," she said.

"Of course not," I said, though from that time on I did. In my head.

"The neighborhood Gloria Swanson and Rudolph Valentino inhabited during the 1920s is called Whitley Heights," Frank said. "Any relation?"

"I don't think so. Sorry. And sorry again about the piano."

"What do you say, Frank?" Mimi prompted him.

"Is that your natural hair color?" he asked.

3

"That son of hers," Mr. Vargas said when he saw me off at the Newark airport the day I left for California. "Do you think he's adopted? Because she got rid of that ridiculous Malibu Ken I told her not to marry ages ago."

This wasn't the kind of conversation Mr. Vargas and I had regularly. "I don't know," I said. "Why don't I ask her?" He looked so horrified I had to say, "Mr. Vargas. I'm joking."

"Of course you are. I'm sorry, Genius. I've misplaced my sense of humor." "Genius" was the nickname Mr. Vargas gave me once we'd relaxed enough to kid around with each other. He plunged his hands into his pockets as if he thought he might find his sense of humor there. "Oh," he said. "I almost forgot. I have something for you." He handed me a small wrapped package.

"What is it?" I asked.

"It's nothing much," he said. "It's silly. Open it when you get on the plane. Keep me posted, Alice. Take care of yourself. Take care of Mimi. Take notes."

Take notes? Before I could ask Mr. Vargas what he meant by that exactly, he gave me an awkward hug that made me think this must be what it felt like to have your father send you off to college if you happened to have a father to send you off to college. "Go Big Red," he said, and left me at security without looking back once. I know because I watched him walking away until I lost him in the crowd.

When I unwrapped the package I found a U-shaped inflatable travel pillow emblazoned with the seal of my college, the University of Nebraska. I got a full scholarship to study accounting with a minor in studio art, receiving an education there equal to anything you'd get at Harvard, though not much of anybody I'd met in New York would agree with me on that. Except Mr. Vargas, SUNY New Paltz class of 1969. We'd bonded at the computer store when he passed this chestnut along to me: "You can always tell a Harvard man, but you can't tell him much."

Go Big Red. Ah, Mr. Vargas. It said so much about him that he'd know the name of your college team even if he never watched football. Not that I watched football, either.

For the first time in my life, I slept on an airplane. Of course, before that night I'd never been on an airplane.

After Mimi showed me to my room, I got in my pajamas and crawled into bed with my laptop to e-mail Mr. Vargas. *Her son,* I wrote him, *has the same brown eyes and auburn hair so I doubt he's adopted. Frank's exquisitely handsome but—*

But what? My eyes wandered the room while I considered my next sentence. It was nicer than I'd expected after the fugitive decor of the living room. Beige walls, nubby beige carpet, fluffy white double bed, blond bureau, big closet, minimalist console desk. The one colorful touch, a scarlet love seat arranged in front of the floor-to-ceiling blond curtains, was a bright, true red that stood out like lipstick on a woman so rigorously elegant that she refused all other makeup. There wasn't a framed photo or a book anywhere. So when I say the place was nice, I mean hotel nice, not homey nice. And way too quiet. Outside as well as in. What kind of city doesn't grumble to itself at night? Even Omaha was noisier than this.

Then I heard someone bumping around out in the hall and voices murmuring and, softly, the piano. I got out of bed and crept to the door to listen. I heard Frank's drone, mostly, interrupted now and then by Mimi. I couldn't hear what she was saying, but by the cadence I was pretty sure she was trying to herd Frank back to bed.

I felt sleepy and my feet were cold, so I got back in bed myself. I erased *Frank's exquisitely handsome but,* pressed "send" and lay back and closed my eyes. What else was there to say? His fingernails are dirty? He stumbled into our century through a wormhole in the space-time continuum? I'm worried he'll julienne me in my sleep?

That last bit occurred to me thanks to what Mimi said as she bid me good night. "If you get hungry, help yourself to anything in the kitchen. Plates are in the cabinet by the sink, silverware in the drawer underneath. Big sharp knives in the drawer next to that in case you need to cut something up. Just don't open an outside door or any windows at night. I set the alarm before I go to bed and I won't turn it off until morning."

I'd been looking forward to opening a window to let in the night breeze. Even the air smelled rich here, with top notes of jasmine and ocean and orange blossom, without bottom notes of garbage and cat urine. "Is this a dangerous neighborhood?" I asked.

"It's Frank," she said. "He sleepwalks. Well, not 'sleepwalks' so much as 'roams the house when he should be sleeping.'"

Holy Bluebeard's castle. How could I sleep with the kid wandering the halls swinging his bat or maybe a big sharp knife he'd borrowed from the kitchen drawer? Yes, okay, I confess, too many late-night horror movies when I was old enough for the TV to babysit me while my mother typed legal documents because the night shift paid better than days. When I finally told her why I was having trouble sleeping, she said, "Alice, you're too smart for that. Learn how to take care of yourself and silly things like zombies and escaped psychopaths won't scare you quite so much." I hoped that meant karate lessons, but what I got instead was my own toolbox and electric drill. My mother showed me how to rewire lamps and tighten loose doorknobs and to examine broken things closely to understand how they could be fixed. She trained me to collect random screws and extra buttons in baby food jars so I'd always have extra on hand in a pinch. After that, she taught me how to balance her checkbook and keep track of her tax receipts. Then she tuned our ancient television to the cooking channel, pulled the dial off, and pocketed it, handed me her splattered copy of *The Essentials of Classic Italian Cooking* and left for work. From then on I was the family cook, handyman, and accountant. When I was done with my chores I got in bed and went straight to sleep. I was too tired to do anything else.

So that first wakeful night in California, I unpacked my suitcase. Brushed my teeth and flossed. Made a list of meals I might cook for Mimi and Frank in the next week and ingredients I would need to do it. Filed my nails. Read some more of Mimi's book. Drew a funny little sketch of Frank on the first page of my unicorn notebook, under the heading I'd scrawled earlier: "Who is Frank?" I had no clue who Frank was yet, but in my drawing he looked like a grade-school Charlie Chaplin who'd misplaced his hat, shoes, and cane.

After what seemed like an eternity the murmuring stopped and I heard a door click shut. I locked my door then and tucked the notebook under my pillow with my cell phone.

Every bed I'd ever slept in before that night had been a couch, a cot, or a twin bed, so I woke up around 3:00 A.M. disoriented by the wasteland of mattress on either side of me. This time when sleep wouldn't come I got up and opened the curtains. In my microscopic studio in glamorous Bushwick, Brooklyn, I had a view of an airshaft, its sooty brick opposite so close I could lean out and touch it if I were crazy enough to try. Now I had Los Angeles, serene and twinkling, shot here and there with parti-colored neon signs and snaking lines of red that were taillights of cars crawling home from places exciting enough to make staying up past three in the morning seem worth it.

I sat on that love seat for what seemed like forever, just looking, the way those old immigrant ladies in the City with black babushkas and hairy moles on their stevedore arms put pillows on their windowsills and park themselves all day to take in everything streaming along the sidewalks of their new world. From that high up, language or the lack of it didn't matter much. The swirling currents of people were way better than anything on TV. Even on cable. Except, possibly, the Armenian Channel.

Which made me wonder then if my hotel-ish room came with television. I got up and checked the cabinets. Empty. So I crawled in bed with my cell phone and typed in *Fred Astaire Broadway Melody* 1940. Fred's jaunty artistry didn't translate to a playing-card-sized screen. I remembered that later, when Frank introduced me to *Sunset Boulevard,* starring Whitley Heights resident Gloria Swanson as washed-up silent film star Norma Desmond. "I'm still big," she said. "It's the pictures that got small."

I opened my bedroom door the next morning at six and smothered a little shriek. Frank was on the floor in the hallway, staring at his hands. "I'm sorry," he said. "Did I wake you?"

"No, you just surprised me. I didn't think anybody else would be up. I'm still on East Coast time. Have you been out here long?"

"About an hour."

"Where's your mom?"

"Asleep. Your door was locked."

"You tried to come into my bedroom?"

"I knocked first. You didn't answer. I got worried."

"Why?"

"The raccoons around here big enough to scramble over a ten-foot wall are notoriously acquisitive and sometimes rabid. Also, there are coyotes. Dangerous to pets and snack-sized people."

"I'm from the Midwest," I said. "Nobody from the Midwest is snack-sized."

"There are people out there, too," he said. "Fanatics. One of them climbed the wall to get at my mother before I was born. Which explains its crown of razor-wire thorns."

"These fanatics," I said. "Are you talking about your mother's fans?"

"*Fan* is a derivation of the word *fanatic*," Frank said. "An overzealous follower of a person or thing. She has millions. Maybe billions. My mother says she doesn't like to drive because the fanatics used to rush the car every time she pulled out of the driveway. There aren't as many now, but that doesn't seem to provide her the comfort you would expect."

"I don't think your mother's fans would hurt her," I said. "They probably just want to talk, or get her autograph."

That didn't seem to provide him much comfort, either. Frank was wearing a straw boater tipped onto the back of his head, and two pieces of his hair had fallen forward on either side of his part, forming a parenthesis around a forehead gone rumpled with concern. An expression, I realized later, he'd borrowed from the tool kit of Jimmy Stewart, circa *It's a Wonderful Life*. I could see his cuff links today were little green and silver shamrocks. The pants of his blue and white seersucker suit, also rumpled, were hiked up so that his yellow and blue argyle socks showed. A navy bow tie with white polka dots dangled untied from his buttoned shirt collar. He looked like he'd been up all night, either policing the perimeter with his yellow bat or hanging off the back of a streetcar with Judy Garland, singing.

"I was probably sleeping," I said. "I understand your concern. But no walking into my room uninvited. Ever. Got it?"

At the private school where I'd taught third grade math after being kicked upstairs from kindergarten when the pretty teacher who'd preceded me ran off with the father of one of her students, I could never get over how many of the children I'd been put in charge of had never had anybody say no to them. One girl used to walk up to my desk during class to go into my purse looking for cough drops. At the age of eight some of them were cheating off other kids' papers with a sense of entitlement that took my breath away. I could imagine any number of them ending up in the slam. A nice white-collar joint where, after getting over their surprise at being not only caught but also punished for stock fraud or fudging their income taxes, they'd recast the whole jailbird experience as time well spent polishing their racquetball game and networking. I hadn't been the least bit surprised to learn that the investment adviser who'd rooked Mimi had a grandchild at that school.

I'm just saying, you have to set boundaries with these privileged kids or all is lost.

"Yes, ma'am," Frank said. He sat up straight and tied his bow tie with impressive quickness and precision. Frank's eyes couldn't quite scale the heights to my face so they'd come to roost on my kneecaps. He looked at his hands again and cut his eyes to my nostrils for the briefest of moments before finishing his sentence with "Alice." I noticed then that he'd written my name on his left hand, spelled *Alis*. He saw me looking and slipped that hand into his pocket. "As family archivist, I have brought this album of photographs for you to look at," he said. I hadn't noticed it propped against the wall, one of those old-fashioned leather-bound volumes that must have weighed twenty pounds.

"I'd love to see that," I said. "How did you know I'd want to?"

"I have uncanny intuition unencumbered by the editorial reflex," he said. "I heard Dr. Abrams explain it that way to my mother when I pressed my ear to the door during one of their marathon discussions. My mother's response was, 'Where I come from we call that tactless.' Can you tell me what she meant by that? I have tacks. Quite a nice collection, in many colors. I understand that thumbtacks have fallen out of favor since the invention of the Post-it note, but my mother knows I am still a fan. When I asked her why she said I was tackless, all she did was sigh. Can you explain that to me?"

"I can try," I said. "The kind of tacks you have are spelled *t-a-c-k-s.* What your mother was talking about is spelled *t-a-c-t.*"

When I paused to think about the most diplomatic way to proceed, Frank said, "Oh. It was a case of homonym confusion. I see. Well, do you want to look at these photographs or not?"

"I do," I said, glad to be off the hook. "Very much."

He patted the floor beside himself. "Can I offer you a seat?"

I slid down the wall to sit next to Frank and he laid the album across our knees, opening it to a crumbling newspaper clipping showing Elvis Presley being kissed by a beautiful young woman in a swimsuit and a tiara.

"You like Elvis?" I asked.

Frank shrugged. "I don't know much about Elvis, other than that his middle name was Aaron and he had a stillborn twin named Jesse Garon and he drove a truck for Crown Electric Company in Memphis before he cut his first record, a single called 'That's All Right.'" His voice had just enough tincture of Mimi's Alabama in it to make him pronounce Memphis as *Mimphis.* He tapped the woman in the photo. "I do know something about this lady, though. She's my mother's mother."

"She's your grandmother?" I asked.

"Indeedy."

"Let me see." I leaned closer and read the caption aloud. " 'Crawfish Carnival Queen and Ole Miss student Banning Marie Allen welcomes Elvis.' Wow." Banning. I couldn't decide whether I was more surprised to find out that Mimi's mother was a beauty queen, or that a beauty queen was the source of Mimi's pen name.

Frank's grandmother may not have looked like his mother but there was a lot of her in Frank. "Do you see her much?" I asked.

"Not when I'm awake. She died in a car wreck when my mother was pretty young. Not a kid still, but not old like you."

"That's terrible," I said. I almost said, I can't imagine, but of course I could. "So, how old do you think I am, anyway?"

"I don't know. Old enough to know better?"

I laughed. "Indeedy,"

"You must be twenty-five then," Frank said.

"Close. Twenty-four. How did you know?"

"Dr. Abrams says that's when the prefrontal cortex usually finishes developing. That's the part of your brain that controls impulsivity. According to her forecast, by the time I'm twenty-five I'll be old enough to know better. If we're lucky. It might happen later, when I'm thirty. Or never. Some people's prefrontal cortexes mature earlier than others. Women's, mostly. Debbie Reynolds was a teenager when she made *Singin' in the Rain*, for example. Look at this." Frank stopped flipping pages to show me a photo of a gray horse. "That's Zephyr. He belonged to Uncle Julian. My grandmother said that while there was breath in her body Julian would never get behind the wheel of a car, so she got Zephyr to take him everywhere he needed to go. I wish I had a horse. Horses were native to the North American continent until the last Ice Age. The Spanish conquistadors reintroduced them and the Native Americans were glad. Until they got to know the downside of horses."

"What's the downside of horses?"

"The Spanish conquistadors."

"That's funny," I said.

"What's funny?"

"What you just said."

"Why?"

"I thought you were going to tell me something else about horses. I didn't see 'the Spanish conquistadors' coming."

"Neither did the Native Americans."

"Good point. Hey, want to hear a joke my boss in New York told me about a horse?"

"Yes."

"A horse walks into a bar and the bartender says, 'Hey, buddy, why the long face?' "

When I didn't elaborate, Frank said, "Then what?"

"Then nothing. That's the whole joke. 'Hey, buddy, why the long face?' "

"I don't understand."

"Horses have long faces." I motioned with my hands to stretch my own face to a horsier length that ended someplace around my belly button. "Get it?"

"No," Frank said. "If I had a horse, I would name him Tony."

So much for jokes. "Tony?" I asked politely.

"Cowboy star Tom Mix's horse was named Tony. His hoofprints are in the cement outside Mann's Chinese Theatre. My grandparents fenced their yard and turned the garage into a stable for Uncle Julian's horse. Then my grandmother wrecked her car into said fence. She was going fast and wasn't wearing a safety belt so she went through the windshield and died. Zephyr ran away through the broken place in the fence. They found him the next day standing in somebody's peony bed all the way across town." Frank turned another page. "Since he was in a bed I imagine Zephyr asleep and wearing a flannel nightcap. Horses sleep standing up, did you know that? This is my uncle Julian." He pointed to a photo of a young man in a pair of embroidered jeans and a bead necklace, no shirt, a cigarette tucked behind his ear, sitting on a fence I suspected of being said fence. He had a tooled leather bag strapped across his muscular chest and long blond hair with sideburns like people wore during the Summer of Love, plus an incandescently beautiful face a lot like Frank's grandmother's, circa Elvis.

"Wow," I said. "He's a handsome guy."

"Was. He's dead, too."

"What happened to him?"

"He fell out of a window when he was visiting my mother at college."

"Oh," I said. Ohhh. "How?"

Shrug. "I don't know. He got kicked out of the college he was going to for making all Fs. He was probably so busy thinking about how he'd tell his mother that he didn't notice the floor had ended. In my head it plays out kind of like Wile E. Coyote stepping off a cliff he hadn't seen coming. Do you want to see a picture of my mother's father? He's dead, too, just so you know."

He showed me a picture of a distinguished-looking young man in a military uniform. "My grandfather was a doctor, also named Frank. Which is a nickname for Francis. My mother named me after my grandfather and my uncle because she says she has always had a hard time coming up with names. Dr. Frank

volunteered as a field surgeon in World War I before
the United States entered that war, then known as the
Great War. Because nobody could foresee the Second
World War coming yet, although given the enormous
reparations the world community forced on Germany
after it lost the first war and the resentment that finan-
cial burden engendered, the world community should
have known."

"What happened to Dr. Frank?"

"Cerebral hemorrhage. In layman's parlance, his
head exploded. My mom's whole family died within a
year or so of each other, but her father lived the longest. He was born in 1894 and died in 1976. It was a
first-in, last-out kind of a thing."

"In 1894, huh?" I said. "He'd be one hundred and
fifteen years old if he were alive."

"He's probably glad he isn't, though I wish he were.
I suspect we'd have a lot in common." Frank paged
past a series of black-and-white photos: Mimi's mother,
in a two-piece bathing suit that looked like bulletproof
underwear, a kerchief on her hair and red lipstick that
showed black in the photo. Dr. Frank smiling at his
wife as he settled his tuxedo jacket around her shoulders at their wedding, his young bride staring straight
into the camera and grinning. Alongside that, another
yellowed newspaper clipping, no picture, with the

headline "Banning Marie Allen weds Julian Francis Gillespie" and a first line that read, "Under an antique veil of finest illusion—"

Before I could read any further, Frank turned the page.

After that, toddler versions of Julian and Mimi with chocolate-smeared faces, holding hands and squinting across a battlefield of ruined birthday cake. Preteen Julian and Mimi in a photo Christmas card, sitting back to back on the horse, Mimi facing the mane and Julian the tail, all three wearing Santa hats. Printed across it the line "We don't know if we're going or coming this Christmas!"

The color shots hadn't aged as well. A Polaroid of Julian in his pitcher's uniform on the mound, hair and face faded to a pale green. A prom portrait of him in a sky-blue tuxedo, face and hair yellowed out, a necktie knotted around his head like a kamikaze pilot's, his arm around an empty space where his date should have been. Mimi at what must have been her high school graduation, dressed in a shiny black gown and mortarboard and looking worried.

Frank closed the album and put it on the ground beside him. "The end," he said. "Everybody in these pictures is dead except for my mother."

"Well," I said, "who's hungry?" But what I was thinking was, What about your daddy? Where's his picture? Is his photograph not in there because he's not dead yet?

The kid was right about having uncanny intuition because just then he said, "My mom has pictures of my dad somewhere, but she says he doesn't belong to our family so they don't go in this album."

"Because your dad's not—" I couldn't figure out a tactful way to finish that sentence.

"Dead? I don't think so. Maybe. I've never met him."

"Have you seen the pictures?" I asked.

"Yes. But we keep our photos put away because otherwise they make my mother feel too sad. We don't talk about him, anyway." Frank picked up the album and tucked it under his arm. "I know how to make waffles. I'm very good at not spilling the batter."

"I love waffles."

He offered me a hand up. I knew I was allowed to accept it because he'd offered his hand to me, as stated in the Second Rule of Frank. "Of course you love waffles," he said as he hauled me up. "You aren't crazy."

"How do you know that?" I asked as I followed him down the hall to the kitchen.

"The kids at school say I'm crazy and you don't remind me much of me. Also, I just know things. For example, Thomas Jefferson had a waffle iron he bought in France."

"You're lucky. When I want to know something, I have to look it up. You've got so much stuffed in your cranium, Frank, I don't know how you remember anything."

"My mother says my brain is so full of facts that there's no room for nuance. Our waffle iron is from China. We ordered it from a catalog called Williams-Sonoma. There was a sale for very special customers." He dragged a stool to the counter, climbed onto it, and stood on his toes, straining to reach the waffle iron, still in its somewhat-battered original box, stored on the top shelf.

"Here," I said. "Let me get that down for you."

Everything happened fast after that. Frank shrieked, "NO NO NO NO NO NO NO," swatted the box and sent it flying toward me. I covered my face with my arms and ducked. The box crash-landed someplace behind me and I lowered my arms and looked over my shoulder to see where. When I turned back, Frank was laid out on the linoleum like a corpse on a mortician's slab, his eyes closed and hands bunched into fists. His straw boater rolled toward me in slow motion like a freed hubcap in the aftermath of a car crash.

"Frank?" I asked. "Are you all right?"

Mimi bounded into the kitchen in her nightgown then, one side of her face still creased by her pillow and her hair in two messy braids. She picked up his boater, stepped over the waffle iron box and knelt beside Frank. "Did he bang his head?" she asked.

"Bang his head? I don't think so. I don't know what happened. Does Frank have some kind of seizure disorder?"

"No, Frank does not have some kind of seizure disorder. For god's sake. You've upset him somehow. Obviously."

"But I didn't do anything," I said.

"She," Frank said, eyes sealed, elevating an undead fist and switchblading its index finger free to point in my direction, "wanted to touch my waffle iron."

"I offered to help him get it down, that's all," I protested.

"No touching Frank's things. I told you that." Mimi picked her son up, set him on his feet, and put his hat on his head again. "There we go. Are you okay, Monkey?"

"I might be someday," he said. "According to Dr. Abrams."

When Mimi turned her attention to me I understood how a rabbit must feel when the headlights hit him, just before the car does. "We don't have a lot of rules around here, Penny," she said to me. "If you don't think you can follow the ones we do have, you might as well leave now."

"Alice," I said. "My name is Alice."

But she was halfway down the hall already. After I heard her door slam, I put my freezing hands to my hot cheeks. Don't let her scare you off, Alice.

Frank, meanwhile, had freed the waffle iron from its box and bubble wrap, plugged it in and opened the refrigerator. "I love chocolate chips in my waffles," he said with all the ardor of the voice on a telephone answering tree. He took out a carton of eggs and promptly dropped it. Then picked up the carton, checked inside, and said, "Good. None broke this time. Well, well, well. I guess today is our lucky day."

4

We don't get out much, I scribbled in my unicorn notebook ten days after I'd arrived. I was in the laundry room, waiting out the last few minutes of the dryer cycle so I could grab the sheets before they wrinkled and hide the notebook in between the folds to smuggle back into my room. I was also keeping an eye on Frank outside as he plunged into and out of a rosemary hedge brandishing a big plastic machete. Frank's psychiatrist Dr. Abrams was out of town for all of July. There would be no school to trundle the boy off to until well after Labor Day. Everything that was needed to keep body and soul together—groceries, office supplies, Frank's clothing—came to the gates in a delivery van. Even drinking water, despite the fact that it flowed free and sweet from every spigot in the house. With no solid reason to go anyplace, we didn't.

Frank a very special customer, I wrote. *As for Mimi, I never see her. Always locked in her office.* What I didn't add, but wanted to was, *Because she hates me.*

Mimi shut herself away as soon as she ate breakfast and stayed gone until dinnertime. After dinner, she'd read to Frank or they'd play Clue, his favorite board game; or they'd watch a movie together while she plowed through a stack of bills, groaning audibly from time to time. Mimi averted her eyes whenever we had to talk. You couldn't call what passed between us conversation. An exchange of information was more like it, though there wasn't even much of that.

Frank and I, however, seemed to be getting along well enough after our early episode with the waffle iron. When I apologized for my infraction, he said, "That's okay. You hadn't learned your lesson yet. I don't care what people say. Ignorance is not bliss."

After that, he explained and reexplained and then explained all over again the byzantine Kremlinology of rules chez Frank Banning. His laundry, for example, I could wash, fold, and put away with impunity; but once an item was clean, pressed, and shelved, hands off. I could feather-dust the surfaces in his bedroom, but under no circumstances was I allowed to touch anything on them with my hands. A lesson I had to relearn the hard way when I made the rookie mistake of resetting the old-fashioned windup alarm clocks on his desk and bedside table. Those clocks drove me crazy. Both ticked loudly and out of sync and neither showed the correct time in Los Angeles or anyplace else on earth. Frank watched me without comment or changing his expression, then took the reset clocks and winged them across the room. Once that was done he banged his forehead against his desktop like a gavel.

"Frank!" I gasped. "Stop!" Miraculously, I remembered not to touch him—Rule Two—and put my hands on the desktop over the spot he was pounding. I guess the feeling of his forehead hitting flesh wasn't as satisfying as hammering it on wood, so he quit. When he straightened I saw a coin of red blooming on his forehead. I hoped it wouldn't turn into a bruise.

"No touching my things," he'd said matter-of-factly. "Rule One."

"I'm so sorry, Frank. My bad. Please don't ever hit your head like that again. I can't bear it."

"Most people can't," Frank said. "My mother in particular. She says the cheap histrionics I use to test boundaries with new authority figures will give me a concussion someday."

"You're testing me?"

"According to my mother. In my opinion, I'm trying to keep my head from exploding."

I struggled with Rule Two as well. While it was okay to encourage Frank to chew with his mouth closed and use a napkin, brushing away a bit of egg that dangled from his chin for most of a morning without asking was absolutely unacceptable. On his voyage to the floor and rigor mortis post-Egg Dangle Incident, Frank somehow managed to take me down as well.

At first I suspected he was the kind of demon spawn who'd take malicious pleasure in "accidentally" using me to cushion his fall. But to make amends for knocking me over, that night Frank surprised me with a juice glass filled with gardenias for my bedside table so, he explained, I could enjoy the smell of them last thing before I went to sleep and first thing when I woke up. I decided then that the kid was not so much evil as a clumsy, sweet-natured boy whose whole body seemed to be made of thumbs. More oblivious than obnoxious, a sleepwalker both night and day. I was convinced he meant well. Even after his acting out of the trajectory of fragrance to my pillow knocked the glass over moments after its delivery. I had to strip my bed pronto before the water soaked into the mattress.

By the time our first week was out, we'd established a routine. After breakfast I'd tidy up while Frank selected his wardrobe. You had to give him credit: He might not bathe or wash his face or brush his teeth without prompting, but Frank could put an outfit together. The high point of my day was seeing Frank emerge from the chrysalis of his closet to unfurl his sartorial wings.

The low point came hard on the heels of that, when I looked past him to the piles of rejected clothing shed on the floor. Getting him to return everything he'd nixed to a hook, hanger, or a drawer was usually a job of work.

"It's not enough to dress like a gentleman," I told him. "You need to act like one, too. Gentlemen do not disrespect their clothing by leaving it crumpled on the floor."

"You can pick it up," he said.

"Rule One says I can't. You know that."

"Then my mother can do it."

"Your mother most certainly cannot do it. She's working on her book."

If he continued to balk, I'd pocket the remote to the house's only television, saying, "No cinematic education for me today until those clothes are put away." In the spirit of "ignorance is not bliss," Frank had undertaken schooling me on film. Threatening to deny him the joy of lecturing me on his favorite topic worked every time.

Not that he didn't protest. One day he'd be the un-tamed Helen Keller pre-Annie Sullivan in *The Miracle Worker,* dumping out drawers and kicking the contents around the closet, or tearing his hair and banging his head against the wall; the next, he was Boy Mahatma in *Gandhi,* lying stiff and motionless on the floor, the only thing folded up and put away being Frank's connec-tion to the outside world. If I ignored all that, sooner or later the kid caved. Once he'd taken care of the task at hand, though, he needed to spend some time wrapped in his comforter, rolling on the floor and muttering to himself before he could calm down enough for us to move on.

I tried to project the serenity my mother had when she'd dealt with my own bad behavior. But it was ex-hausting work. I lay awake at night, trying to come up with some developmentally appropriate Montes-sori way of inspiring Frank to discover the restraint buried somewhere deep inside him so I wouldn't have to strong-arm him anymore. One night as I drifted off I had what seemed to me a brilliant idea. Frank was a devotee of film. We'd watch those two tales of the triumph of self-control, then discuss. He was an intel-ligent young man. He'd get the picture.

"I've got two of my favorite films for us to watch next," I said, holding the DVDs of *The Miracle Worker* and *Gandhi* out for Frank to inspect as soon as they were delivered to our door.

"But I didn't select them."

"I know. I thought it could be my turn to pick."

He looked dubious. "Is there dancing?"

Dancing in a movie about Helen Keller or even, let's face it, Gandhi, seemed like the preamble for some particularly tasteless jokes. "I don't remember," I said. "Maybe not."

"If you can't remember, then they can't be very good."

"I'm not like you, Frank," I said. "I forget stuff."

I outlined plots. He listened solemnly, giving my eyebrow his full attention while I talked. When I was done he said, "No thank you please."

I confess. I caved. We watched what the kid wanted to watch. Which, for Frank, meant starting with the special features, "making-of" addendums on DVDs or broadcast specials that explained how the stories had been hammered out, which actors had by some twist of fate or ankle been cast or not cast in a role, and why the characters they played on-screen said or didn't say the things they really had on their minds. Only after we'd watched those a few times did we see the movie itself.

Frank talked all the way through, drowning out the dialogue as he explained how an actor could open a living room door in one location and step onto a porch on the other side of the real, nonmovie world. As if I hadn't sat through the same making-of documentary many times over, too, he'd explain to me why a particular make of car or member of the cast was parked in the corner of a frame, or how it was a failure on the part of the script supervisor if an actor held something in one scene that vanished in the next, only to reappear again in the one after that. Sometimes Frank sidled up to the screen, arranged his features to match the actor's expression, and delivered the next line of dialogue in sync with the character.

With so much extracurricular stuff going on, there were times during our movie marathons when I found it hard to follow the film's plot. Not so Frank. Though he seemed to have no interest in the narrative he still knew it intricately. Revealing the twist moments before it untwisted, telling you who was about to get it right between the eyes—nothing gave Frank more pleasure. When I tried to explain to him that giving away the plot was considered bad form even among film critics, he refused to believe me.

"If you could know what was about to happen, why wouldn't you want to?"

"Because it ruins the surprise," I said.

"But I don't like surprises."

"Well, most people do. At the movies anyway. So put a sock in it." Which, during our *Sunset Boulevard* screening, translated into Frank crouched beside me, rocking and looking miserable even before the opening credits were over. He started to speak and I shushed him, which prompted him to rip off his shoes, fling them across the room, and start tearing at his socks. The look he had on his face frightened me a little.

"What are you doing, Frank?" I asked.

"I'm putting my socks in it. It being my mouth. Otherwise I will tell you that Gloria Swanson shoots William Holden before the movie even gets going, though she's decades past old enough to know better than to do something impulsive like that."

And then, like magic, Frank relaxed. For someone who'd just been all but frothing at the mouth, he was now remarkably serene. I think that must have been the first time I understood how impossible it was for Frank to bottle up information. He had so much knowledge trapped inside that giant brain of his that if he didn't let some out from time to time, his head might explode just like his grandfather's had.

"So, wait, William Holden is dead?" I asked.

"William Holden is dead," Frank confirmed. "I was confused by that cinematic technique at first myself, as William Holden is a corpse as well as the movie's narrator. By 'William Holden is dead' of course I mean Joe Gillis, the character William Holden plays, not William Holden himself."

"Of course."

"William Holden himself died November twelfth, 1981, after falling and striking his head on a coffee table."

"Got it."

"May I continue?"

"Please."

"In the scene where Joe Gillis meets Norma Desmond she thinks he's come to show her caskets for her dead chimpanzee. When the cinematographer asked director Billy Wilder how he wanted the chimp scene framed, Wilder is quoted as saying, 'You know, your standard monkey funeral shot.' Some connoisseurs of film believe that scene prefigures Joe Gillis's death. I don't understand why you'd need to prefigure Joe Gillis's death when we've already figured out he's dead. Can you explain that?"

"Search me."

"Search you? Why? Do you have the answer on a piece of paper tucked in your pocket? Is that the sort of thing you're writing when you're scribbling in that notebook?"

"What notebook?" I asked, disingenuously. Had Frank seen me taking notes for Mr. Vargas?

"The one you're always writing in. The pink one, with the unicorn on the cover."

I changed the subject fast. " 'Search me' is a way of saying 'I can't answer that.' Do you want me to pick up those shoes for you?"

"Yes thank you please."

I handed them to him and didn't say another word. He hugged his shoes against his chest in a way I couldn't imagine him hugging me and rested his head on my shoulder. "You're bony," he said, but left his head there anyway.

While it was true that I couldn't touch Frank, that didn't keep the kid from becoming an honorary citizen of my personal zip code. He especially enjoyed pressing his face against my shoulder blade, as if I were a pane of glass he needed to see through.

"Don't let him do that," Mimi said the first time she saw him at it. "He needs to learn to respect your personal space."

But the thing was, I didn't mind. I knew Frank missed his mother pretty desperately. He didn't see why a book that didn't even exist should take her from him, even though he tended to ignore her when she was around and preferred talking to himself over anybody else in the room. If he slipped away from me during

Mimi's workday I knew I would find him outside her office, a drinking glass held between his ear and the door that separated them.

One morning Frank threw himself down and starting pounding his head against the carpeted floor outside her office. He ignored me when I asked him to get up. Also when I asked if it would be okay for me to help him up. I don't think he even heard me. I decided under the circumstances that no answer was an answer and that I had to do something before Mimi came out and turned the high beams of her contempt on me again. I grabbed Frank by the ankles and dragged him to the kitchen, where I waved an unwrapped chocolate bar under his nose until he came around.

"I know what we'll do," I said when his eyes were able to focus on the exterior world again. "We'll write a book, too."

"Good idea," he said around the chocolate bar he'd stuffed whole into his mouth. "Then I can offer my mother pointers from the position of a knowledgeable technician rather than that of a dilettante."

"Dilettante, huh?" I said. "You know what I like best about you, Frank?"

"My cravats?"

"No. Well, yes, I like your cravats, of course. But I love that you know so many interesting words. Is it all right for me to touch your face and hands with a damp towel now to clean the chocolate off it?" I hoped he'd say yes. Otherwise he'd use the shoulder of my T-shirt as his freelance napkin.

"If you must." He screwed his eyes shut tight and grimaced as I wiped his face and hands. "I read the dictionary for pleasure as it's always easy to find a stopping place. Also I hope my perambulations there will improve my spelling, but that hasn't happened yet."

"I see," I said. "So, what are we going to call your book?"

"As *Webster's Third* is taken, I will call my book *I Shall Commute by Submarine*."

I wasn't surprised to hear that. The kid loved being bundled up and pressed against things; he was a big fan of tight spaces. He wedged himself between cushions on the family room couches, played Clue on the floor of his closet, and chose the inside of the station wagon as a play space over the wider world of the yard. We'd crawl under the kitchen table to read a book, him inside and me outside the cocoon of his sleeping bag, pretending we were traveling in an overnight compartment of a Pullman train.

We wrote his book on my computer, sitting at the kitchen table. We finished it by lunchtime. *I Shall Commute by Submarine* chronicled the adventures of

Adult Frank, a guy with some kind of amorphous job that required constant undersea travel between his hundred-square-foot apartments in Tokyo and New York City. Frank used one of my graphic design interfaces, untutored by me or the computer help program, to draw tall buildings and tight cubicles and a little man dressed in a tux that he dropped into the text as if he'd been doing that all his life. All this work on his book made me wonder what the real Adult Frank would do for a living one day. Graphic designer, maybe? Maître d' on a cruise ship? Understudy James Bond?

After we stapled his book together, we lay on our backs under the kitchen table as I read it to him.

"I must confess that I've never been inside a submarine," Frank said, taking his book back from me and flipping through the pages.

"That's okay," I said. "It's fiction."

"But it could be about me someday."

"I suppose. But you understand nobody can see into the future."

"Cassandra could. Also, my mother."

"Your mother can't see into the future."

"Yes she can. She's always telling me I'll end up living out of a shopping cart if I don't learn the multiplication tables. She can't fathom how numbers could elude me. I tried explaining that I lose my way among a series of digits like Hansel and Gretel lost among the trees in the forest after the birds have devoured their trail of crumbs. She said I was too smart for that. I tend to agree, as I would use gravel to mark my way instead of something as evanescent as bread crumbs. I like my gravel in the utilitarian gray of gray flannel suits, though I suppose white marble chips might be a better choice in the chiaroscuro of a forest."

"Your mother doesn't mean the part about the shopping cart, Frank," I said.

"Maybe not. Sometimes she says I'll end up in jail. But that's usually after I've broken something or somebody."

"When have you broken somebody?"

"I slammed a taxicab door on my mother's hand once and broke her finger. Also, there was an unfortunate incident with a jump rope in preschool that sent a girl flying across the playground. But I was exonerated of that. I've never understood why the girl got upset. Doesn't everyone dream of flying, Alice?"

While the way he said it made me think maybe somebody shouldn't have been exonerated, I have to confess I was thrilled to hear Frank drop my name. After *Alis* wore off his hand he'd been saying "Excuse me?" to get my attention.

"Here," Frank said, handing his book back to me. "Take this book in lieu of the one my mother promised. You can leave today. I will call a cab while you pack."

It seemed our relationship wasn't progressing as well as I thought.

As for Mimi's book, it was hard to know how it was getting along. Around noon each day Frank and I would eat together, then I'd arrange her lunch on a tray while Frank went outside to pick a flower to go with it. We'd put his offering, often badly mangled, in a juice glass on the tray and I'd carry the whole thing to her office and leave it on the floor just outside her closed door. I always made Frank swear to wait for me in the kitchen, but he'd trail me in the hall like Cary Grant in *To Catch a Thief,* pressing himself into doorways to hide if I happened to look over my shoulder. After I put the tray down and knocked, I'd hear a mad scramble behind me as Frank hotfooted it back to the kitchen. I'd count to ten before I returned to give him time to arrange himself under the table with a book and catch his breath. Then we'd have a cookie.

He wasn't the only one trying to fake me out, though. As soon as my knuckles connected with her door I'd hear a burst of typing from the other side— Mimi didn't use a computer—which always made me think of those recordings people have of dogs barking in place of a doorbell. I guess she was worried I was keeping tabs on her output. Which, in fairness, I was. Mr. Vargas had worked up a schedule to keep her on track, and part of my job was to somehow make sure she turned in pages, however rough, once a week or so. I was supposed to enter her typescript into "Mimi's computer," a tool that lay fallow as far as I could tell except for when she used it to order things online or trawl eBay for Frank's outfits. Then I was to e-mail the pages to Mr. Vargas. He wasn't looking for high polish or even any polish. Just evidence of a story, coming together, not coming together, whatever.

Except Mimi hadn't surrendered pages yet.

When I texted Mr. Vargas to confess as much, he answered with one word: *Patience.*

PART II
Our Adventures Begin

5

After much of June spent under house arrest, I decided it was time Frank and I staged a jailbreak. I put a note on Mimi's lunch tray that said: "May I borrow the car keys?" Frank and I had climbed in the Mercedes a few times to watch a movie on my computer and pretend we were at a drive-in. Other than using it as a stage for imaginary adventures, though, no one had touched the car since I'd been there. The crud accumulated on its windows and dead leaves puddled under its wheels were a testament to how long it had been since it had moved. "Does this thing drive?" I asked Frank.

"Yes. But not by itself, in the way my piano plays itself. I would be an enthusiastic supporter of such technology except that the self-driving car gives my mother less incentive than ever to buy me a horse."

Mimi emerged from her office while Frank and I were having our after-lunch cookie. Frank jumped out of his chair so quickly he knocked it to the floor and flung himself into her arms with such force that she staggered back a few steps.

"Careful, Frank," she said. "Where did you get the black tape?" Frank was wearing his alternate, un-ragged tailcoat and intact morning pants, and had applied black tape to his eyebrows and upper lip in the manner of Groucho Marx.

"What black tape?" he asked.

"The black electrical tape that I hid from you so that you wouldn't put it over your eyebrows again. Remember how much it hurt getting it off last time?"

"Oh, that black tape," he said. "You can have it back." He started peeling it delicately from his upper lip.

"Where do you need to go, Penny?" Mimi asked.

"Alice," I said as automatically as you would say "God bless you" to a stranger sneezing. "I don't need to go anywhere. But I thought Frank would enjoy getting out. I figured we could find a playground where Frank could hook up with other kids and—"

"—No!" Frank and Mimi all but shouted in unison.

I must have looked startled because Mimi was quick to explain, "Frank doesn't like waiting his turn at the swings."

"Waiting your turn isn't fun," I said to Frank. "But it's something you have to do in life if you're planning on getting along with other children."

"Something I have to do in life is bang my head against the metal pole when people tell me to wait my turn at the swings," Frank said. "And I don't plan on getting along with other children. No thank you please." Mimi closed her eyes and grimaced in a way that made me suspect they'd been through all this a few times already.

"Well, how about this?" I said. "Frank and I could go on a drive. Feel the wind on our faces. Sniff the salt air. If I'm going to chauffeur him to school in the fall, now's a good time for us to get used to being out in the world together."

"I would like to feel the wind on our faces," Frank said. "I'd better get these eyebrows off." He jackrabbited down the hall.

"I'm not so sure about this," Mimi said. "You don't know where anything is. You'll get lost."

"I won't. The beach is downhill."

"So is the Valley."

She made that sound like a bad thing. "True," I said, "but my phone has GPS."

She looked at me blankly.

"Global positioning system," I said. "It's a—"

"I know what GPS is," she said. "I'm thinking. You don't know how difficult Frank can be out in the world."

"I supervised twenty-five third graders on a field trip to the Bronx Zoo on my own and lived to tell the tale. I'm not worried."

Mimi ran her hand across her mouth while she pondered all this. I noticed her nails were gnawed to the quick. "Frank and I used to go on adventures all the time," she said finally. "He was the cutest little boy you've ever seen. I was so worried somebody would kidnap him that I thought about hiring a bodyguard. But Xander was around more then."

"Xander?" I asked. "Who's Xander?"

As if she hadn't heard my question, she continued, "Somehow Frank's pediatrician got wind that I was worried some lunatic might snatch Frank, so she gave me a card for a psychiatrist who deals in anxiety issues. For me! Like I was crazy to think somebody would want to kidnap my son. I gather she's not much of a reader, that one. Not familiar with my book. Too busy saving lives."

"I haven't read your book," I said. I don't know what possessed me to say that.

She must have stared at me for a full minute before she responded. "Did it occur to you to read it before you came to work for me?"

"Bad enough to have me underfoot," I said. "I thought you might not want me inside your brain." Dear god, I prayed, keep Mimi out of my bedside table drawer. If she opened it, she'd find the dog-eared, food-stained copy of *Pitched* I'd bought in the New York airport and had read twice on the flight out and had dipped into many times since, when writing in my notebook left me too rattled to sleep.

Mimi, who usually avoided looking at me at all, eyed me like my mother had after I presented my pajama-clad self to her, claiming I'd bathed when I'd only run water in the tub and stood at the sink making fashion-model faces in the mirror until I thought enough time had passed for her to believe I'd soaked and scrubbed. Mimi had to know I was fibbing. My mother always did.

"That's the most idiotic thing I've ever heard," she said.

I shrugged. "I majored in accounting. I guess I'm not much of a reader, either."

"I don't believe you. Why would Isaac hire an assistant who doesn't read?"

"I'm good with computers."

"Good with computers. That's all that matters now, isn't it?" The funny thing was that she seemed more pleased than angry. "The car keys are on the hook by the door. Bring Frank home right away if he bites anyone or pulls his hair out or bangs his head against anything." She went to the counter and scribbled some things on a pad of paper there, frowning intensely as she wrote. When she'd finished writing she tore the paper from the pad and handed it to me. "Take this with you."

She'd written out Dr. Abrams's phone number at her beach house, along with the names and numbers of her emergency room of choice and Frank's pediatrician, Dr. Not-a-Reader. "Frank doesn't swim well, so if you stop at the beach, stay in the car." She thrust her cell phone at me. "Here. Take my phone, too, in case you lose the paper. All the numbers are in there."

"I don't lose things," I said. "What if you need to call somebody?"

"Who would I call?" she asked. "Take it."

I was halfway down the hall to gather Frank when Mimi called after me, "Alice. Thank you." Alice, not Penny.

After Frank got the tape off his eyebrows, he'd refreshed himself with a pass through Wardrobe. Now he was wearing an outfit more suited to an afternoon's motoring: white canvas duster over chinos and a white shirt, leather aviator's cap and goggles, a silk scarf and old-school binoculars around his neck. He had his plastic machete stuck in his belt and his pith helmet under his arm. "Is that what you're wearing?" he asked.

"What's wrong with it?" I had on a T-shirt, Bermuda shorts, and tennis shoes, my New York-via-Nebraska idea of standard Southern California daywear.

"Everything," Frank said. "I know just what you need. Tartan! Let me get you my plaid cravat."

"That's okay," I said. "I'm not big on plaids."

"What's wrong with you?" he asked. He launched into a brief-for-Frank disquisition on the importance of tartans as clan signifiers in Great Britain from ancient times forward, which segued into a history of the evolution of the striped necktie as a means of differentiating university rowing teams from afar. He paused to take a breath and I groaned, figuring this might go on a while. Instead, Frank used the air he'd taken in to bellow, "Gentlemen, start your engines!" Then he whipped the machete from his belt and charged the station wagon, carrying the pith helmet in front of him like a shield in his left hand and brandishing the machete in his right.

After I got over my surprise at his enthusiasm for our adventure I was pleased to see how eager he was to go. So of course the car wouldn't start. "Why?" I asked the ozone.

Frank, mouthpiece for the ozone, answered me. "The battery's dead. If an automobile isn't driven for weeks or months, the cables should be disconnected to prevent the charge leaking out. However, my mother refused to allow me to perform the necessary operation. She said disconnecting the battery was abject capitulation. And that I would get grease on my cuffs."

"Abject capitulation to what?"

"To her not driving."

"Does she ever drive?"

"Sometimes not for weeks or months. As if the driving weren't bad enough, once you reach your destination you have to find a place to park. God help you if you end up in a parking garage because chances are you'll never find your car again. If you do find your car, then you've lost the stupid parking ticket. That's it. You're doomed. Why did you ever leave the house? Better to stay home. According to my mother."

"Don't you ever go anywhere?" I asked.

"We do," he said. "In taxis."

After an eternity—or maybe what just seemed an eternity to me, as Frank was lecturing, not briefly, on the ins and outs of internal combustion engines, which segued into an explanation of Nikola Tesla's alternating current (A.C.) engine, which, I don't know if you know this, revolutionized the delivery of electricity over long distances, much to the chagrin of Tesla's archnemesis and purveyor of the direct current (D.C.) delivery system, Thomas Edison—a guy from roadside assistance showed up at the gate carrying a briefcase-sized battery to shock our engine back to life.

"Drive your car at least half an hour before you turn the engine off again," he said once he got it up and running.

"It's not my car." I signed the papers on his clipboard while he unclamped the jumper cables. "But don't worry. We may not stop driving until we get to Belize."

The guy eyeballed the pair of us. "Not yours either?" he asked, nodding toward Frank.

"Nope," I said. "I'm the chauffeur."

"Nice gig," he said. "Enjoy Belize. Don't forget your sunscreen."

After the gate clanged shut behind the guy, Frank said, "I don't think my mother would like it if you took me to Belize."

"I was joking."

"Your jokes are not funny. I wish you would say 'knock knock' when you're trying to make a joke so I would know."

"Great idea," I said. "Listen, Frank. I was going to take you to a museum today but since it's getting late, let's just go for a drive along the beach. No getting in the water, though. Okay?"

"Just as well. The lifeguards say I swim like a drowning man. I don't see why that matters as long as I don't in fact drown." He handed me the pith helmet. "This is for you, Alice. Sir Howard Carter didn't wear sunscreen in the Valley of the Kings."

In that small gesture I saw another leap forward in my acceptance into the Banning household. "Thank you, Frank," I said. "That's sweet of you. Let's leave the machete at home, okay?"

And without complaint or hesitation, he flung the machete straight up into the air. I cringed and covered my head with my arms—I know it was plastic, but that sucker looked heavy. When it didn't thunk to earth again I peered at the sky, wondering if he'd somehow launched it into orbit. But there it was, lodged in the upper branches of a tree where, I noticed for the first time, a number of other items hung camouflaged by leaves and branches. A pair of kid's sneakers I couldn't imagine Frank ever wearing tied together by their laces, a Hula-Hoop, a tennis racket, a jump rope.

"We ought to get a ladder out one day and take all that stuff down," I said.

"No," Frank said. "It's art. My mother and I hold hands and look at it together sometimes. We enjoy its random nature."

We drove out the big Banning gates, south to Sunset, then looped west through all the fancy neighborhoods with Tudor mansions and Italianate palaces and faux Norman farmhouses tucked away behind clusters of palms and groves of citrus trees or stretches of lawn and rose garden. Sometimes you could see just a gatehouse here and a turret there peeking over a high wall or hedge. Lots of those big giant houses had FOR SALE signs posted out front. I couldn't imagine who had enough money to buy even one of them, and we must have cruised past a dozen.

When we hit the Pacific Coast Highway we hung a left, away from what my phone told me was Malibu and back toward the city of Los Angeles. As I drove I kept stealing glances right, to the beach, where I caught flashes of bikers and Rollerbladers and volleyball nets strung close to the highway. Closer to the water I saw bright beach umbrellas and blue lifeguard shacks on stilts and deep white sand and gray, cold-looking water. Which surprised me. I'd never seen the Pacific in close-up and I'd expected it to be blue and clear, like a kid's crayon drawing of a tropical paradise.

In the side-view mirror I could see Frank behind me, oblivious to the beach's half-naked activity. He was leaning out his open window to enjoy the feel of the wind in his eyebrows and eyelashes and on his fingertips. His scarf snapped in the wind behind us.

"Watch out for your scarf."

"Isadora Duncan met an untimely end in France on September fourteenth, 1927, when her scarf got entangled in the wheels of the convertible she rode in."

"That doesn't sound like fun, does it?"

"No. Thank you. Please."

"So watch out for your scarf."

Frank tucked it under his jacket and rolled the window up again. We drove along in silence for a while after that, slipping past the Santa Monica Pier with its miniature amusement park, complete with Ferris wheel and a little roller coaster pinned there against the sky.

"You know what does sound like fun?" Frank said about then.

"Lay it on me," I said, thinking he was checking out the rides.

"Lay what on you?"

"Nothing. Tell me what sounds like fun."

"Going to the little airport where the antique planes take off. It's around here someplace, but I haven't been there since I was very young."

"But now that you're practically antique—" I said.

"I'm not antique," he said. "Things fifty years old

or older are considered 'antique.' Anything thirty years old to fifty is called 'vintage.' So I'm not even close to vintage, although of course you are swiftly approaching that."

"Thanks. So what does that make you?"

"I'm a child. My mother, however, is antique."

"Well, let's not tell her that, okay?"

"Why not? It's true."

"Lots of true things aren't polite to say. If you're not sure whether something you're about to say might be rude, it's better to keep your mouth shut. That's the kind of tact your mother was talking about, by the way. Having tact, *t-a-c-t*, means knowing when to keep your thoughts to yourself."

When he didn't have a comeback to that I checked him in the mirror and saw I'd upset him. His face, of course, was as impassive as ever; his shoulders were the tipoff. They'd risen to his ears, which I knew by then was step one to Frank going stiff and wordless on me. "What do you say we look for that airport?" I asked.

"I would like to see it again," he said. I pulled to the side of the road right away and found the place on my cell phone.

When we got there I parked in the lot by the airfield and Frank climbed over the seat to get the windshield view of all the private prop planes and petite jets coming and going. The thing that got us out of the car finally was a bright yellow biplane that kept taking off and circling back to land again. Frank got out first and stood there with his goggles pushed up on his forehead and the binoculars pressed to his eyes, watching until it just kept going and lost itself in the horizon. There was something so poignant about Frank standing there with the wind blowing his coat and scarf around him that I got out to photograph him with my phone.

It occurred to me I should take a picture with Mimi's phone, too. So I fished it out of my pocket and snapped the photo, and then I did something unfathomable. I scrolled through her list of contacts. It was the same kind of awful impulse that makes people inventory bathroom medicine cabinets when they're using the facilities at someone else's house. Until that moment I'd always considered myself above that kind of thing. But there I was, my eyes flicking down the list, past several Drs. This and That; Emergency Room, two listings; Home; and Hospital, a few selections there, too.

Had she handed me her own personal cell phone or one she'd gotten as a free bonus gift with a year's subscription to *Accidents Waiting to Happen Weekly*? Where were her people, the Ellens and Eds, Dianes, Dicks and Sheilas most of us carry around in our pockets in case we really, really need to tell someone we're in line at the grocery, waiting to pay for cat food? Or had she deleted the names of anyone who mattered to her, anticipating my snoop through her connections when I never would have suspected something like that of myself?

I spun through the entire list. I told myself I'd come across Mr. Vargas's name at the end of it, and that finding his name would validate me, the only person in the world Mr. V. trusted enough to send to M. M. Banning's aid.

There it was. *Isaac Vargas.* And after that, one more name. A name I'd heard before. *Xander.*

"What are you doing?" Frank asked. He'd materialized at my elbow. I was so startled I dropped the phone.

"Nothing," I said. "I was just taking a picture of you with your mother's cell phone. Look." In one movement I picked the phone up and exited Mimi's address book, feeling hugely relieved to have something as innocent as Frank's photograph to show him.

Frank studied the picture. "I look like the Little Prince," he said. "My mother and I used to look at that book together when I was a kid."

"Of course you look like the Little Prince," I said. It was something I'd noticed when I'd worked in the kindergarten. On the day kids brought their favorite books to class, you could see the Pippi Longstockings and Cats in the Hat and Corduroy Bears coming from a mile away. Bedtime Story as Destiny, I used to call it. And here we had another case in point: Frank, a snappy little dresser given to mood swings, scarves, and non sequiturs, just visiting our world from a small, eccentric planet of his own.

Me? *Harriet the Spy*. Of course.

6

Back in the car we decided to try the freeway for the full-on traffic experience, driving toward the jagged cluster of downtown Los Angeles with the mountains propped up behind it like cardboard scenery. Though the "driving" I was doing felt more like being parked in Omaha at the Seventy-Second Street Wal-Mart, waiting for the store to open for its post-Thanksgiving Day sale. The freeway was so packed it was hard to believe there could be anyone left driving cars anywhere else in the world.

"In the winter it doesn't get very cold down here in the Los Angeles Basin but that far mountain is covered in snow," Frank said, leaning forward between the seats to point it out to me.

"Fascinating. But listen, Frank, gentlemen don't point. Although I guess it's all right to point at mountains. Mountains don't have feelings like people do."

"You aren't supposed to point at people? How else are your eyes supposed to find them?"

"Not that way. Nobody likes to look up and see people pointing and staring."

"Yes. That I know from firsthand experience."

"Have you ever been up there to play in the snow?" I asked.

"Up there? No. I can see it from my school. Just before winter break they truck snow in from there and spread it on the playground for our Winter Festival. It's more convenient that way."

And to think I'd been surprised people had their drinking water delivered. "That sounds like fun," I said. "Back in Omaha, we have to get our snow the old-fashioned way. Falls on us out of the sky."

"Here, when the hills are on fire the ash falls like that, like snow. Or the mashed-potato flakes they use in movies as a stand-in for falling snow. Last summer there was a huge brushfire and no wind so this giant mushroom cloud of smoke hung in one place on the horizon for a week."

"Like an atom bomb mushroom cloud? That sounds scary."

"Exactly like that. Except it wasn't scary. It was in the Valley." Frank said "the Valley" as if it were a world away instead of a few freeway exits. "Did you know that Einstein's one regret—you know Albert Einstein, don't you?"

"Mr. *E* equals *mc* squared? Everybody knows him."

"They do?"

"Not personally. Since, you know, he's dead."

"Yes, as of April eighteenth, 1955. Einstein's regret was that he signed the letter a scientist named Leo Szilard wrote to Franklin Roosevelt in 1939 warning of the danger of the Nazis inventing a nuclear fission bomb many linked to the secrets unlocked by Einstein's famous equation. That bomb would be capable of unimaginable carnage. Einstein, who was a pacifist, felt the letter Szilard wrote also linked him to the creation of the fabled Manhattan Project—"

"That's the one where the scientists tried to invent more affordable apartments in New York City, right?"

"I don't know what you're talking about." Frank sounded troubled by this, like a guy who hadn't noticed an open manhole at his feet until he'd fallen into it.

When would I learn? "Knock knock. Keep talking."

"—The Manhattan Project, which led to the American invention of the atom bomb dropped on Hiroshima and Nagasaki at the end of World War II. Did you know that the *Enola Gay,* the airplane that dropped the first atom bomb, was built in Omaha in 1945?"

"I didn't know that," I said. "So, Frank, you must love school. You know more than most grown-ups I've met."

"The other kids say I'm retarded."

"I thought they said you were crazy."

"They say that, too."

"They're probably mad because you're smart and make good grades. Kids are stupid like that. The teachers love you, though, right?"

"I'll tell you what my mother says teachers don't love," Frank said. "Being corrected."

Sheesh. "You don't do that, do you?"

"Only when teachers make factual errors." In the mirror, his shoulders hadn't tensed up, but he'd put his goggles over his eyes again. "Winston Churchill failed the sixth grade," he added.

"Oh, yeah?"

"Yes. Frank Lloyd Wright never finished high school. Neither did Cagney or Gershwin or Ansel Adams or Irving Berlin. Charlie Chaplin and Noël Coward never even finished grade school."

"Is that true?"

"My mother keeps a list in the drawer of her bedside table. You can go look at it sometime if you don't believe me."

"I believe you."

"I want to go home now."

"You're the boss," I said and crept off the highway at the next exit. Neither one of us said anything for the rest of the trip. The next time I stole a look at Frank in the mirror, he was sleeping like a baby, his goggles down around his neck and his face pressed against the window.

When we pulled into the driveway I could hear Mimi hammering away on the typewriter through an open window. Frank started awake when I turned off the engine and ran for the house like an electrified rabbit with a live greyhound at its heels. I found him crouched outside Mimi's bedroom door, rocking in a little chair invisible to Earthlings like me.

"Are you okay?" I whispered.

"I just want to sit here with her for a while."

I got that. I would have given anything to sit with my own mother again for a while. "That's fine. Just don't bother her while she's working, all right?"

He nodded and I decided to trust him. I went to the kitchen and hot-potatoed Mimi's cell phone out of my pocket and onto the counter so she would see and relieve me of it as soon as possible. Then I took the list of emergency contacts from another pocket and entered them into my phone so I'd never have to touch hers again, ever.

After all that guilty business was taken care of I sorted through the mail I'd picked up from the box as we came in, separating trashable junk from the bills. There was rarely much of anything else in her mailbox, though sometimes Mimi got fan mail, recognizable by virtue of being hand addressed and stamped. Or, more unsettlingly, stamp free, saying only "M. M. Banning" on the rumpled envelopes, missives clearly shoved through the mail slot by one of her fanatics. Every time I handed her one of those pieces of somebody's heart sealed inside an envelope, she tossed it in the trash unread.

Today, however, there was a postcard. It showed a shack with big stuffed animals—the kind you win at a fair and then lug around regretfully for the rest of the day—nailed all over it like lumpy and disheveled siding. I flipped the card over, thinking it might be some kind of nutty advertisement for a roofing company or maybe an invitation to check out an unusually depressing day care center. The card was addressed to Frank. I didn't mean to read it, but there was so little written there, my eyes couldn't help taking it in.

Outside Salt Lake City. Xander.

Xander again. Who was Xander? I put the card, writing side down, by Mimi's phone, pulled a big knife from the drawer by the sink and started savaging basil for tomato sauce. I put a pot on to boil and slopped some olive oil and crushed garlic into a saucepan, and after that, cherry tomatoes. By the time I had the noodles draining in the sink, Frank wandered into the kitchen and said, "I'm hungry."

"Lucky you," I said, and put a plate of pasta in front of him.

"Can I eat this on the couch?"

" 'May' I eat this on the couch. No. Gentlemen do not eat on couches."

"Why not?"

"Because mankind went to all the trouble of inventing tables to save good trousers from bad stains. Couches deserve the same consideration."

"That makes perfect sense," Frank said. Then, "She's never coming out, is she?"

"She will. She has to eat, too. Look, you got a postcard."

Frank ignored the postcard, too caught up in the thrilling fork pursuit of tomato around the velodrome of his pasta bowl. I nudged the card toward him when he was done.

"Look, I got a postcard," he said.

"You did? Spectacular. Who's it from?"

"Xander. He's back on our side of the Continental Divide."

"Who's Xander?" I said, hoping I sounded more innocent than I felt.

"Xander is my piano teacher. When he's around."

"Oh, yeah? How long have you been taking lessons?"

"Off and on since I was little."

"You know, I've never heard you play."

"I don't like playing much. I'd rather listen."

"So why do you take lessons?"

"Because my mother says my gifts shouldn't be squandered. Also, Xander is my friend. He's been coming here to play our piano since before I was born. He tried to teach my mom to play. She says she wasn't any good because she was too old to learn, but she liked him and he likes our piano, so she gave him a key to our house so he could let himself in and play it anytime."

I had to turn to the sink so he wouldn't see the avid look on my face. Not that Frank was much for reading facial expressions, but it shamed me to show my evil twin, Nosey Parker, to anything more sentient than a crusty skillet. "So, Xander stays here?"

"Sometimes. When he's in town. He makes money teaching piano lessons. He plays in restaurants, too, and fancy department stores until he gets a wad of cash up. Then he wanders all over the place until the money is gone. In my gallery I've mounted a retrospective of his postcards. Would you like to see?"

As someone who had vacuumed every inch of the house outside the forbidden zone of Mimi's office, I had to wonder where this gallery might be. Frank led me through the sliding doors, blasted right past the art installation in the tree and stopped in front of the garage. I'd seen the garage a million times, but had gone so far past not noticing it backed up close to the stucco security perimeter that I'd never even wondered why the car wasn't parked in it, ever. Unlike the house, it had a shake roof with moss growing on the wood shingles shaded by a eucalyptus tree, and stucco walls instead of floor-to-ceiling windows. All the better, I supposed, to stuff it floor to ceiling with junk.

Frank threw the door up with one hand and swept a bow to the interior, like Aladdin welcoming me to his cave. But it was neither cave nor junkyard, and in fact so not of a piece with the house that it took my breath away. The walls were whitewashed boards and exposed studs with a bank of windows on the backside tucked under the rough beam-and-plank ceiling that was also the floor to the loft spanning much of the garage. More light spilled in through skylights set on either side of the peaked roof. The concrete floor must have had some kind of seal on it because it shone like marble and there was neither oil stain nor faded memories of leaking radiator fluid to be seen anywhere. The oddest part was that there was nothing in the bottom floor at all, no old bicycles nor toys nor rusty tools nor screens to windows that didn't exist anymore. Not even a rake or a hose. I'd never been in a cleaner garage in my life. Or a bigger one. It could have housed a dozen tractors.

"Look how nice it is in here," I said. "You could eat off the floor."

"Even gentleman could?"

"No, gentlemen could not. I didn't mean you could literally eat off the floor. That's just something people say when a floor is really clean. Most garages look like Dagwood Bumstead's closet, with junk falling out all over the place every time you open the door."

Frank lit up when I said that. "Fibber McGee had a closet like that, too, but since it was a radio program they had to convey its overstuffed nature through the medium of sound. My mother is not an archivist like I am and doesn't believe in keeping things. She says the more you have, the more you have to lose. So if she doesn't have any use for something, it's gone before you can say 'Fibber McGee's Closet.' Come on. The gallery is up here." Frank scrambled halfway up a ladder of two-by-fours nailed between a pair of studs. There was a trapdoor up top that he pushed open and climbed through. He poked his head back into the frame of the hole to watch me ascend. "Careful," he said. "The old lady fell off this ladder. And she was way closer to the bottom than you are."

"What old lady?"

"The old lady my mother bought the house from. She built it when she was young. This garage went with the original house and the old lady couldn't get a permit to build a new one, so she never tore this one down. She turned it into her painting atelier."

Once I got up there I could tell the old lady was an amateur, because she had everything a real artist could ever dream of in a studio but can seldom afford. Here there was not just light and space but wide cabinets with shallow drawers for storing drawings and slotted racks against the wall for canvases and an easel. A sink for cleaning brushes and counter space alongside it and even more drawers under that. A couple of sunflower-yellow straight-backed chairs arranged around a yellow table I couldn't imagine anyone getting up there in the first place, and a yellow wooden day bed and bedside table.

"Van Gogh at Arles meet Barbie's Dream House," I said.

"Yes," Frank said. "Or somebody got a very good deal on yellow paint. Look, here's the bathroom." He opened a door and showed me a tiny bathroom fitted with a teacup-sized copper tub and a demitasse sink and one of those old-fashioned high-tanked toilets with a chain I couldn't resist pulling. It flushed with a sound like a jet taking off from an aircraft carrier. Frank covered his ears and grimaced.

"Sorry," I said when he uncovered his ears again. "It's just that I've never seen a toilet like that."

"Van Gogh would have done the same thing," he said. "He never saw one, either. Or these." By the sink, he twisted the knob on the top of what looked like a vertical row of drawers. The lot swung open as one and presto—a tiny concealed refrigerator that released a puff of stale, chilly air. Another drawer by the fridge pulled out to reveal a little two-burner electric stovetop.

"Wow," I said. "You could live up here. Does your mother come here a lot?"

"Not so much. The ladder scares her. When the son moved the old lady out, he just left all her stuff, see?" He opened another drawer to show me brushes with dried-paint evidence of use on the handles but whose bristles had been so well cared for they were as soft and immaculate as they must have been in the shop. There were tubes of paints and pastels and balls of string and wire and clamps and a hammer and nails and many blue tin cups of tacks segregated by color, all laid out in their drawers as if they were in a shop window in Paris. I say that like I've been to Paris. I haven't, except in movies, or my dreams.

"I don't know if it was too much trouble to move out, or if it made the old lady too sad to bring it with her. She didn't want to sell the place but her son didn't want her anywhere near that ladder again. My mom said she couldn't bear to pitch everything because the old lady had it all arranged so beautifully and she was about to be dead but her materials were still so alive with potential. Then of course I came along and by the time I was three my mother was pretty sure I was going to be famous for something someday. Since that something might be painting, she kept everything like it was. My mother bought a lot of art back then, too. We don't have that anymore. But thanks to us keeping all the old lady's stuff here, the potential for us having it again is alive even if the old lady is dead."

I reached for one of the brushes. "Oh, don't touch," he said.

"I'm sorry. I forgot to ask. Is it yours?"

"I told you all this stuff belongs to the old lady."

"I thought she was dead."

"She is, probably. A lot of the pieces in museums used to belong to people who are dead but you aren't allowed to touch them, either. Here, let me show you my favorite thing up here." He darted across the loft to a big wire basket on the top rail of the waist-high fence that separated us from the concrete floor a dozen feet below. He flung the basket over the edge, and I gasped. "Don't worry. It's attached to this pulley, see? It's how you get groceries and stuff up and down, since the ladder is so dangerous."

I came to the fence and peered over. "That's quite a drop. You be careful," I said. "If you fell over you'd break your neck, and probably every other bone in your body."

"I couldn't fall over that. It's too high. I'd have to jump it." Frank leaned his elbows on the top of the fence and looked over.

"Don't even think that," I said. "And please, don't lean on it. What if it gives way?"

"My mother says the same thing. She doesn't like it when I come up here because she's sure I'll manage to find a way to fall like my uncle Julian did. So I have to curate my collection when she isn't looking."

Uh-oh. "Wait. Are you not allowed up here?"

"I'm not not allowed. I'm just strongly discouraged from coming here alone. And besides, you're here. Now step this way, please, to the gallery." He backed away, palms up and fingers waggling like a tour guide, to a corner of the loft where he'd put his tack collection to good use attaching a crazy quilt of postcards to the studs. He took a magnifying glass from a hook on the wall by the exhibit and handed it to me. "Use this," he said, "to savor the details."

So I did. Had to, almost. There were so many details in every four-by-six-inch card that it was hard to appreciate the whole of any of them. There was a sidewalk mosaic of the *Mona Lisa* which, when magnified, proved constructed entirely of buttons. A tower built of every crazy, broken-down material delight a city dump offers—bicycle parts and rusted bedsprings, discarded water tanks and twisted pipes, limbless dolls and worn-out brooms. There was a multilevel tree house constructed of scrap lumber and lengths of firewood, with windows of bottle butts and crystal punch bowls and a door made from a metal highway sign that read REST AREA, THIS EXIT. NEXT EXIT 47 MILES. I moved from postcard to postcard, increasingly boggled by the too-much muchness of it all. At last I lowered the magnifying glass and stepped away from the wall. "What a trip! I want to meet your Xander."

"No you don't," Frank said. "He'll only disappoint you."

"How would he disappoint me? I don't even know him."

He shrugged. "That's what my mother says about Xander. Also, that he's too good at too many things to ever succeed at anything."

I was going to press him for details, but he held a finger up. "Shhh."

After a moment or two of intense listening, I said, "I don't hear anything."

"She's stopped typing," he said, and was through the trapdoor, down the ladder, and out the door like a shot. I hurried after him and cleared the garage door just in time to hear Frank shout "Mama!" with all the joy and intensity and sweet, pure love that makes a woman's womb ache if she doesn't have children of her own. Mimi had just stepped outside the sliding glass door. She smiled at Frank as he hurtled across the yard. Frank launched himself into her arms.

It's kind of unimaginable the carnage caused by the locomotive force of one slight nine-year-old boy traveling at the speed of light, colliding with his tiny mother, midfifties, a little off balance because she was twisting around to close the door behind herself. He hit her with enough velocity to explode that antique sheet of cracked glass into about a million lacerating diamonds.

I've seen a lot of blood in my day, but never quite that much.

7

Frank and I had been in the emergency room for a couple of minutes, listening to the symphony of shushes, clicks, and beeps coming from all the monitoring equipment hooked up to Mimi and other unseen patients sequestered in curtained-off cubbies. I'd told the expedient fib that I was Mimi's daughter and Frank was my brother so they would let us come see her together. I was more than a little nervous about Frank blowing our cover.

"Is she asleep?" Frank asked, not in a whisper.

"Shhh. Looks that way."

An emergency room nurse whisked past us. "Don't worry. She's okay. Just tired."

Mimi didn't exactly look okay—one of her eyebrows had been shaved off and the skin seamed back together there, and her head was wrapped in a wimple of bandages. Frank put his goggles on and gripped my hand like it was the only thing tethering him to this earth.

"You all right?" I asked.

"Mama," he said with all the urgency that odd, flat voice of his could summon. Mimi's eyes popped open and I held his hand more tightly, just in case he was thinking of rushing her again. "What's that thing you're wearing?"

"They gave me this nice clean gown to put on when I got here," Mimi said. "My other clothes were dirty."

"You call that a gown? I'd better check you for brain damage."

"What?" The emergency room nurse had reappeared by then.

"One of the EMS guys taught Frank how to check for brain damage," I said.

"He gave me his special little flashlight, see?" Frank said, pulling a penlight from his pocket and holding it forth on his flattened palm for all to admire. "He said I was a natural. He also likes my coat." He was still wearing his white cotton duster, now smeared with Mimi's blood.

"That's nice," Mimi said. She sounded so calm that I suspected the tube taped to her left forearm contained morphine rather than saline. "Please do check me for brain damage, Monkey. The doctors might have missed something."

Frank handed his goggles to me, moved the visitor's chair to the head of Mimi's bed, and climbed up so he'd be tall enough to shine his light down into her pupils. "Nurse," he said. "Come closer. Let me show you how this is done."

I was about to suggest to Frank that maybe the nurse knew already, but from the indulgent way she smiled and came to his elbow I imagined she had lots of experience with people in bloody white coats showing her how to do things she already knew how to do.

"See her pupil contract when I do this? That's a good sign," Frank said. "With brain damage, I get no response when I flash the light. If the pupils are different sizes, then we've got real trouble. The injuries we have here are minor. Superficial scalp lacerations, swelling and bruising, maybe a concussion. We'll keep tabs on her for the next twenty-four hours to make sure she doesn't show evidence of an intracranial bleed." Frank hopped down without turning anything over or bringing the bed curtain down with him. So that was a relief.

"Is that so?" the nurse asked. She winked at me.

"That's what the paramedic said," Frank said.

"Pretty much word for word," I added. "Frank has an incredible memory."

"Maybe Frank should go to medical school. The triage nurse says he's told her plenty about cholera outbreaks in London in the nineteenth century."

"John Snow proved it a waterborne illness by tracing the 1854 outbreak to London's Broad Street well," Frank said. "He removed the pump handle and within days the outbreak ended. Would it be all right if I checked you for brain damage, too?"

"Sure," she said, and settled on the chair Frank had carried over.

Holding that penlight somehow freed him to study her face closely. "You look like Tinkerbell," he said, then snapped his light on. It was true. She had blue eyes, a pert nose, and pink lipstick, plus lots of blond hair done up in an elaborately casual topknot.

"Thank you," she said. "Does that mean I'll live forever and never get old?" I wasn't surprised by her question. She had a smooth, unworried brow that looked suspiciously younger than her hands.

"I'm just saying you don't have brain damage," Frank said.

"Well, if I'm not going to be young forever, then I'd better get back to work." She checked the bag of fluid flowing into Mimi's arm and made notations on her chart.

"My father was a doctor," Mimi said. "Frank would love medical school. But first he has to make it through elementary school."

"Winston Churchill failed the sixth grade," Frank said. "Noël Coward—"

"Frank," I said. "The nurse is busy."

"Oh, that's okay," Tinkerbell said. "I'm done. So, Frank, just to be extra sure your grandmother's brain is in good shape, we're sending her upstairs for an MRI. That stands for magnetic resonance imaging. It's a way of taking pictures inside her brain without actually having to poke a hole in her skull to see how everything looks on the inside."

"My grandmother?" Frank said. "My grandmother died in 1976. You could look inside her skull through one of the eye sockets without having to poke a hole, but I doubt there'd be much to see in there anymore." He plunged both his hands into his hair, as if he needed to make sure his own brain was still under there someplace.

"It's okay, Frank," Mimi said. Then, to Tinkerbell, "He's my son."

"Oh." Tinkerbell's eyes flicked from Mimi to Frank to me. "I thought—oh, forget what I thought. Doesn't matter."

By then Frank had uprooted a tuft of hair. I took it from him and slid it into my pocket, but not before everyone else had seen it, too. "Stop that," I murmured, aiming for the tone my mother used on me when I cracked my knuckles in church. I didn't want to make a big deal of it.

"I'd better see where we are on that MRI list," Tinkerbell said, hanging Mimi's chart on the end of her cot and smiling overbrightly before slipping away.

"You two should get going," Mimi said.

"I don't want to leave you here alone," I said.

"This is not a negotiation. You and Frank need to clear out. Now."

"You aren't coming with us?" Frank asked.

"The doctors need to keep an eye on me here tonight. Alice needs you at home. She's afraid of being by herself."

"It's true," I volunteered. "I'm terrified of the dark."

"There's nothing in the dark to be afraid of," Frank said. "It's out there, and we're in here. You're safe as long as I'm with you."

"I'm lucky to have you then, huh, Frank?" I said.

"Yes," he said.

"So am I," Mimi said. "I love you, Frank."

Frank didn't answer. I could see his shoulders rising. "We need to go, Frank," I said. "You heard your mother."

Frank threw his shoulders back when I said that, saluted smartly and said, "Aye-aye, Alice! Tell me, do you have the stupid parking ticket, or are we doomed?"

"Do you need me to fly out?" Mr. Vargas asked when I called the next night, after Mimi had been released from the hospital. It was pushing midnight in New York. I'd hoped he'd still be awake but I could tell by the groggy sound of his voice that he must have been asleep for a while already.

"No. Don't worry. I have everything under control now. Sorry to call so late, but I wanted to give you a heads-up in case word leaked out."

"Did anybody recognize her?"

"I don't think so."

"Is she okay?"

While I was formulating my answer, Mimi asked, "Who are you talking to?" I was in the living room, alone I thought, watching a smeary-looking evening settle over the city through the plastic I'd taped over the hole where the door used to be. By some miracle Frank was sleeping, and had been since just before Mimi got home from the hospital in the late afternoon.

As for the patient, I'd convinced Mimi to change out of the blood-encrusted cardigan and jeans she'd worn to the hospital and into a set of my sweats. From my dealings with the laundry I gathered Mimi didn't own gym clothes. She slept in lacy white cotton nightgowns that I worried would be ruined if her bandages oozed. Mimi was surprisingly okay with wearing my sweats but refused to let me help her change into them. She did let me tuck her into bed, though, where she'd conked out right away. But like Lazarus, she had risen again and materialized behind me, her hands swallowed by my sweatshirt's overlong sleeves, her hollow-eyed, bandaged head shrouded in its gray hood, a crimson NEBRASKA emblazoned across her chest. I almost fainted when I saw her.

"It's Mr. Vargas," I said. "I didn't want him to worry, in case word got out you'd been hurt. The nurse told me I should fix an ice pack for you to hold to your stitches to keep the swelling down. Now that you're up I'll do that."

"Give me the phone."

I helped Mimi settle on the sofa and handed her the phone. My hands were shaking as I put a soft pillow behind her back and covered her legs against the draft leaking in the taped-up door. I hustled off to the kitchen to scoop cubes from the ice machine into the ice pack Frank had found for me the night before. It was a pink plaid bag—tartan!—with a metal screw top that looked like something used to cure hangovers in a Doris Day movie. "Why do you even have this?" I'd asked him.

"I requested it for my sixth birthday."

"Why?"

"It was so hot that year. I wore it to school tied to my head with a burgundy Hermès scarf that belonged to my grandmother. Shall I get the scarf?"

"I think we can make do without it," I said. "Thanks, anyway."

As I stood at the sink adding a little tap water to the bag so it would shape to Mimi's face more easily, I stared out the window at Los Angeles in the first stages of its nocturnal twinkle. To the east I saw fireworks splayed across the sky, over by the Hollywood Bowl or maybe Dodger Stadium. I thought it might be a concert or a ball game, but then I noticed explosions down at the beach near Santa Monica, and then to the west, above the hills of Malibu. I realized then that it was the Fourth of July.

By the time I was back in the living room Mimi was off the phone and tears were dribbling down her face. I put the ice pack down fast and rustled up a box of tissues.

"Where's Frank?" she said.

"Sleeping," I said. "Are you okay?"

"Sleeping? Still? How is that possible?"

"I wrapped him up tight in a comforter, put him on the floor in the family room, piled couch cushions on top of him, and turned the TV to the Korean language channel. Is anything wrong? Does anything hurt?"

"Everything hurts."

"Here's your ice pack. I'll check and see if it's time for another pain pill."

"It's not that kind of pain." Mimi pushed back the sweatshirt hood and tilted her less-swollen eye at the ice pack in her hands. "This is Frank's," she said. "He wanted it for his birthday. First I bought him one of those blue gel packs you keep in the freezer, and he was so disappointed. It took forever to find this one. I almost didn't buy it. 'What's wrong with pink?' Frank asked me when I told him how I'd hesitated. 'Pink is the navy blue of India.'" She took a tissue from the box and mopped her face. "I can't stop wondering what will happen to Frank if something happens to me."

"But you're fine," I said. "The doctors said so. And I'm here."

"Now. I'm fine now. You're here now." She collapsed against the back of the couch. "When I had money, I didn't worry so much about Frank. Someone will take in a rich kid, even if he's weird."

"I'm not leaving. You'll have money again. Frank's not weird. He's different."

She snorted, then winced and pressed the ice pack to her eyebrow. "At least you didn't say 'special.' Isaac was so right about you. You're quite the Pollyanna." The way she said it didn't sound flattering. Sometimes it was hard for me to fathom why Mr. Vargas was so fond of her.

"How did it go last night, anyway?" she asked. "I was too wrung out to ask you when I got home from the hospital."

"No complaints."

For some reason that made her cry again. No leaking tears this time, though. Gut-wrenching sobs.

"Is there anybody you want me to call?" I said. "Relatives? Frank's dad?" Alice, I thought. Shut up already.

She pulled herself together enough to say, "My relatives are all dead. Frank's dad is not an option." She put the pack in her lap, blew her nose gingerly, then stared, glassy-eyed, out the hole where the sliding door had been. She got so still I couldn't see her breathe. I was a little worried she'd slipped away with her eyes open, like people do in the movies, and was fighting the urge to go find a mirror to hold under her nostrils when she said, "Fireworks."

"Yes," I said. "It's nice that they're high enough to see over the wall."

"I bought this house for the views. Can you believe that? Also I knew my mother would hate it."

"Did she?"

She put the ice pack back on her eyebrow and sighed. "She was dead by the time I bought it. But every day I hear her complaining about one thing or another, so it's like she's still right here with me. I've lived here more than half my life now. I'm older now than my mother was when she died."

She seemed to expect me to answer, so I coughed up, "Well, if you've stayed so long, you must really love it here."

"I hate it here. It was crazy to buy this place. I laughed when the real estate agent showed it to me. 'I'm too famous to live anywhere that has windows where walls should be,' I said. He assured me this house would work for me because the driveway was so steep and the road that led to it wasn't on maps thirty years ago. 'If you were still married to a movie star, your privacy might be a concern. But nobody cares about writers. You'll be fine.' Ha! I don't know why I listened to him." She held the ice pack to her brow again. "Not that many people care about writers, but for the ones who do—no driveway is too steep."

"Why did you stay?"

"I didn't want to give my mother the satisfaction of being right."

"Wasn't she dead by then?"

"Yes. Anyway, I called somebody from the studio and they came with a crew and finished that wall in two weeks. Anybody who says you can't build Rome in a day has never been to Hollywood." She lowered the ice pack and groped for another tissue. "This is leaking. You didn't screw the top on tight enough." She tossed the ice pack at my head.

I caught it, checked the seal, and dried it on my shirt. "It's not leaking. The wet is from condensation."

"It's leaking," she insisted, and hauled herself up off the couch. I tried to give her a hand but she shook me off and vanished down the hall. The doctor had been very clear that using the ice pack was important to her healing quickly. But Mimi slammed the door and started typing before I could talk myself into going after her. If the swelling didn't go down in a timely fashion, too bad. I wasn't her mother. I let her go.

8

As noted, I am not one for complaining, so I wasn't about to tell Mimi how my night alone with Frank really went. Our night together went more like this:

It was late and we were exhausted when we got home. We tottered in through the hole where the door had been but only made it as far as the living room couch before collapsing.

"You need to take a bath before you get in bed," I said after an eternity slumped there. I hoped the little boy on the outside would wrestle down the insomniac old man trapped inside Frank and that both parts would tumble into bed together and fall asleep.

"Why?"

"Because you're—dirty." I'd wiped his face and hands before we went to the hospital, but neither of us had bothered to change our clothes. We looked like fugitives from *The Texas Chain Saw Massacre*, a movie I'd never seen and prayed Frank hadn't, either.

"I don't want to take a bath," he said. He reached into his duster pocket. "Cigarette?"

"What?" I thought I couldn't have heard him right, but he produced a cellophane-wrapped rectangular pack with a label written in French. I was about to hit the ceiling when I noticed the word *chocolat*. "Where did you get these? I thought they stopped making candy cigarettes."

"I exchanged them for letters of transit."

"*Casablanca*," I said.

"I think this is the beginning of a beautiful friendship."

I drew one from the pack. "Here's looking at you, kid."

"We'll always have Paris." Frank looked very pleased with both of us. He shook a cigarette from the pack and arranged it between his third and fourth fingers before palming it to his face. Happiness, I'd noticed, was a facial expression that almost came naturally to him. Fear, discomfort, confusion—those made him roll down the shades and bar the door. Which said a lot for Frank, if you ask me. Say you had to pick just one emotion you could convey to others easily. I'd like to think I'd go with happiness, too.

"You know what I've always wondered?" Frank said. "Why anyone would join the French Foreign Legion. Aside from the uniform. I like those hats very much. I wish I had one. I have a fez."

"I'm not surprised."

"The fez is named after Fez, the town in Morocco that had a monopoly on its production."

"Uh-huh," I said. "Wait, I don't remember a character from the Foreign Legion in *Casablanca*."

"There isn't one. But my father is."

"Your father is in *Casablanca*?" Geez, his dad had to be about a hundred years old by now. Maybe that's why Mimi didn't like to talk about him.

"Not in the movie," Frank said. "In the French Foreign Legion."

I sat forward. "Your dad is in the French Foreign Legion?"

"I imagine he might be. Otherwise, why doesn't he visit?"

Oh. "Have you asked your mom about that?"

He exhaled a plume of imaginary smoke and nodded. "What did she say?" I asked.

"Nothing," he said. "Nada. Bupkis. Diddly. Zip. Zero. Zilch—"

"I get it, Frank," I said.

"There are a lot of words for nothingness,'" Frank said. "Love means nothing."

"That's not true."

"Yes it is. In tennis. What's your father like, Alice? Is he the gentleman you're always referencing?"

I ran my cigarette under my nose like a Havana cigar. "No. I mean, I don't know what my father's like. He's been gone since I was eight."

"Is he dead?"

I peeled the paper off my cigarette. "No. Maybe. I don't know. He's just—gone."

"Maybe he's in the Legion with my dad."

"Maybe he went out for a pack of chocolate cigarettes and never came back," I said. I wasn't up for talking about my father.

"People do that?"

"I imagine they do. Now let's get you in the tub and then into your pajamas and bed." I ate my cigarette on the way to his bathroom. Frank stood there, mesmerized, watching water cascade from the faucet. "Get undressed," I said. "I want to soak your clothes overnight so the stains won't set."

He turned his face from the water to commune with my elbow.

"What are you waiting for?" I asked.

"Some privacy," he said.

"I won't look," I said. "Come on. Hand over the clothes."

"Please," he said. "If you don't mind."

I sighed. "Fine. Wash your hair. Scrub your nails. I'll be outside if you need me."

I lay down across the doorway in the hall. He'd be okay in there by himself. As long as I could hear him splashing around I'd know he was alive. I'd have to be deaf not to hear him. It sounded like he was wrestling an alligator in that tub.

But lying down was my first mistake. The hall was carpeted, so of course I fell asleep.

I think the quiet woke me.

My first thought was that Frank had made a break for it. Stepped over me while I was snoozing, wandered through the living room door hole, jumped the wall, and now lay at the bottom of the hill in a million pieces. Bleeding. Which was a good sign, we'd learned from the paramedics earlier in the day, because bleeding people aren't dead yet.

But Frank was the kind of kid who left a trail—wet footprints, chocolate hand-tracks, scuffed walls, broken stuff. There was no sign of his passage in the hallway.

Oh, no. I yanked the bathroom door open and all but fainted on the spot.

Frank was in there all right. Fully clothed, goggles pushed on his forehead and toy submarine clutched to chest. Eyes closed, pale as death, halo of floating hair. Imagine Jules Verne, Angelic Shipwreck Victim. Angels, of course, are known for many things, one of them being that they are dead. How was I going to tell Mimi I'd let her kid drown in the tub while she lay in her hospital bed?

I fell to my knees alongside the tub. "Oh, Frank," I gasped. "Oh, no, no, no."

His eyes slitted open. "Is it morning already?" he asked sleepily.

I sat back on my heels, dizzy with relief. "You almost gave me a heart attack, Frank," I said. "I thought you were dead. What are you doing in the tub with your clothes on?"

"Sleeping. I thought it would save you work if I soaked my clothes while I soaked myself."

"Are you insane?" I regretted saying that instantly.

"No," he said. "See? I took my boots off first." He lowered his goggles over his eyes and went under. He watched my chin while I watched the water fill the goggles.

"Those aren't watertight," I said when he came up for air and pushed his goggles up his forehead.

"I know. I was just confirming earlier research."

"Listen, Frank. I'm sorry I said that you're insane."

"You didn't say I was insane. You asked. One is a statement and the other is a question. You're not the first to ask me that, either."

"Okay," I said. "You need to get out of that tub. I'm going to hold up this big towel to give you some privacy. I want you to take off those wet clothes. And leave them in the tub to keep soaking. That was a good idea, by the way. Just what I would have done, although I think I might have gotten out of them first. Then let's get you dried off and into your pj's."

" 'Let's get out of these wet clothes and into a dry martini,' " he said. "Robert Benchley."

I laughed. I was so relieved he wasn't dead that I would have laughed at anything.

"I've been waiting all my life to say that," Frank said. "Robert Benchley was a famous wag who belonged to a group of Jazz Age writers known as the Algonquin Round Table. What you may not know is that Robert Benchley's grandson Peter Benchley wrote *Jaws*. Book and screenplay."

When Frank stood it sounded like Niagara Falls as the water cascaded from his clothing. If all the grunting coming from the other side of the towel was any indication, getting out of the wet clothes was about as easy as going over those falls in a barrel. "Do you need a hand?" I asked.

"No thank you. Almost finished. Archimedes discovered the way to measure volume of irregularly-shaped items when he stepped into the bathtub, did you know that? The water level rose an amount commensurate with the volume of his body. He was so excited by his insight that he shrieked 'Eureka!' which means 'I have found it!' Then he ran through the streets naked. I have never been excited enough about anything to consider doing that."

"That makes two of us," I said.

Frank took the towel moments later and wrapped it around himself like a burka. "Now into my pajamas," he said. "Alice, could you put yours on, too? I've always wanted to host a pajama party. I've never had a friend to invite before."

I didn't want to leave Frank alone for even a minute but I wasn't about to decline that invitation. So I sprinted to my room, changed, and dashed back to the kitchen. There I found the pajamaed Frank at the breakfast bar, cocktail music oozing from the piano and two full martini glasses in front of him. Frank held one out to me.

"Thanks," I said, cradling the glass in my palm and sniffing it. Club soda.

"I asked for martini glasses for my ninth birthday," Frank said. "So my mother got me plastic ones."

"Your mother is a smart woman."

"You're supposed to hold your glass by the stem, like this, see?" Frank demonstrated. "That way the warmth of your hand won't ruin the chilly deliciousness of your cocktail."

"My hands aren't warming up anything right now. It's freezing in here."

"It's because we're missing a door."

I looked at the hole that had once been sliding glass. "We should cover that, huh? We could use blankets, or a big piece of plastic if we had one."

"Dry cleaner bags," Frank said. "I have a lot in my closet."

I knew this to be true. "We'll piece them together," I said. "You get the bags, I'll find the tape."

After ransacking the kitchen drawers—bupkis—I found packing tape in a laundry room drawer. When I emerged, Frank was on the kitchen floor swaddled in dry cleaning bags. He was indulging in a much more transparent and dangerous version of his favorite game, rolling-around-in-a-comforter.

"Stop that," I said, grabbing the plastic and rolling him free. "What are you doing?"

"Playing."

"You can't do that with a dry cleaning bag, Frank. This is not a toy. Look, it says it right here on the bag. 'This is not a toy.' You could suffocate. And we can't use these now. You've shredded them."

"I've got more."

"That's not the point," I said. "The point is, you're a smart boy, and this would be a dumb way to die. Come with me, please." I herded him to his closet to harvest more bags. "Don't touch the bags. Do you hear me? Do. Not. Touch."

"What can I do then?"

"You carry the tape. I'll get the tape measure. Meet me in the living room."

When I got there, Frank was sitting on the floor, behaving himself. I measured the hole and lay the bags on the floor so we could piece together something big enough to cover it. "Come and give me a hand with this," I said. "Please."

"I can't."

"Why not? I said please."

"Look what I've done this time," he said. I looked. The kid had manacled his hands together with the tape. The almost-empty roll dangled from his wrists like a charm on a charm bracelet.

"How'd you manage that?" I asked.

"With my teeth," he said. "It was easy at first, and then harder."

"I believe you. I'm going for more tape. Don't touch anything while I'm gone."

"I don't think I could if I wanted to."

"Good." I ran back into the laundry room and came back with a second roll of tape and a pair of round-edged children's scissors to cut Frank loose.

"Vive la France," he said when I'd freed him.

"Vive la France," I said. "Now hold the plastic still while I tape it together." When we had a sheet that was big enough I took it and stood by the door. "I'm too short," I said. "I need something to stand on."

"I know just the thing," Frank said. He disappeared for a minute and returned rolling his mother's big rubber yoga ball.

"You've got to be kidding me," I said.

"You can stand on it," he said. "I've done it. It's exciting."

"I don't want exciting, Frank. I want stable."

"Why?"

"Because I'm boring that way. Listen. Bring me that chair over there instead. Please."

Once the plastic was up, I said to Frank, "Now go to bed."

"I'm not sleepy yet. I'm cold."

"You'll warm up in bed."

"I'll warm up, but I won't go to sleep."

I thought about all the times I'd heard Frank knocking around in the middle of the night. "Okay," I said. "Let's build a fire then."

Frank's eyes lit up. "Where?"

"In the fireplace, idiot." Bad. I know. I was tired. "I'm sorry, Frank. I'm the idiot, not you."

"I know," he said. "My IQ is higher than 99.7 percent of the American public. For some reason it makes the children at school laugh when I tell them that. Can you explain the joke in that to me?"

"There isn't one. Some kids laugh at people smarter than they are to make them feel stupid."

"That doesn't make sense. Why do they think laughing at me will make me feel stupid?"

"Because they're stupid," I said.

I'd never lived anywhere that had a fireplace before, so I was more excited than an adult person ought to be to put my Girl Scout training to use arranging the logs and twigs from the alcove by the fireplace on top of wads of crumpled newspaper. "Now, matches," I said. "Where does your mother keep them?"

"I wish I knew," Frank said. "She hides them from me."

I believed that. "How about candles? I could light one on the stove and use it to start the fire."

"She hides those, too." Of course she did. I'd never seen one anywhere, ever. Not even a lousy birthday candle. "You could call her and ask," Frank said.

"Your mother is in the hospital," I said. "I'm not calling her. Let me think. You know what? We could light a twig on the stove and—"

"You cannot walk through this house carrying a stick that's on fire," Frank said. "My mother has said that to me at least a million times."

I was tempted anyway, but knew I shouldn't be modeling bad behavior for a lit firecracker like Frank. Also, without meaning me ill, it would be the first thing he'd tell his mother when he saw her again. "I guess we can't have a fire then," I said.

"I have an idea," Frank said. He disappeared down the hall. I gave chase as he beelined to the laundry room drawers where—Eureka!—he found a nine-volt battery and a roll of wire. Then he beat it back to the living room, where he took the round-tipped scissors from his bathrobe pocket—when did he palm those?— and cut a couple of pieces of wire, wrapped one around each of the batteries' terminals, and touched the loose ends against each other. The touch produced a spark that made the paper catch fire.

"You're a genius, Frank," I said. "How did you think of doing that?"

"Oh, I do it in my room all the time," he said.

We watched the flames reduce the logs to ember, then ash. I was so afraid of nodding off that I would have taped my eyelids open if there'd been any tape left. This had been the longest day of my life. How did Mimi function if all her nights were like this? How did Frank? One night alone with the kid and I was practically reduced to ash myself.

When Frank piped up with, "I'm tired now," I jumped the way mothers catapult from chairs when their toddlers say, "I need potty."

"Off to bed then," I said, giving him the bum's rush to his bedroom.

"I don't sleep much in my room. If you want me to sleep, put me in my mother's bed."

I sighed. "All right."

In Mimi's room I pinned him tight under her blankets. "Go to sleep," I said.

"You aren't leaving me, are you?"

"Do you want me to sit here until you fall asleep?" The thought of staying awake any longer made me want to cry.

"I thought we were having a pajama party. You have to sleep in here with me."

"I'm not sleeping in your mother's bed without her permission. It's not polite."

His face went blank. Blanker, I should say. Tired as I was, I hurt for him. "How about this?" I said. "I'll sleep on the couch in the family room. I'll be close enough to hear you if you want to talk. That's what makes a pajama party a pajama party, you know. Being able to talk to somebody else until you fall asleep."

"That may be so. But what you may not realize is I have a hard time falling asleep. And when I fall asleep, I wake easily. And since I slept some in the tub already—"

"Frank," I said. "I realize. Close your eyes. Close your mouth. Go to sleep."

I crept out of Mimi's bedroom, leaving the door open and a light on in the hall. I fell on the couch and was out maybe fifteen minutes, maybe fifteen days. When I opened my eyes Frank's face hovered inches above mine. I was so exhausted I couldn't muster the strength to be startled. "What's up, Frank?"

"I am," he said. "I couldn't sleep."

"I gathered. So now what?"

"We could watch a movie."

"It's too late to watch a movie. Or too early. What time is it?"

"Four A.M."

"Have you always been like this?"

"Like what?"

I tried to think of a word that wouldn't wound his psyche for keeps. "Nocturnal," is what I came up with finally.

"Nocturnal? That implies daytime sleep. I don't do that much, either. My mother says my brain's lack of an 'off' switch is a sign of unusual intelligence."

"Unusual," I said. "Uh-huh." I rubbed my eyes, sat up and yawned.

"You're tired," he said. "Go back to sleep. I'll sit here and watch you. Or I could borrow your phone to make a movie of you asleep. Like Andy Warhol. His first movie was called *Sleep*. It was about—"

"Sleep. I get the drift. No thanks. I didn't come to California to be in the movies. Let's watch *Casablanca* again."

Frank did a quick soft shoe—soft slipper, really—of joy that was so unexpectedly charming that it put me right back in the palm of his hand. He'd never spent a night away from his mother in his life, poor kid. She wasn't with him now because his hug had turned into a tackle that had landed her in the hospital with twenty-nine stitches in her scalp. You couldn't blame him for not sleeping. But you had to wonder what his excuse was every other night.

Frank slid the movie in the DVD player and the two of us rolled up in comforters, shoulder to shoulder but individually shrink-wrapped in our own little movie-watching cocoons. Frank fell asleep sometime during the mushy part, where Rick and Ilsa reminisce about the good old days in the Paris apartment when they thought Ilsa's husband was dead. I stayed awake watching all the way to the end.

PART III

In the Manner
of Apollo

August 2009

9

It had seemed six months long but July was finally over, which meant Frank was seeing his shrink every other week again. Mimi and Frank were in the two chairs available in the psychiatrist's outer office— Two chairs? Don't both parents ever come?—while I lounged against the wall, unsure whether in my role as chauffeur I should stay or wait in the car. When the doctor came to fetch Frank back into her inner sanctum, her eyes flicked to me; but Mimi didn't make a move to introduce us, so I didn't say anything, either.

Frank was done up in a three-piece glen-plaid suit, bow tie and pocket square, gold knot cuff links and watch chain strung across his vest. Very *Clarence Darrow for the Defense*. Mimi had on a turban she must have filched from Frank's closet, or maybe

Gloria Swanson's, accessorized with a pair of the gigantic black sunglasses favored by very young and very old women in Hollywood who weigh less than a hundred pounds and carry yappy dogs in their purses as ballast.

"What happened to you?" Dr. Abrams asked Mimi. Because not even those jumbo look-at-me/don't-look-at-me glasses were big enough to cover the greening bruises gravity had started to dribble down her cheekbones.

"Eye lift," Mimi said.

"Ah," Dr. Abrams said. "Well, Frank, come on in. I like your suit."

"Thank you. My mother's computer bought it for me."

"Well, your mother's computer has excellent taste. Are you starting to think about getting ready for school?"

"Did you see my cuff links? My friend Xander gave them to me. They represent the Gordian knot, which—" The door closed behind them.

"Getting ready for school? That's rich," Mimi muttered. "For a kid like Frank, hell is other children."

Either Mimi could read minds, too, or all the time I'd spent with Frank had made me slack about managing my facial expressions because Mimi took one look at me and said, "I didn't tell Dr. Abrams about the accident because it really isn't any of her business. She's not my psychiatrist. Have a seat. Read a magazine. Here's one I loved when I was your age." She handed me a copy of *Highlights for Children*, then helped herself to a travel magazine. She started snapping through its pages like somebody looking for a Jell-O coupon she was pretty sure she saw, dammit, in that issue when she read it six months ago and she meant to find it if it was the last thing she ever did. "I don't need a psychiatrist," she added.

Like a good lackey, I kept my mouth shut, busying myself solving children's puzzles, looking for the thing missing from one picture that could be found in the other if you just looked closely enough.

"That's why Xander calls me 'Jeopardy,'" Frank was telling Dr. Abrams forty-five minutes later, when the two of them emerged from the inner office.

"Because you know all the answers."

"Yes. Also because I am dangerous to be around. That's what is known as a *double entendre*, a French term meaning 'a word or phrase that can be taken two ways.' If he were referring only to the scope of my knowledge, Xander said he'd just call me 'Quiz Show.'"

"What did you and Dr. Abrams talk about?" Mimi asked Frank in the elevator.

"Buster Keaton," Frank replied. "Also Xander."

To stay out of Mimi's hair, Frank and I spent most of August revisiting the L.A. sights he'd seen in the good old days of adventures with his mother. Stir-crazy as both of us were, I was all for adventures. On one condition: I could take Frank's hand and hold it without asking first.

"Why would you need to do that?" he asked.

"I get scared," I said. It was the first thing I thought of.

"Is it the fanatics at the gate?" Every now and then as we left on an adventure, we'd encountered one or more of Mimi's faithful lying in wait outside the walls. College students, usually, or older men and women who must have been my mother's contemporaries. They carried cameras or copies of Mimi's book, and leaned down to peer at our faces as we drove out. I'm sure they were harmless, but it was a creepy business anyway. They hardly ever spoke, which was frightening enough. When they did say something, it tended to be along the lines of, "Oh, it's nobody." Never in my life have I felt more relieved to be a nobody.

"Yes, it's the fanatics," I said. I had underestimated how Mimi's fans terrified poor Frank until I dropped the gate-code Post-it one day as I leaned out the driver's-side window to punch it in. Frank saw me drop it and started howling. It took a while for him to calm down enough to explain the problem—that he was afraid a fanatic might find the code fluttering down the street and use it to breach the walls and come for us. Once I understood what was upsetting him I chased the piece of paper down, then chanted the litany of 1's and 2's and 0's under my breath all the way up the driveway and into the house. Once we were safe in the kitchen I asked the kid to quiz me on the code and when I got the sequence right three times running—21 22 00 0—I ate the Post-it note in front of him. I'd hoped that would make the kid laugh. Instead, he thanked me.

Anyway. Frank's introduction to the city's cultural hotspots was not for the faint of heart. The Los Angeles County Museum of Art and the neighboring La Brea Tar Pits led to the Museum of Contemporary Art, which segued to the Norton Simon Museum, which brought us to the Gene Autry Museum of Western Heritage, the Gettys Bel Air and Malibu, the Adamson Tile House, the Gamble House, the Jesse Lasky Hollywood Heritage Museum, the Hollywood Walk of Fame, the Petersen Museum of Automotive History. Then there was the Ahmanson, the Geffen, the Dorothy Chandler Pavilion, Disney Hall, the Hollywood Bowl, the Bradbury Building, the Greek Theater, the

Griffith Observatory, the California Science Center, the Los Angeles Museum of Natural History. Who knew so much was stuffed between the beaches and the Hollywood sign?

When I dared suggest that we, meaning I, might be getting tired, Frank exclaimed, "Poppycock!" He was done up in Teddy Roosevelt Rough Rider regalia that day for our visit to the Los Angeles County Museum of Art—cavalry uniform, pince-nez, puttees, boots. The pince-nez had lost their grip on the bridge of his nose and fallen to the ground several times already. After lunch he'd stepped on them. I held my breath, worried he'd go into a tailspin. But Frank picked the frames up, shook out the broken glass, and balanced them on his nose again. "Ah, that's better," he said. "No fingerprints. Carry on!" I did, after I'd brushed up the bits of glass into a paper napkin I'd saved in case of emergency. As I'd gotten better acquainted with Frank, I'd taken to hoarding random things in my pockets, thinking to myself as I did so, "in case of emergency." It was only a matter of time until I got my own subscription to *Accidents Waiting to Happen Weekly*.

I'd expected frank to lollygag in museum galleries, ogling every line and squiggle. Instead he dashed from room to room, doing an entire exhibition in the time it took me to consider one wall of paintings. The crazy thing about it was that he took everything in. I know this because I quizzed him. It was really kind of incredible how much the kid could assimilate in thirty seconds or less.

"What's up with you?" I asked after an early sprint. "You're going through this place like a dose of salts." I was terrified of losing him. I wanted to hold his hand every minute, but I had to catch him first.

"If I slow down, I get too close. And if I get too close, I want to touch things. That's why I can't go on school field trips unless my mother comes, too. And sometimes not even then. Museum guards don't like it when you touch things."

"I bet they don't," I said.

Mimi had warned me that Frank was like a magpie, nabbing anything that attracted his attention and making off with it. When my hairbrush vanished early on, I came out to fix breakfast looking like someone who had combed her hair with a pillow.

"Sorry about the hairdo," I said. "I can't find my brush."

"I'll order you another," she said.

"You don't have to do that."

"Frank probably took it."

"Why would he do that?"

"He's got sticky fingers. Although his psychiatrist prefers calling it 'insatiably curious.' He sees something unfamiliar and spirits it away for further examination."

"Surely he's seen a hairbrush before."

"Of course. But never your hairbrush. Put away anything you value if you want to see it again." That's when I'd decided I'd better start keeping Mr. Vargas's notebook in my purse instead of in my bedside table drawer.

"On the bright side," Mimi added, "living with Frank has forced me to be tidy."

Although, honestly, she didn't seem very cheered up by that at all.

Two weeks into our cultural odyssey I'd awakened from a bad dream brought on, I suspect, by my aching feet. In it, I'd lost Frank at the Getty Museum, Malibu. He'd been transformed into one of the spooky white-eyed black statues that people its courtyard. But which statue? I'd been rushing from one to the next, telling each stony face that endless unfunny knock-knock joke that ends with "Orange you glad I stopped saying banana?"

I didn't want to slip back into that nightmare

again, so I got out of bed and went to the kitchen for a snack.

Which is how I happened on Mimi in one of her girlish white nightgowns standing in the mirrored foyer, brandishing a big sharp knife.

You can imagine the confusion that followed.

In case you can't, it went like this: I screamed, she screamed, the knife clattered to the floor, and from somewhere down the hall, Frank started howling. Both of us rushed toward the sound, bumping into each other in our urgency to get to him. "Everything's okay, sweetheart," Mimi said as she gathered Frank into her lap. "I startled Alice, that's all. She saw me trying to cut my hair. I couldn't tolerate this mess another minute." She gestured to her half-shaved, stitched-up head.

"You were going to cut your hair with a butcher knife?" I asked incredulously. "Have you heard of scissors?"

"I couldn't find any scissors. I hide them because, you know." Mimi nodded toward Frank. "I needed to do it someplace where I could see what I was doing. I didn't want to hurt myself."

It occurred to me all over again to wonder why the knives weren't hidden, too. Or why a woman who hated to show her face in public lived in a house where even the ceiling of its entranceway was mirrored. That foyer made me crazy. There was no way to avoid seeing yourself from every angle every time you passed through it. Frank, naturally, loved it. He had some of his most satisfying conversations with himself there while examining his outfits from every angle.

"Why didn't you wait until morning?" I asked Mimi. "I would have cut it for you."

"I wanted it done already. It wasn't like I was going to make my hair look any worse."

Frank slid out of her lap.

"Where are you going?" Mimi asked.

"Bathroom," he said. That night he was sleeping in a scarlet union suit, the kind with the back flap that buttons. "Do you need help?" Mimi and I asked in unison.

"I'm not a baby anymore," he said.

After he left, Mimi and I sat there just looking at each other. "When my brother was a teenager he decided to shave with a hunting knife, like in frontier days," she said.

"How did that end up?" I asked.

"In stitches. But my father was home so he was able to sew him up in the kitchen. He was a doctor, you know."

"Yes. Frank told me."

"He did? What else did he tell you?"

"That famously parsimonious eccentric billionaire J. Paul Getty dressed in threadbare clothing so people wouldn't realize he was rich, and that he had pay phones installed in his mansions for his guests to use so he would stay that way. In 1957 Getty was quoted as saying 'A billion dollars isn't what it used to be.'"

"I was born in 1957," Mimi said. After a pause she added, "Frank's psychiatrist says it runs in families."

"Says what runs in families?"

"How Frank is. Dr. Abrams says there's a genetic element to his kind of eccentricity."

Frank chose that moment to come back from the bathroom. Both his hands were busy behind his back, probably buttoning that panel. Mimi said, "I didn't hear you flush."

"I didn't use the bathroom," he said.

"Then what were you doing?"

He brought his hands from behind his back, and held out a pair of scissors in his right hand. In his left was my kidnapped hairbrush. "Quite by accident I found these at the bottom of my laundry basket."

I'd done the laundry yesterday, and they hadn't been there then.

Mimi sighed. "Well, I guess I didn't look everywhere for those scissors after all."

10

He's here," frank said.

"Who's here?"

"Xander."

That day I'd left Frank in his Teddy Roosevelt rig on a bench outside the ladies' room at the Los Angeles County Museum of Art for probably less than a minute. We'd decided he was too old to go in with me and stand outside my stall just so I could be comforted by the sight of his puttees while I peed, so I transacted my business, washed my hands and dried them on my shorts as I rushed out the door. I was so relieved to find him where I'd left him that at first I couldn't take in what he was telling me.

"Xander?"

"XYZ," Frank said.

"Huh?"

"Examine Your Zipper. Xander. Given name, Alexander. My piano teacher. Not Alexander the Great, although there is a sculptural representation of that Alexander here as well."

I yanked up my zipper and sat beside him. "Your Xander? Where?"

"He was over there. He's gone now."

It was hard for me to believe anyone could appear and disappear so quickly, unless Xander just happened to be as fast on his feet as Frank. I have to confess I'd been doubting Frank's overall score on the truth-o-meter that day already, ever since we'd paused on our gallop long enough to examine an early Picasso together. I'd figured out by then that to slow the boy down all I had to do was ask questions. Question, really—one was usually enough to root him behind an imaginary lectern long enough for me to catch my breath. I may have mentioned that the depth and breadth of Frank's knowledge was as dazzling as it was tedious.

"What do you know about this painting?" I asked.

"Picasso executed over twenty thousand works of art during his lifetime," Frank said. "I use the word *executed* in the sense of 'creating' rather than in the cigarettes-blindfold-and-firing-squad-at-dawn sense. Most of Picasso's paintings are considered brilliant.

Some, mediocre. A few, tiresome. Take this one, for example. It used to hang over our fireplace until just before you came to stay with us. My mother got sick of looking at it so she gave it back to my father and he had so much Picasso already that he decided to give it to the museum."

"What?" I felt like I'd jerked awake in one of those snooze-inducing stadium lecture halls in college moments after the professor finished outlining the answers to every question on the final. "Your father? What are you talking about?"

"Anonymous Donor. My father doesn't like calling attention to himself." Frank held his busted-out pince-nez in front of his eyes like a lorgnette and peered at the label posted on the wall by the painting. "That's why he's listed here as 'Anonymous Donor.' He's a major collector. When he gets bored with stuff, he gives it to museums."

I couldn't get any more out of him, which was frustrating as heck, since Frank generally left no fact unturned. I'll say one thing for the kid. When he was done talking about something, he was done.

But I wasn't done with Xander yet. "Okay. If Xander's here, where is he?"

Frank shrugged. "I called his name and waved like this," he said, throwing his arms around as if he were having a seizure from the waist up. "But he was wearing a headset. I don't think he heard me."

"Why didn't you get up and go tap him on the shoulder?"

"Because I was under direct order to stay on this bench. Can we look for him now?"

"Of course. Except I don't know what Xander looks like."

"Oh, I can fix that. Follow me."

The Rough Riders would have had a hard time keeping up with Frank. A couple of guards on the other side of the esplanade called, "Hey, kid, no running!" I prayed I'd catch him before he knocked somebody over or palmed something he wasn't supposed to touch.

I caught up to him in the sculpture gallery, standing unruffled in front of an ancient statue of a young, curly-haired god some fisherman had netted in the 1920s in the Aegean Sea. One of the statue's hands was raised like a footsore New Yorker flagging a cab; the other touched his chest lightly in a not-to-brag-but-check-out-this-body kind of way. I found myself wondering if the fingers on the raised hand had broken when they snagged that fisherman's net. Maybe losing those fingers had been the price of finding his way out of the ocean again.

Frank took off his cavalry hat and dabbed his brow with one of his buckskin gloves. "Xander looks like this guy, 'In the Manner of Apollo, Greek, 300 to 100 B.C.' Except Xander isn't missing any of his fingers. His hair is blond, like yours. He isn't made out of stone. He's wearing more clothes."

Which wasn't saying much, since the statue wasn't wearing any clothes at all. Although if I were built like that, I probably wouldn't want to, either. In real life, and by that I mean life outside of Los Angeles, you might come across one or two people in a lifetime with a physique like that topped with such an exquisite face and hair that begged you to run your fingers through it, assuming you still had fingers. In L.A., of course, guys like that worked as busboys in family restaurants and manned the checkout counter at health food stores. I have to admit, though, looking at that statue made me want to meet this Xander all over again.

"Let's go," Frank said.

"Wait. I'm still looking."

What intrigued me was that the statue's chiseled face and upraised arm were pitted and dark compared to the unblemished marble of everything else. What happened to you? I wondered as I leaned closer to read his display card. What happened was this: After In-the-Manner-of-Apollo sank to the ocean floor, the tides gradually covered his nakedness in a blanket of sand so that only his face and arm were exposed to the friction of currents and nibbling undersea creatures. The price of his salvation, it seemed, was centuries of that face and hand being worn down by the elements.

I got this crazy rush of longing then for my life back in Manhattan. I missed the unpredictable cocktail of people everywhere you looked. Missed flushing pink and looking away quickly when one of those insanely gorgeous guys I'd sit across from on the subway sometimes caught me staring. I even longed for the earnest, geeky boys who worked at the computer store and stuttered when I said hello and sometimes brought me lunch, a cold slice they'd saved from their pizza the night before. I wanted to see Mr. Vargas, who always had something nice to say or a silly joke for me and had stepped into the hole my father kicked open when he left. In that glass box on the hilltop with Mimi and Frank, I'd gotten lonesome for the everyday friction of ordinary life.

Without thinking, I let go of the vise grip I had on Frank's wrist and reached out to touch the broken stumps of In-the-Manner-of-Apollo's fingers. I probably would have gotten busted for it if Frank hadn't chosen that moment to crash to the floor at my feet.

I knelt over him. "Frank?" I said, my hand hovering over his shoulder. His eyes were closed, but not that squeezed-shut closed of a kid who's faking. His face was smooth and stony. If his cheeks hadn't been so pink, he would have looked dead.

"Is he all right?" the guard asked, looking at my crumpled pile of boy. "Do you need an ambulance? Does he have epilepsy? My cousin Rick had epilepsy. When we were kids he would fall over like that, boom, right in the middle of a kickball game." The guard was old enough to be my father and had a sincere face that was as worn and pitted as In-the-Manner-of-Apollo, but not nearly as pretty.

"I've never understood the allure of kickball, although polo has always appealed to me. Will Rogers had a string of polo ponies and a playing field on his Malibu estate, where games are played to this day," Frank said. He rolled onto his back and opened one eye to look at me. "I was leaning."

I sat back on my heels. "What do you mean, 'I was leaning'?"

"I was imagining the statue tipping over the side of a boat in a storm. Because otherwise how did he end up at the bottom of the Aegean Sea? He's made of marble. He can't swim much better than I can."

I grabbed Frank by the scruff of his cavalry uniform and hauled him to his feet. "Don't do that, Frank. It worries people. What's wrong with you?"

"The jury's still out on that one," Frank said.

I hid my exasperation by dusting him off and retrieving his hat, touching both him and it without bothering to ask permission. I think Frank decided to roll with it because even he could tell I was irate. I thanked everything holy that we were in Los Angeles rather than New York, which meant the gallery was empty aside from the three of us.

"Don't be so hard on him, Mama," the guard said. "Boys just don't think, right, pal?" He gave Frank a conspiratorial poke. Me touching the kid without his okay was one thing, but I couldn't imagine what would happen when a stranger broke The Second Rule of Frank. I braced myself for whatever massive wigout lay ahead. The plank, the hair snatch, or a full-on headbanging extravaganza?

But as I had explained to Frank, nobody can foretell the future, particularly not me. The Student of All Fabrics in Frank was so fascinated with the guard's jacket that he hadn't seemed to notice the poke. "What kind of fabric is that?" Frank asked.

"Washable," the guard answered.

"May I?" Frank asked, pointing at the guard's sleeve. I opened my mouth to remind him not to point, but I figured that in this instance pointing was better than touching the guy without asking. Or pressing his cheek against the man's lapels, the way he did with me.

"Knock yourself out," the guard said.

Frank fingered the fabric. "Hmmm," he said. "The texture is interesting. Rough. Scratchy. Stiff. Is it flammable?"

The guard guffawed. "A hundred percent polyester, so yeah, I'm thinking it would probably go up like a Roman candle on the Fourth of July."

"I had the misfortune of sleeping through the July Fourth display this year," Frank said, "so I suggested we purchase a few Roman candles for home use. I refer to the delayed ignition fireworks, of course, not the beeswax-dipped papyrus wicks the Romans invented as portable sources of illumination. 'Not in this lifetime,' my mother said."

"Mom's probably right about the fireworks," the guard said. "Better leave that to professionals. Those things are dangerous to play with. Even for a smart kid like you."

"My mother says I have a very large brain, which is, however, not always a corollary of genius. Einstein left his brain to science. It wasn't any bigger than average but did feature an unusual number of grooves and fissures. That suggests an abundance of connections and agility of thinking not common in the general public."

"Let's go, Frank." I wanted to leave before he launched a lecture on brain anatomy. "Thanks for your help," I said to the guard.

"You're welcome," the guard said. "Have a wonderful day."

"Thank you," Frank said. "We will."

"Nice kid, Mom," the guard said. "Smart. Polite. You need to fill the house up with more like him. You need to fill up the world."

I surprised myself by getting choked up by that. All I could do was nod and smile and hustle Frank out of there, making sure this time to keep a tight hold on his wrist. When we were out of earshot Frank said, "What a nice gentleman. Do you think that guard is a good painter?"

"Huh? What makes you think he's a painter?"

"Someone needs to use his nailbrush more diligently. And turpentine. Gasoline might work, too. Oil paint is notoriously difficult to remove."

If you never looked a person in the eyes, I guess it made okay sense to look them in the cuticles. "Maybe he paints houses," I said.

"Roy G. Biv," Frank said.

"Roy Who?"

"Red, orange, yellow, green, blue, indigo, violet. Roy G. Biv. It's a mnemonic for recalling the colors in the visual spectrum."

"Oh, *that* Roy G. Biv. Remember, Frank, I studied art in college."

"How could I remember something I never knew? As I was saying, a house painter wouldn't have that many different colors under his nails. Either he's an artist or he goes up to the paintings in his galleries when nobody's looking and gives them a good scratch." Frank pondered his own fingernails. "I would like to try that sometime."

"Don't," I said, a little more forcefully than I meant to. I was tired. I needed a day off. I hadn't had one since I'd gotten there.

Mimi, of course, hadn't had a day off since Frank was born.

"Why did the guard keep calling you 'Mom'?" Frank asked on our way out of the museum.

"I guess he thought I was your mother."

"Why do people keep assuming that?"

"Because I'm lucky?"

"Probably," he said. "My mother always tells me before I go to sleep that she's lucky to be my mom."

The next time I dreamed of statues, In-the-Manner-of-Apollo was bent over my bed, evidently surprised to find me there. The full moon was shining through my open curtains, and in its silvery light his skin wasn't pitted and worn at all. It was like alabaster. I couldn't resist reaching up and laying my hand against his cheek. He put his hand on top of mine and curled his fingers around my fingers. "Who are you?" he asked. "And what are you doing in my bed?"

"Keeping it warm," I said. When I said the word "warm" I awakened to the fact that the cheek my palm lay on was neither cold nor the least bit stony, and the hand that grasped mine had all its fingers intact.

That's how I came to meet Xander.

11

Y ou're wearing a skirt," Frank said the next morning as I put a plate of French toast in front of him. "Why are you so dressed up?"

"I could ask you the same thing," I said.

"But I'm not wearing a skirt," he said. It was true enough. He'd suited up that morning in a severe charcoal pinstripe number, complete with pocket square, wing tips, and a monocle on a chain threaded through the buttonhole of his vest. I sat across the table, fighting the urge to tell Half-Pint E. F. Hutton what, exactly, I felt I could bring to his corporation and where I saw myself five years hence, in 1934.

"No," I said, "but it looks like you've made a special effort to look nice for the first day of school."

"That's today?"

"Did you forget?"

"No. Although I tried my best to."

"Well, I put on a skirt because I wanted to make a good impression on your teacher," I said.

"Do you have to take me to school?"

"Kids have to go to school if they want their mothers to stay out of jail."

"You're not my mother. I'd rather have my mother take me to school today."

"Of course you would."

"Or Xander."

I felt my face get hot so I opened the refrigerator door and shuffled around the cartons of milk and orange juice. "Xander?" I hadn't seen any sign of him this morning—no unfamiliar car in the driveway, no blanket-bundled form sleeping on the couch—so I was starting to wonder if I'd only dreamed last night's encounter. In which case I'd gotten up half an hour earlier than usual to put on a skirt and eyeliner for no good reason. Frank, not being one for eye contact, hadn't noticed the eyeliner.

"Xander is my sometime piano instructor and itinerant male role model. The one I saw and you didn't at the museum. Remember?"

"In-the-Manner-of-Apollo. Of course I remember," I said. "If it's any comfort, your mother is coming to school with us."

"It is an enormous comfort. Just as it would probably be an enormous comfort to her to have me with her right now to select her outfit." Frank jumped from his chair, knocking it over backward again and sweeping his plate to the floor. This time I didn't chase down the hallway to drag him back. I stayed behind to clean up his mess.

They sat in the back for the drive, clutching hands. Glancing at the two of them in the mirror made me so nervous I worried I'd drive the car over the edge of one of the steep hillside switchbacks that make the Bel Air views so spectacularly gorgeous and driving there so spectacularly terrifying.

It was hard to resist the urge to look. Mimi had on the kind of outfit you'd expect Audrey Hepburn as Holly Golightly to wear to cocktails or maybe a funeral: little black dress, big black sunglasses, white gloves, pearls. In place of the chignon she didn't have the hair for anymore, she wore black fabric wrapped tightly around her head. While I couldn't remember what my mother had worn on the first day of my fourth grade year, I'm pretty sure it didn't look anything like that.

"What's that on your mother's head?" I asked Frank before we set out, when Mimi skittered back to her room to fetch her cell phone.

"A stylish head wrap I made by cutting up one of her ex-husband's black T-shirts," Frank said.

"You're kidding," I said. "She has his T-shirts? She hasn't seen him in twenty years at least."

"It's quite possible she saw him last week."

"Last week? Where was I when all this was going on?"

"Sleeping, probably."

"He came in the middle of the night?" Which, it struck me, was when Xander had put in his appearance. Maybe it wasn't Frank I'd heard out there stumbling around every night since I'd arrived.

"My mother's ex-husband was an actor in the moving pictures," Frank said. "I noticed one of his films showing on the classic movie channel last week, Tuesday night at three A.M. and again Thursday at twelve A.M. It's possible she saw him there though I don't think she really likes bumping into him even on the classic movie channel. That's why we only have the one television set. To minimize such chance meetings. Also why she told him he had to stop coming to our house."

As noted, I'd started tuning out during some of Frank's long-winded harangues, but now he had a hundred and ten percent of my attention. "Her ex-husband kept coming to your house after they divorced?" I asked. I tried to remember what the guy looked like. Like Frank, maybe, a little? But I couldn't call up his face or for that matter his name. Only the torso. "How long did that go on?"

"For years."

"So, wait, have you met him?"

"Not in real life, though I'd like to. Reviewers of my mother's ex-husband's oeuvre say his smolder and physical presence were genuinely Oscar-worthy and that when he opened his mouth his acting was on par with Pinocchio's. Quite a compliment in my book, since *Pinocchio*, the eponymous Academy Award-winning film released in 1940 by the Walt Disney Studios, is one of my favorite animated movies."

"That is quite a compliment," I said.

"I'll say. I wonder what's keeping my mother? If we're too late setting out for school, there isn't any point in going at all."

"Hold on. I don't understand. Why did her ex-husband keep coming back?"

"For the T-shirts."

"You lost me."

"No, I didn't. You're standing right in front of me."

I sighed. "Yes, Frank, I know. But the T-shirts. I don't understand why your mother's ex-husband kept coming back for them."

"Oh," Frank said. "When he was a movie star, my mother's ex-husband didn't wear shirts much. But when he did he was famous for wearing tight black T-shirts. In fact, he got his actor name out of the collar of a shirt he was wearing."

"His actor name? What was his real name?"

"Milton Fuller, but his friends called him Milt. Or, if they were pals from his Muscle Beach days, Milt the Built. Even though that sobriquet was well earned, you can see why as a serious actor he opted to change it to Hanes Fuller. Changing one's name was a common practice among entertainers in the olden days. Fred Astaire's original moniker was Frederick Austerlitz and his friend Benjamin Kubelsky was known to the world as Jack Benny. Why Hanes aka Milt would go to the trouble of changing his name but then go out in public in a shirt meant to be worn as underwear is baffling to me." Frank grimaced at his shoelaces, which were, of course, untied.

I knelt down and double-knotted the laces for him. "Can't be tripping on these bad boys on the playground," I said. "So why are his shirts still here?"

"Once Hanes aka Milt became famous and the story about how he selected his actor name got out, the underwear company that provided him with his inspiration sent him boxes of their shirts gratis. After he wasn't such a big movie star my mother suspected the underwear company wasn't mailing them anymore, but that Hanes aka Milt was. My mother started marking the boxes 'return to sender' and told him not to come over ever again. Even though there were about a hundred shirts in boxes here he'd opened and forgot. In this context, my mother accompanies the word *forgot* with this gesture." He made air quotes with his fingers. "Under normal circumstances my mother would have thrown something like that out, but as you can see, they're very handy to have around. I like to use them for polishing silver. I wish we had a goat."

"A goat?"

"If we had a goat we could strain its milk through his T-shirts and make ricotta cheese. My mother and I could sell it at the farmer's market. To make money."

"Sell what at the farmer's market to make money?" Mimi asked. She was standing in the doorway by then, looking distressed.

"Goat cheese. You and I could man the booth together, although of course neither one of us is technically a man. We would need aprons. The long white kind, like waiters wear in restaurants in France."

I could just see it. I could also see that Mimi was working herself into a state. "What's wrong?" I asked.

"I can't find my cell phone."

"I've got my cell phone," I said.

"I can't leave the house without my cell phone," she said. "I need it."

"Oh, well. If we can't leave the house it follows that I'll have to stay home from school today," Frank said.

"Should I call your phone?" I asked.

"Yes," Mimi said.

I called her cell and within moments we heard a tinny, muffled Cab Calloway singing "hi-de-hi-de-hi-de-ho" from the neighborhood of Frank's pocket square.

"I think your phone is in Frank's pocket," I said.

Frank fished it out. "Ah, yes. I changed your ringtone, Mommie. It was on a default setting so if you happened to be in a crowded room when it rang you might not recognize it as yours. Now you won't have that problem. Are you glad I changed it?"

"Of course I'm glad, Monkey," Mimi said, though she didn't look it.

"But you're making the angry face," he persisted. "Are you angry with me?"

"What angry face?" Mimi asked.

"Dr. Abrams has a chart in her office. We've been using it to prepare me for the resumption of school. The oval that looks like this"—Frank lowered his eyebrows and pressed his lips into a thin, straight line—"is the 'angry' face. If you raise one eyebrow on the angry face like this"—he demonstrated—"you're 'skeptical.' 'Pleased' looks like this." He relaxed his eyebrows, crinkled his eyes, and shaped his mouth into a smile. "I thought the whole exercise tedious until Dr. Abrams pointed out that the greats of the silent era were masters of these subtleties of facial expression."

"Is that why you were talking about Buster Keaton?" Mimi asked.

"Yes. I countered by saying that Keaton was known as The Great Stone Face for his ability to convey so much with so little facial movement. To which Dr. Abrams replied that while Keaton was a genius most elementary school students are not, so for my own sake I'd better learn how to be more overt in expressing what I am feeling. What you're doing now," Frank told his mother, tipping his head to one side as she had, "turns 'pleased' into 'tender.'"

Mimi wrapped her arms around Frank and kissed the top of his head. Ah, Mimi. So what if she didn't like me? Every bit of affection she had she channeled to Frank, who needed it more than I did. Particularly today. After she'd wrangled Frank to bed Mimi must have been awake all night worrying about what would happen to him at school. She had to be exhausted. That explained a lot, I decided. Mimi was exhausted. Not mean.

Mimi lay her cheek on the top of Frank's head and caught me considering the two of them. "What are you looking at?" she snapped. Correction: exhausted and mean.

"I don't belong here," Frank said when we got to his school.

"Of course you do," Mimi said with a conviction I had to wonder if she felt. "You'll be fine. I'm going in there with you, so there's nothing to worry about. Now that you're in the fourth grade, no excuse for throwing things, okay? No head banging or pulling out your hair. Please. No matter how upset you get."

We all got out of the car in the parking lot behind the playground. Frank looked my skirt in the eye and said, "You heard her. My mother will walk me to class. You stay here."

"Oh. All right." I'll admit I was disappointed. I'd been looking forward to meeting his teacher. Teachers always liked me. Once a teacher's pet, always a teacher's pet.

"Don't just stand there staring at us," he said. "Get back in the car."

I felt my face get hot.

"That's not nice, Frank," Mimi said. "Alice is your friend. Is that how you treat your friends?" I managed to keep from laughing at the shock of having Mimi defend me.

"Alice is staff," Frank said. So much for my status as his friend and first pajama party invitee.

"It's fine," I said. "Don't worry about me. I'll wait in the car."

I watched them walk away in the rearview mirror. They were easy to track, since they were the only pair on the playground dressed like they were going for drinks at the Algonquin after a funeral.

Mimi was gone for almost an hour.

There was an awkward moment when she opened the back door of the station wagon, then closed it and got in the front with me. "I'm so used to riding in the backseat of taxis," she said. "I've almost forgotten what it's like to sit up here. I really ought to drive more."

"Do you want to drive now?" I asked.

"No." She looked out the window. "Did you see how alike they all are?"

"Who? The kids?"

"The mothers. They're all so perky and inter-changeable. 'Isn't it a beautiful day?' Please. Every day here is a beautiful day. I guess they didn't move here because they're geniuses. If you ask me, I think every small town mean girl in America who's pretty but not much else comes out here to die. Which they start to do the minute they realize there are a million girls already here who look just like them but have more talent. Even the ones who don't even pretend to be actresses think they'll show you what good actresses they are anyway by pretending they aren't bitter. The ones who smile like lunatics and wear yoga pants all day are the worst. At PTA meetings they're like those chickens that have to wear tiny eyeglasses in poultry barns so they won't peck each other's eyes out."

Yikes. Still, it was the most Mimi had said to me at once and I'd been trying to engage her in conversation since day one. So I ran with it. "You go to PTA meetings?" It was hard to imagine M. M. Banning sitting on a folding chair, accepting a handout on peanut allergies from the person on her right and passing the pile along to the person on her left.

"Not anymore."

"So," I persisted, determined to keep her talking. "How did it go in Frank's classroom?"

"The fourth graders are proud of being big kids, so I was the only mother in the classroom. But Frank gets so anxious." Mimi seemed pretty anxious herself. She kept looking out the window, as if she was afraid some perky mother might jump from behind a hedge to peck our eyes out.

"He's getting pretty big himself," I said.

"You say that like it's a good thing."

"Isn't it?"

"Not for someone like Frank. Kids like him have their charm when they're little. But they grow up, the magic wears off, and they're just bigger and lonelier and living in their mother's basement. If their mother still has a basement for the kid to live in."

"Frank will be fine," I said.

"You need to stop talking now."

So much for Mimi opening up.

School was three miles away as the crow flies, but the crow didn't have to deal with rush-hour traffic. We pulled into the gate half an hour later.

"Be prepared to pick up Frank later today," Mimi said before she got out of the car.

"Of course," I said.

"I gave them your cell phone number."

"Okay. The school day ends at two-fifty-six, right?"

"Something like that." Mimi slipped off the heels Frank had selected for her, tucked her gloves inside them, and walked into the house in her stocking feet, shoes in one hand, unwrapping her T-shirt headdress with the other as she went.

I'd harbored this fantasy that Mimi and I would really get down to work together now that Frank was tucked away in school. But the way she banged her office door shut just as I reached it made me think maybe not. I stood there for a few minutes, wondering if I should knock anyway so I could assure Mr. Vargas I was doing everything I could to keep the whole writing process moving. I took a breath to steel myself, then another and another. Just as I raised my knuckles, Mimi yanked the door open and said, "Why are you still here? I can hear you breathing. Are you waiting to be invited in? Then let me spell it out for you. You are not welcome in this office, ever. You're bothering me. Go away." Slam. Then I heard the tumble of typewriter keys.

Fine, I remember thinking. I will never knock another unscheduled knock on that door. Not if I could help it. Not even if the house were on fire.

A superstitious person might say I brought that down on us just by thinking it.

Back in my bedroom I washed my hands and held a damp cloth over my face and counted to a hundred. After that I changed into a pair of shorts, slipped my cell phone into my pocket, and headed for Frank's closet. He'd gone through a major growth spurt lately and I'd been eager to purge clothing he shouldn't wear in polite company anymore. Which had been out of the question while Frank was in the house.

I should note here that Frank's bedroom was surprisingly austere for a little boy who dressed like a

Savile Row version of the Artist Formerly Known as Prince. White walls. A simple bed and nightstand that wouldn't have been out of place in a monk's cell, with a studio portrait of Buster Keaton hanging over the headboard where the crucifix would be. A desk furnished with a battered dictionary and Dr. Frank's copy of *The Merck Manual*, circa 1917. The windup clocks, out of sync again and staying that way.

Frank's closet was more what you'd expect. It was outfitted with a dazzling array of built-ins, all stuffed to capacity: cupboards and shoe racks and shelves with cubbies for hatboxes and a dressing table with a mirror that had folding panels you could adjust to check your side and rear views. The cupboards were fitted with little brass rings in the drawer fronts that flipped out to pull open. It was the kind of hardware used in the outfitting of yachts, Frank had explained, since a random wave could fling an unsuspecting yachtsman against a plain old outie knob and thus mar the smooth perfection of his yachtsman tan. Also a nice feature for a young man in a thrashing rage unable to find the cummerbund he'd had his heart set on wearing that day. Another excellent platform for the tantrum-tossed was the Oriental runner on the floor, a thick, soft rug that was the only nice one in the house, really. In place of a porthole a skylight spilled natural light into the closet, a key feature when distinguishing navy socks from black from charcoal.

But all that sunshine spilling in, plus Frank's enthusiasm for heavy jackets, long sleeves, and woolens made the place a hot box. After twenty minutes I would have traded all that closet's fabulousness for my pathetic window opening onto the airshaft back home in Bushwick. I needed water.

Mimi had stopped typing, so I stood at the kitchen sink, wondering what she was up to. Reading her manuscript and making notes? Napping? Wishing she could enjoy having her house all to herself now that Frank was in school but knowing she couldn't leave the office without bumping into me?

As I rinsed out my empty glass it struck me that something was different about the yard. No station wagon. I checked the front door for the keys. Also MIA. Mimi was driving again? How about that. Good for her. I hoped she had a valid driver's license.

There was a time—yesterday, for example—when I might have been tempted to dash into her office and give it a quick vacuum and dust, with a heaping side of snooping. But after the way she snapped at me for breathing outside her office door, no thank you. Imagining the look on Mimi's face if she reappeared while I was pretending to straighten up the pages of her manuscript—I pictured something steps beyond "skeptical"—sent me scuttling back to Frank's closet.

I was so in the purging zone that I yelped when a coyote howled from what sounded like its nest in my hip pocket. It took me a minute to realize it was my cell phone. Frank must have changed its default ring so I'd recognize it as mine in a crowded room. Like, for example, a room crowded with all his clothing, and me.

The call was from Frank's school.

"This is Paula in the office," a scratchy, friendly-sounding voice on the other end said. "You need to come and pick Frank up."

"What's going on?" I asked.

"His teacher says he's disrupting class. Wait. What? Stop crying, honey, and use your words." She hung up abruptly. Was she talking to Frank? Was he hurt? Had he hurt another kid? Set a vexing math textbook on fire with sunlight and his monocle? Anything was possible.

I scooped up the pile of too-small clothing I'd winnowed from Frank's wardrobe, ran to my room, and stuffed it under my bed. In the hallway I could hear Mimi's typewriter clacking away again, which meant the car was back. I checked my watch. Eleven-thirty. I slapped a sandwich together and wrote a note that said, *Picking up Frank a little early.* I sped Mimi's lunch tray

to her office door where I slid the note under the door
and left without knocking.

I was at school by eleven-forty. I must have looked
pretty wild-eyed when I got there, because the first
thing the woman behind the desk said when I lurched
into the office was, "Calm down. It's not a bad break.
We've got her arm iced down and splinted with a vo-
cabulary workbook and an Ace bandage. That should
hold her until she gets to the emergency room."

"She who? He broke somebody's arm?"

"Who are we talking about here? Aren't you Fiona's
mother?"

"I'm nobody's mother," I said. "I'm here to pick up
Frank Banning."

"Oh. I thought you might be the new third-grader's
mom."

Again? I was twenty-four years old. Twenty-four.
Did I really look old enough to be the mother of a kid
more than halfway out of grade school? Oh, wait. This
was Hollywood. So, yes.

The office lady was still talking. "Tough start at a
new school, getting her arm broken the first day."

"Frank broke a third-grader's arm?"

"Fiona was pretending she was an astronaut and
jumped off a swing. You'd think she'd be old enough to
know better. Frank had nothing to do with it. But that

boy, bless his heart, is the best argument for life insurance I ever met. Are you Alice?"

I recognized Paula's scratchy voice then. "Yes. And you must be Paula. Is Frank okay?"

"Oh, honey, did I not tell you that? When I call I usually say that right after 'hello. I'm calling from school, blah blah isn't hurt.' I'm so sorry. Fiona came in with her arm at a crazy angle right as I was dialing you and it threw me off my game. You have to pick Frank up at Room Five. Sign him out here first." Paula handed me a pen. She had a big smile and glasses and fluffy caramel hair and was wearing a macaroni necklace like the ones my kindergarten students made me.

"Can you tell me what happened?" I asked.

"Not exactly. Nothing bad, I know. Some days are just harder than others for Frank. You tell him I'll miss him at lunchtime. He sits right here at my desk with me every day and we eat together. I love him to death."

I'd wondered how Frank made it through the days at school. Now I had a much better idea.

I guess I was meeting Frank's teacher the first day of school after all.

I found Frank on his back across the doorway just inside Room Five, looking like a cross between a pinstriped doormat and a felled statue of a deposed

Communist dictator. "Oh, hello," his teacher said. "I'm Miss Peppe. You must be Alice."

We stood just outside the classroom so we could talk while she kept one eye on the children inside. "We were worried you wouldn't get here before lunch," she said.

"What happened?"

"His circuits overloaded. His third grade teacher warned me this would happen. When Frank gets overwhelmed, he jumps out of his seat and heads for the exit. I think he wants to keep running, but being out in the open makes him more anxious than being in here. So he lies down across the doorway and goes stiff. Then the children can't get out. They don't like stepping over him."

"I can't blame them." I went and crouched alongside Frank. His eyes were closed and he looked remarkably serene. "Frank," I said. "What are you doing?"

"I was on my way to the gentleman's room when quite by accident I ended up here. I suspect myself of having fallen asleep, as we were doing mathematics at the time. If my mother should ask, Alice, please tell her the only thing I threw today was my body onto the floor."

"Get up, Frank," I said. "Right this minute."

"No thank you please," Frank said. He opened his eyes. "I see you changed your mind about the skirt," he added, and closed them again.

"You have to move him," Miss Peppe told me. "We aren't allowed. His mother is so small, I don't know how she manages it. She said she'd tell you that you might have to come pick him up before the day was out."

I replayed the morning in my head and realized that Mimi had said that very thing. I knelt beside Frank again. "To pick you up, Frank, I'm going to have to put both my hands on you," I said.

"That will be all right," he said. "Until you master the art of levitation."

By the time I got to the car, mastering the art of levitation seemed like a great idea. Carrying a fourth grader impersonating a statue is like trying to get an armload of two-by-fours from the checkout counter at Home Depot to a parking spot in the farthest corner of the lot without using one of those orange metal carts. My arms were shaking when I put Frank down to unlock the car. Frank brushed off his jacket, hopped into the backseat, and strapped himself in as if it was just the end of another of our adventures.

"Thanks for all the help, Frank," I said.

"You're welcome," he said. He held his monocle to his right eye socket and regarded me through it. "You're sweating."

"It's hot," I said. "And you're heavy."

"Not according to the charts at my pediatrician's office, where I rank somewhere in the fiftieth percentile for weight among boys in my age group. That places me firmly in the 'average' category."

When I didn't respond, Frank added, "If the warm weather inspires you to change clothes again today, consider the Bedouins. They dress in flowing black robes to maximize air circulation on their skin. The heat absorbed by the fabric rises, taking body heat with it. That's why I opt for dark suits even in the warmest weather."

"Thanks for the advice," I said. "So if your suit was keeping you so cool and comfy, why didn't you walk across the playground yourself?"

"Because you were carrying me."

"I don't want to go home yet," Frank said when we turned into his street. I peered through the windshield to see if any of Mimi's stalkers were huddled by her gate. It hadn't happened often, but it had happened.

The point is, whenever we came home to a lurker I'd drive on past, park at the end of the block, and let Frank play with my cell phone until the poor slobs got bored with the vigil and left. This time, however, I didn't see anyone waiting.

"Why?" I asked.

"I'd rather my mother didn't know I left school early."

I pulled over and turned around to look at him. "Do you think she'll be angry?"

He shrugged. "She worries. Her worried face scares me more than her angry face."

I could understand that, though I was surprised he did. "What do you want to do instead?" I asked.

"Let's find a playground."

"I thought you hated playgrounds."

"I love playgrounds except for the times when I hate them. The times I hate them are summertime, during the school year after three P.M., and on weekends."

"Too many kids?"

"Too many big kids."

"Fair enough," I said, and hung a U-turn. This was the kind of adventure I'd been waiting for. Museums are fine in moderation and I've had some refreshing naps at the opera, but I was kind of desperate to see for myself how Frank interacted with other children. Even if it was just the pre-K brigade.

"You hungry?" I asked after we got out of the car and walked past a hot dog cart at the edge of the parking lot on our way to the sandpit.

"Not really."

It was getting close to lunchtime, so I bought each of us a hot dog anyway. We sat on a bench together while Frank wolfed down both his and mine. Then he bounded up and began circling the field of play, clockwise, monocle gripped in his right eye socket and hands clasped behind his back. He peered at the sky and muttered about the Kaiser, not the sandwich roll I'm guessing, while platoons of sweet, pudgy babies got pushed in those little swings that look like inverted leather biplane helmets and legions of toddlers dug tiny ramparts in the sand.

By the time we left the playground it was evident Frank had marshaled a successful campaign inside his head against the forces of evil, armed only with hope, pluck, and the ragtag playground troops circumstance had dealt him. Also, I saw that his preferred mode of interacting with other children was not interacting with them at all. The little kids, the ones who weren't too busy hitting each other on the head with plastic shovels to notice Frank, were thrilled to have such a colossus walking among them. That the colossus wasn't about to get down in the sand and play with them didn't diminish their excitement in the least.

Back home, frank made a mad dash for his bedroom and slammed the door. Like mother, like son.

I stood listening to the faint fusillade of Mimi's type-writer keys sounding in the distance, enjoying a sweet-scented breeze rearranging the wisps of hair around my face.

Then it struck me that the breeze meant one of the flattened-out cardboard delivery boxes I'd taped over the door hole when the dry cleaner plastic tore must have slipped loose. I hadn't quite gotten around to finding workmen to fix that door. Frank and I had driven to the nearest Home Depot a week or so ago to ask for recommendations and pick up some supplies. But when I pulled into the lot, the station wagon was besieged by a scrum of out-of-work day laborers who elbowed each other aside and pressed their desperate faces against the car windows, shouting you need help lady you need help you need help in half a dozen differ-ent accents. Frank started screaming and we'd had to beat it out of there fast.

I hung up the car keys and went to the living room to retape the cardboard. But it had all been taken down and folded in a neat pile. The door hole was framed out in raw wood and a brand-new set of sliding doors leaned against the living room wall.

I stood in the framed-out doorway. In the yard, bent over two-by-fours laid across sawhorses, his back to me, a man in a tight black T-shirt was going at the lumber with a handsaw. Old school. I was so mesmerized by the ticktock rhythm of his arm going up and back, up and back, that I didn't hear Frank coming.

"There he is," Frank said.

"There's who?" I asked. "Don't tell me that's Hanes."

"I won't," he said. "Because it isn't." He ran across the yard and grabbed the guy by the biceps and pressed his face against his shoulder blade. Black Shirt lay the saw across the two-by-fours, turned around and swept Frank up as if he still weighed no more than a toddler. Frank's face went pink and he giggled wildly. I'd never seen him laugh like that.

Xander set the kid on his feet again and looked at me. "Long time no see," he said and smiled in a way that made me feel noticed for the first time since I'd come to California.

Frank ran across the grass, grabbed my hand and dragged me forward. "Inside the Hanes T-shirt you will find Xander." It dawned on me then that Xander, Frank's sometime piano instructor and itinerant male role model, must also be Mimi's Mr. Fix-it who did things around the house whenever he was in town.

"Xander was wearing an Egyptian cotton shirt with French cuffs and a spread collar this morning," Frank continued, "but we decided for his trip to the lumber yard and subsequent carpentry, a T-shirt would be more appropriate. As you know, we have many boxes on hand."

Ah. Then it was Xander who took the car, not Mimi. Now I remembered I'd noticed the faint tang of milled lumber in the station wagon when I'd gone to rescue Frank. In my panic I'd mistaken it for the smell of my own desperation. Thank god I hadn't decided to investigate Mimi's office.

"Who's your girlfriend?" Xander asked Frank.

"Alice is not my girlfriend," Frank said. "She's way too old and bony."

"I don't know," Xander said. "She looks pretty good to me."

12

ho is this Xander, Xactly? Mr. Vargas texted. I
W worried for his editorial dignity if he ever discovered emoticons.

Xander Devlin, I typed back. *Julliard graduate and
general handyman. Seems harmless.* After I pressed
"send," I deleted our exchange. I was paranoid about
leaving even the most innocent back-and-forth there
ever since Frank had coyoted my phone.

It was Saturday and I was in the kitchen making
lunch while Frank and Xander played a game in the
living room with Mimi. The game was called "Frank,
Xander, or Piano." It was a sort of combination of
pin-the-tail-on-the-donkey and name-that-tune, in
which Frank and Xander sat on the piano bench while
Mimi, on the couch and blindfolded with one of the

ubiquitous black T-shirts, listened to a few bars of a song. When it stopped, Mimi had five seconds to name the player manipulating the piano's keys. Frank was the official timekeeper, which meant he got to shout "TICK-TICK-TICK-TICK-TICK-TIME'S UP!" like the world's happiest time bomb.

You might think this an easy game, since one of the players was a Julliard graduate, one a computerized piano, and one a nine-year-old boy, but Xander had come up with a way to mix up the material—some ragtime, a little classical, and a few choruses of "Row, Row, Row Your Boat" that kept Mimi guessing, or pretending to guess. I could hear her laughing, as well as Frank's monotone "ha-ha-ha-ha-ha." I had never managed to make Frank or Mimi laugh like that.

Not only was Xander more fun to be with than I was and worked a black T-shirt way better; he'd replaced the shattered sliding glass doors in three days using only the most primitive of tools. When I asked why he didn't use an electric saw to cut the two-by-fours, he'd given me one of those cripplingly gorgeous Jay Gatsby smiles of his and said, "An electric saw? Around Frank?" He'd also snaked every drain in the house, vacuumed lint from the dryer engine and dust from the refrigerator coils, and changed all the fluids in the station wagon. When he wasn't doing something

useful, Xander played the piano with the joyful abandon of a golden retriever fetching an old tennis ball.

What's his story? Mr. Vargas asked.

He just shows up from time to time, says Frank.

Why?

*Started as Frank's piano teacher. Now mostly fixes
things. Far as I can tell.*

Did Mimi send for him?

That hadn't occurred to me, though it made perfect
sense. Which bothered me, since I was the one who
was supposed to be fixing things, or having them fixed.
Dunno. I put my phone down to toss the salad. When
the light started flashing I picked it up again.

How old is this Xander?

Old, I typed. The first time I saw Xander in daylight I'd been surprised by the lines across his forehead
and bunched at the corners of his eyes. Veins mapped
the back of his hands and his blond hair was a little silvery at his temples. But then I realized I sounded like
Frank when he decided I was older than Methuselah
for being in my twenties. I changed *Old* to *Older than I
expected. Forty at least. Midforties, maybe. Not fifty.*

So. Young, Mr. Vargas wrote. *Mind the feelings of
your geriatric audience.*

I was about to write *You'll never be old.* But I flashed
on the most wrenching thing Mr. Vargas had said to

me at his wife's funeral. "She never got to be old. We were going to be old together."

Sorry, I wrote instead.

Forgiven. Keep an eye on him.

If Mr. Vargas only knew. With Frank finally settled in at school, I'd been taking my lunches that week over the sink to give me a clear view of Xander working in the yard.

Xander seems okay, I wrote. *He's a charming guy. Fun. Frank loves him.*

Nonetheless. Remember, your job is to protect Mimi from cads and swindlers.

And here I thought I was supposed to be transcribing Mimi's manuscript, of which I hadn't seen a page. I was thinking about how to answer that when I felt somebody's eyes on me. Frank stood in the doorway, wearing a deerstalker hat and a tweedy caped overcoat, with one of those pipes that blows soap bubbles clenched between his teeth. He was staring at my kneecaps with such concentration it's a wonder they didn't spontaneously combust.

I pocketed my phone. "What's up, Sherlock?"

Frank took the pipe from his teeth and said, "I'm Frank."

"I know, Frank."

"What you may not know is that Sherlock Holmes has been depicted on film hundreds of times, perhaps more than any other fictional character. My favorite on-screen Sherlock was portrayed by Basil Rathbone, a cadaverous Brit who popularized the deerstalker hat, Inverness coat, and pipe. His films were made between the years of 1939 and 1946, a time when a war-torn world took solace in the idea of a lone gentleman of towering intellect rescuing the world from its demons. What does *cadaverous* mean? I tried to look it up in *Webster's* but I am not a good speller. When I find a word I'm looking for there, it's usually serendipitous."

"*Cadaverous?* Thin to the point of being skeletal," I said. "Hey, what did the skeleton say when he walked into the bar?"

"I don't know."

"I'll have a beer and a mop."

Xander got to the party in time to award my joke with a chuckle and a rasher of twinkle. "That's one of my favorites," he said.

"Favorite what?" Frank asked. "I don't understand."

"Knock knock," I said.

"Oh. That means it's a joke," he explained to Xander.

"I got it. That's why I laughed, Frank. See, the way a joke works is that it presents you with an impossible situation your brain recognizes as impossible, so you laugh at the absurdity of it. A skeleton, for example, couldn't walk into a bar."

"Franklin Delano Roosevelt walked into a bar," Frank said, "an event rendered practically impossible by a bout of paralytic poliomyelitis he suffered in 1921." Frank acknowledged his own comic gem with a rat-a-tat-tat hahahahaha. "Why aren't you laughing?" he asked when we didn't join in.

Xander ponied up a pretty convincing courtesy laugh.

"Why isn't Alice laughing?" Frank asked.

"I'm slow on the uptake," I said.

"I'm hungry," Frank said.

"Your timing is impeccable," I said. "Lunch is ready. Can you tell your mother?"

"She went back to work," Xander said.

"Oh. Good."

Xander was leaning against the doorway, wearing another of the black T-shirts and unconsciously stroking his opposite shoulder. It was a thing I'd noticed well-muscled guys in T-shirts do sometimes when they talk to women, the way girls with hair like mine toss it back when they're talking to men.

"Can we have lunch together?" he asked.

"Sure."

"Can we sit at the table? Or do we have to stand over the sink?"

So much for thinking a pane of glass rendered me invisible to the outside world. "I have to take Mimi's lunch first," I said, making myself very busy arranging it on a tray. "You boys start without me."

Frank sat at the plate I'd fixed for him. "FDR?" he said to Xander. "More like FD Aren't!"

My braid swung over when I bent to pick up the tray and I swatted it back. Xander turned just as I passed him and our forearms brushed, which was too bad because I knew I'd have a better chance of keeping an objective eye on him if we never touched, ever.

A week later, when I drove home from dropping Frank off at school, Xander was out front of the garage jumping rope with a ferocity that suggested boxing ring more than playground. "There she is again," he said. The sound of the rope striking pavement made an interesting counterpoint to the clacking of typewriter keys floating out of Mimi's office window. I ducked back inside the station wagon for my purse, then occupied myself with getting the keys situated just right inside it. That took all of about thirty seconds. I'd hoped that would give Xander time to get back to his regime.

But Xander had dropped the jump rope and pulled the neck of his T-shirt, stretched out and riddled with the tiny holes from hundreds of washings, straight up over his face to mop his sweat. According to his T-shirt, at The Ritz 21 Club Bar-B-Q in Lubbock, Texas, a person could Dine and Dance in Cool, Air-Conditioned Comfort. I pretty much memorized the street address, zip, and phone number of The Best Meet Market This Side of Mississippi. As long as my eyes stayed on his shirt I wasn't eyeing the kind of ribs Xander had on his menu.

Once his midsection was undercover again I was able to manage, "Yes. Here I am. Again."

"Where have you been?"

"Taking Frank to school."

"In general," he said. "You've been making yourself scarce."

"I've been very busy," I lied, and walked briskly toward the house.

"Doing what?"

With Frank being gone most of the day, the sad truth was that I'd had a hard time keeping myself busy in a way that made me glad I had a college degree. "Working," I snapped. "I work here, you know." I sounded every bit as hostile as Mimi. More.

"Wait a minute, Alice." Xander touched my elbow and stopped me in my tracks. "Are you mad at me for some reason?"

"Why would I be mad at you?"

"I don't know. But it's clear I've made you angry. That, or you just don't like me."

"Do you really need everybody to like you?" I asked.

"Isn't that what everybody wants?"

"Mimi doesn't."

Xander laughed. "Mimi does as much as anybody. She just doesn't want to let on."

"She's stopped typing," I said. "I have to go."

"Why?" he asked. "Whether Mimi's typing or not has nothing to do with you."

"Thanks for the pep talk, Xander," I said. "Now I feel more useless here than ever."

For a second I was sure the inevitable earthquake Angelenos dread but try not to think about had come. But it was just me, crying. Huge, rattling sobs you might expect at a graveside, not standing in a sunny driveway on a Bel Air hilltop with a view of the ocean when the smog didn't get in the way. I felt as surprised by my tears as Xander looked.

"Hey," Xander said. "Hey, I'm sorry. I didn't mean anything by that. Are you okay?"

I couldn't nod or shake my head or anything. Xander took my purse and asked if I had any tissues in it. When I couldn't answer he shuffled through it quickly, gave up on it as a resource for comfort, and put it on the driveway next to his jump rope.

He patted me on the back a couple of times. "Go on," he said. "Let it out."

I am nothing if not obedient so I cried harder. Next thing I knew I was against his T-shirt and his arms were around me and he was apologizing for how sweaty he was. "I'm sorry I said whatever I said that hurt you," he added.

I pushed myself off his chest. "Thanks," I said. I'd left two damp handprints where I'd pressed his T-shirt against his skin, as if I were a starlet leaving her mark in wet cement out front of the Mann's Chinese Theatre. "Wow, look how sweaty you are," I said, tipping over from sobbing into laughing a little. "I can't even sweat as good as you."

"What's that supposed to mean?"

"It's something my mother used to say. It means nothing you can do will make a person like you as much as they like somebody else. Because you can't even sweat as good as that other person does."

Xander used the flat of his palm to brush my face dry and handed me my purse again. "There," he said. "Aren't you glad that's over, Oklahoma?"

"Nebraska," I said.

"I wasn't off by much."

"Just the whole state of Kansas. And yes, thanks, I feel better. I guess I needed that."

"After you've ridden a bus cross-country twenty or thirty times, all those states in the middle start to run together."

"I took a bus from Nebraska to New York once. I remember every mile."

"I bet you do," he said, and smoothed my hair back from my face with his fingertips. "By the way, with all respect to your mother, I have a feeling that your sweat is every bit as good as mine."

That's how it started between us.

13

It's not like I meant for anything to happen.

That first day we were lying in a tangle of sheets in the atelier's big painted bed, me curled up against Xander with my back to him because the fact of him close up was a lot to take in. I had to laugh at the absurdity of somebody like me ending up in the altogether with a guy who looked like him.

Xander propped up on his elbow and wiped the perspiration off his face with a corner of the sheet. "What's so funny?" he asked.

All I could think to say was, "You don't appreciate just how yellow everything is in here until you've lived it for a couple of hours."

"Welcome to the Dream House," he said.

"The Dream House?"

"Frank told me that's what you call this place."

"I do?"

"Barbie's Dream House meets van Gogh at Arles," he said in an uncanny imitation of Frank's monotone.

"Oh. I had forgotten about that."

"How could you?" he said. "It's perfect." He picked up my hair and wrapped it around his wrist. My braid was the first thing he'd undone before we started. It had seemed to take forever, in the very best way possible. "You have the most amazing hair," he said. "You should wear it down more."

"It gets in my way," I said. "It's a distraction."

"Your hair isn't the distraction. You're the distraction."

Later, after we'd had a chance to catch our breath again, I asked, "So, what else did Frank tell you about me?"

"That you're five feet, eight inches tall, weigh a hundred twenty-seven pounds and were born October twenty-fifth. He wouldn't tell me what year because he said a gentleman never discusses a lady's age."

"How does he know all that?"

"He also mentioned you don't need corrective lenses to drive and that you're an organ donor. Make of this assortment of facts what you will."

"Frank's gone through my purse?" I sat up in bed, clutching the sheet to my chest because I felt more naked then than I had a few minutes ago. I guess my purse wasn't the Fort Knox I'd thought it was.

"So what? So have I. How could you not have tissues in that Mary Poppins satchel of yours? Aside from the usual purse stuff, you have a set of tiny screwdrivers and a flashlight and Band-Aids and a box of raisins and a pair of argyle socks and a notebook and dental floss, but no tissues. Explain that to me."

"I ran out of tissues."

"Ah. So I guess you aren't completely perfect after all. Listen, Alice. Don't get mad at Frank. The kid can't help himself. He lacks executive function. Although when I was growing up they called it other things."

"Like what?"

"Impulsive. Irresponsible. Eccentric if you were born rich. Crazy if you weren't."

"There's nothing wrong with Frank that can't be fixed," I said.

"If you ask me, there's nothing about Frank that needs fixing," Xander said. "I'm a big fan of crazy. Without it there'd be no van Gogh at Arles. For all we know, no Barbie's Dream House, either."

"Frank's not crazy," I insisted.

"Fine," he said. "He's eccentric. Come here."

I slid out of bed and started dressing. "I can't," I said. "I have to go."

"What's your hurry?"

"I have to make Mimi's lunch." I turned my back on him while I buttoned my shirt. He sat up on the edge of the bed and grabbed my wrist.

"Aren't you the responsible one," Xander said. He turned my hand over and kissed my palm, then folded my fingers over the kiss for safekeeping and slid his fingers up my arm. If he did that to make sure every follicle on my body was at attention, I'm guessing he wasn't disappointed.

"I really have to go. Right now."

"Not so fast, Suzy Homemaker." He stood up and put his hands on my shoulders, then eased one around to cradle the nape of my neck. I couldn't help noticing that I was dressed but he was still naked. The few boyfriends I'd had in my life, no Apollos they, had always been careful to cover themselves as quickly as I did after they relinquished the sheets. Xander pulled my face to his and kissed me again and then I didn't have any clothes on either. After that, I showered in the copper teacup-sized tub, dressed, and scrambled down the ladder before he could talk me into another round.

When I looked back over my shoulder before I left the garage, Xander was at the atelier railing watching me go. He stood in a shaft of sunshine from the skylight that had turned his hair into a halo but wasn't doing his face any favors. He looked completely different from below, all hollows and tendons and long afternoon shadows. How old was he, anyway? I realized then that I'd paid more attention to Frank's lectures on movie magic than I had realized. For the first time ever I appreciated the importance of flattering angles and carefully orchestrated lighting.

I don't think I'd ever been happier to hear Mimi's typing. It meant she hadn't noticed I was running late. I hoped. I made an omelet and a salad faster than you could say I'll-have-a-double-cheeseburger-with-a-side-of-fries and delivered it to her office. By the time I got there the typing was over so I knocked my lunchtime knock. Mimi must have been just inside the door because she opened it immediately.

"There you are," she said when she took the tray. "Finally."

Busted. "I made you eggs," I said.

Mimi eyeballed me at length, which I only mention because she hardly ever looked at me at all. "I've never seen you with your hair down," she said. "Why are you so flushed?"

Had she looked out her window and seen me running across the yard from the Dream House, giggling? "I was exercising," I said.

"I guess that's why your hair is wet," she said.

"Yes. I took a shower after. I lost track of time. I'm sorry."

Mimi stared at me so long I worried she would fire me on the spot. Had she sent me packing even yesterday I might have been excited. Getting kicked off the mountain today would have been more of a mixed bag.

"I'm so happy," Mimi said.

I hadn't seen that coming. "I can make you eggs more often if you like."

"It's not the eggs, Alice. I just got a call from Frank."

"Oh, no. What's wrong? Do I need to go pick him up?"

"Nothing's wrong. He called to ask if he could stay after school. He's made a friend, and they want to play."

"That's wonderful, Ms. Banning," I said. I meant it, too. If she had been Mr. Vargas and hadn't been holding her lunch tray, I would have hugged her.

"Isn't it?" Mimi said. "One friend is what he needs. One friend is enough for anybody." Mimi's hair had grown out to a ragged pixie by then, and her face was doing something that almost suggested smiling. If you covered up the eyebrow that was growing back in white, she looked like Book Jacket Mimi again. "Alice," she added. "Ms. Banning sounds like some mean old lady who calls the police on the neighborhood kids if they cut across her lawn. Call me Mimi."

I was so shocked and pleased I couldn't answer. Not that she gave me the chance. Her hands were busy with the tray so she kicked the door shut in my face.

"So, how did you meet your friend?" I asked when I picked Frank up after school. I checked him in the rearview mirror to gauge his mood. His facial expression was as inscrutable as ever, but the outfit he was wearing—a navy blazer with a gold insignia over the pocket, shirt plus cravat, captain's hat and owlish horn-rimmed glasses—made him look as jaunty as Tony Curtis pretending to be the rich yachting guy wooing Marilyn Monroe in *Some Like It Hot.*

"I was indulging in one of my favorite pastimes," Frank said, "pretending to be Captain Edward Smith on the bridge of the *Titanic.*"

"Ah."

"Did you know that the Internal Revenue Service, more commonly identified by its monogram, IRS, selected April fifteenth as the date for the annual filing of personal income taxes as a tribute to all the wealthy individuals who died in that tragic event?"

"Is that true?"

"One of the richest men in America at the time, John Jacob Astor IV, age forty-seven, went down with the ship. As did Ida Straus, sixty-three, and her husband, Isador Straus, sixty-seven, a co-owner of the Macy's department store. Also dry-goods retailer and Omaha resident Emil Brandeis, forty-eight. As a fellow native of Nebraska, I thought you might be interested in that fact. When Mr. Brandeis's remains were fished from the ocean, he was still wearing his diamond cuff links. I have often wondered what became of those cuff links."

"I bet you have. But that thing you said about the IRS choosing April fifteenth to commemorate all the dead rich people. Is that true?"

"It's held by many experts that the imposition of the graduated income tax in 1913, hard on the heels of the sinking of the *Titanic*, also sank the ordinary American's ability to amass great personal fortunes. So I imagine it's true."

"You didn't tell me how you met your friend yet."

"As I said, I was indulging in one of my favorite pastimes, reimagining the last moments aboard the *Titanic*. She asked if she could join in."

"What did she want to do?" I asked. "Rearrange the deck chairs?"

"I don't understand. The deck chairs were about to be swept out to sea, so what would be the point of rearranging them?"

"Knock knock."

"Oh. Ha-ha. At any rate, my new friend asked to join in and I told her she would be most welcome if she could hum the melody the orchestra was playing when the ship went down. She asked, 'Song of Autumn' or 'Nearer My God to Thee'? I opted for 'Song of Autumn' of course."

"Why 'of course'?"

"There's some controversy about which the orchestra played. A wistful, minor-key waltz wildly popular in the day? Or the rather too on-the-nose hymn? When I said 'Song of Autumn,' my friend answered, 'Correct!' She knew both and understood which was the better choice. It shows her to be a person of unusual intellect."

Of all the gin joints, she walks into his.

"Anyway, we enjoyed ourselves so much that she asked if we might have another sinking after the school day ended."

"That makes sense," I said. "What's your new friend's name?"

"I don't know."

"How could you not know?"

"I can tell you that my friend broke her arm the first day of school. She is still wearing a cast and a sling, though the cast is supposed to come off in a day or so. She intends to keep wearing the sling after that because she feels it lends her an air of tragedy. Also she can hide snacks in it."

"Fiona," I said, experiencing the kind of exhilaration Frank must feel every time he unearthed a shiny fact he'd squirrelled away in his vast mental warehouse. "I think your new friend is named Fiona."

"That sounds right."

I was dying to meet Fiona. "Invite your friend over to play sometime," I said without thinking. I couldn't imagine Mimi's reaction to a strange child in the house. But a child who was willing to be Frank's friend? I had to think Mimi would be as eager to meet her as I was.

After I retired to my stateroom that night, I fired up my computer and checked the roster of the passengers who did and didn't survive the wreck of the *Titanic*. I'm sort of embarrassed to say it, but I choked up scrolling through the list. I guess I'd never thought about the real people much. For one thing, it happened about a century ago so everybody alive then would be dead already anyway. For another, I'd seen the movie with Kate Winslet and Leonardo DiCaprio, who had zero chemistry if you ask me, so despite all the hoo-ha over it when I was just entering my teens, the film hadn't moved me.

But that list! Just the victims' names, ages, and hometowns. It told you almost nothing, yet so eloquently. Here are the facts, the list seemed to say. Break your heart on them as you will. When I finally went to bed I couldn't stop thinking about Mrs. May Fortune, sixty, and her daughters, the Misses Ethel, twenty-eight, Alice, twenty-four, and Mabel, twenty-three. They survived. Mark Fortune, sixty-four, and Charles, nineteen, didn't.

In the middle of the night I woke up just as Xander or the player piano was working through "Nearer My God to Thee." I decided I had to be dreaming. I didn't know what "Song of Autumn" sounded like, so my unconscious, obviously, had to go with the too on-the-nose hymn. When I closed my eyes again I saw Miss Alice Fortune bobbing in the current in her lifeboat, wondering if she'd ever see her father again and whether her only brother would swim to safety or be swallowed up by the sea.

In retrospect, I wonder if the whole madness with Xander was my way of rearranging the deck chairs at Mimi's house. The two of us had nothing in common but Mimi and Frank, about whom we talked endlessly in a way I'd like to think neither of us would have talked to anybody outside the wall. I learned from Xander that in the old days before Frank, Mimi was freer with her chitchat than I could imagine her being with anybody. Even with Mr. Vargas.

From the way Xander told it, their "music lessons" consisted of Mimi sitting by him on the piano bench with her hands in her lap, staring at the book of scales on the music rack and talking. Part of it, I guess, was that for such a handsome guy, Xander was an unusually good listener. But the rest of it I attribute to Lonesome-Highway Syndrome, a condition familiar to long-range truckers, Greyhound ticket holders, and regular travelers of endless, underpopulated flatlands. That's when two unacquainted people sit by each other long enough to be hypnotized by the white line cleaving highway or the vinyl back of a bus seat and say more than they might have otherwise. Same with two strangers lying next to each other, staring at the rafters.

Which is where we were when Xander told me the story of how as a kid Mimi would ride all over town behind her brother Julian on his gray-white gelding Zephyr. How when they got older and bullies made Julian's life a living hell, Mimi had chalked a target on the side of the barn and taught him to throw. Julian turned out to be a natural, with good speed and dead aim. Mimi took the rap the first time Julian got in trouble for chipping a bully's tooth with a rock, even though Julian was her older brother and all the kids knew she hadn't thrown the stone. The upside of that incident was that nobody bothered Julian anymore, and when he started pitching for the high school teams he became a local hero, even if people still found him impossible to talk to.

There was also the story of how Mimi's mother Banning insisted Zephyr walk in Julian's funeral cortege, saddled but riderless, as if her son were dead Abraham Lincoln or President Kennedy, and how Mimi was so mortified she sat with her head between her knees so nobody would see her in the backseat of her parents' car. Or at least that's what Mimi told herself was the reason she couldn't hold her head up that day.

But sadder than that to me was how Mimi called her mother months after she'd run away from the funeral and college and the rest of it to tell Banning that everything was going to be okay and that she was living in New York City. "Nothing will ever be okay again," her mother said. "Have you forgotten Julian already?" Mimi thought that was the perfect time to tell her she'd written a novel that was but mostly wasn't based on Julian. That, moreover, the novel had been bought by a prestigious New York publisher and was coming out in the fall. She thought the news of her dead son immortalized might make Banning a little happier. Instead she asked, "A book? How could you? Haven't we suffered enough?" Mimi told her mother she'd used a pen name so no one would know she'd written it, unless Banning wanted people to know. When Banning didn't respond, Mimi told her the name she'd chosen. "But Banning's my name," her mother said. "Mine." Then she hung up on Mimi. It was the last conversation they had.

Xander was my Scheherazade. I went to him as much for the stories as anything.

"Frank's not adopted, is he?" I asked him.

"Nope."

"Are you sure?"

"Absolutely."

"Then who's his father?"

Xander shrugged.

"Do you think Hanes might be Frank's dad?"

"I met Mimi before there was a Frank. I don't think she's seen Hanes since I've known her."

"What was the story with Mimi and that guy, anyway?"

"Hanes Fuller was irresistible as long as he was working from her script. Has Frank showed you *Public Enemy* yet?"

"With James Cagney? Of course."

"Remember the scene where Cagney shoves a halved grapefruit into his girl's face because she won't shut up? Hanes unscripted was like that girl. Mimi has a soft spot for lots of human frailties, but being stupid and boring aren't among them."

"I wonder what she hates me for," I said.

"She doesn't hate you. How could she? You're perfect."

Later, Xander said, "It's not about you, you know. What Mimi hates is how her life has turned out. It isn't how she thought it would be back when she was your age and on the top of the world."

PART IV

What Have You
Done with Xander?

14

So we four bobbed along through the fall and winter. Our days went something like this: I delivered Frank to school each morning. Sometimes he said "I don't belong here" and refused to get out of the car. "Sure you do," I said, unbuckled his seat belt for him, pried his fingers free of the car door, and aimed him in the direction of the schoolyard. After breakfast, Mimi disappeared into her office and banged away on her typewriter but never showed me anything. Xander puttered around the yard and house, trimming and painting and hammering and doing whatever else gave him an excuse for being there until I was done with my chores. Then quite by accident the two of us would end up together at the Dream House.

When I went to school to fetch Frank, per his instructions I'd stand by the station wagon in the parking lot, waiting for him to cross the playground and climb into the backseat. Even though the schoolyard was a swirl of kids in bright T-shirts and shorts, dresses and skirts, flip-flops and sneakers, you could spot Frank coming from a mile away. He looked like a peacock in a barnyard full of chickens.

I kept hoping to meet the famous Fiona. "So," I'd ask as casually as I could manage, "what do you and Fiona do when you stay late at school to play?"

"We talk," he said. "Then we join hands and run from our enemies."

Though I kept angling for an introduction, I never got one. "So, what does Fiona look like?" I tried another afternoon.

"She wears argyle knee socks and saddle shoes," he said.

"And?"

"Cardigan sweaters with little pearl buttons. Kilts that look like wool but are actually made of rayon, a wood-based fiber invented in 1855 but not popularized until the 1920s because until then it was highly combustible. Her rayon kilt feels like cashmere but is more suitable for playground wear as it is machine washable."

"Her kilt feels like cashmere? You touched her kilt?"

"Of course not. She let me try on the sling that matches the tartan of one of her kilts. She alternates that one with another she has, in houndstooth. I liked her sling very much. I never realized before what a responsibility it is for the forearm to support the wrist and hand."

"What does Fiona's face look like?"

"She wears oversized hair bows," he said. "I believe they're made of taffeta."

I thought about pressing for more details but doubted Frank could fill me in on the color of her eyes or even her hair. Besides, how many little Los Angelenos who looked like they'd stepped off the set of *Brigadoon* could there be on that playground?

I was proud of summoning that reference from my mental warehouse. In case you're unfamiliar with it, *Brigadoon* is a 1954 film starring Gene Kelly and Cyd Charisse that's about some town in Scotland that doesn't really exist. I'd fallen asleep watching it with Frank back in July.

When we got home in the afternoons, Frank leapt from the car and ran to Xander. The two of them would go indoors to sit side by side on the piano bench, galloping through scales and melodies until it was time for dinner.

None of the stories Xander told were about Xander. For example, when I asked him what he did for fun when he was a kid, he said, "It was a small town in Vermont. I helped my dad fix things around the house. There wasn't much else to do."

"Is that why you ended up playing the piano? Your parents trying to keep you out of trouble?"

He said, "You want to see trouble? I'll show you trouble." Xander put his mouth over mine and after that I was too distracted to ask him anything else.

Another time I asked how he came to have a long thin scar down his right arm. "I broke my arm. In a couple of places. I needed surgery to fix it."

"When did it happen?"

"When I was a senior at Julliard. I never finished school because of it. It hurt too bad."

"Does it still hurt?"

"Every day. Not as much out here."

"Does it hurt when you play the piano?"

"Especially when I play the piano."

"What happened?"

"I was doing something stupid and I broke my arm. I really don't want to talk about it." He sat up and put his T-shirt back on.

"I didn't realize you never graduated," I said.

He shrugged. "It's not the kind of thing you brag about."

"Mimi never graduated from college either, you know," I said.

"I know. I guess that's one reason we hit it off."

"How did you meet Mimi, anyway?"

"I was on the crew that put the wall up around the house. After the crew left, she decided she needed a handyman. I'm handy. I needed money. Simple as that. Any more questions?" He pulled on a pair of shorts, slung his jump rope over his shoulder, and headed for the ladder.

It has been over four months, Genius. Still nothing?

I had just gotten out of the teacup shower and was sitting on the edge of the yellow bed, braiding my hair, when I noticed the message light flashing on my cell. I bound my braid with an elastic I had around my wrist and hunched over my phone. Xander was still in bed, running his fingers slowly up and down my naked back.

Zilch, I typed.

Xander's fingers crept along the crease where my left leg met my torso. "Stop it," I said to him. "I'm texting my boss."

Xander sat up. "Mimi?" he asked.

"Yes. I'm just telling her where we both are in case she's looking for one of us."

His hand fell away. "You're kidding."

I turned around and looked at him. "Are you kidding? Of course I'm kidding. It's Mr. Vargas."

"I was kidding, too," he said. He got up and went to the Lilliputian loo.

My phone flashed again. *How is boy?*

Frank? Speaking of genius. Never met anyone with so much random knowledge at fingertips. Unlike anybody. Have decided he's next rung on evolutionary ladder.

Genius not everything cracked up to be. Intellectual prodigies not known for getting dates to prom. Stumbling block to becoming next rung on evolutionary ladder.

Frank has a girlfriend now.

Isn't he a little young for girlfriend?

Friend who is a girl.

Ah. Well. Everybody needs a friend.

Indeedy.

Heard any good jokes lately? Mr. Vargas texted.

Nope. You?

How do you know when you've met an outgoing mathematician?

Tell me, I texted back.

He stares at your shoes. Instead of at his own shoes. Get it?

Ha. I get it. Frank stares at my eyebrow.

So things are looking up for him.

Yes.

Ask Mimi for pages.

I sat there on the edge of the bed trying to decide how to respond to that. Xander opened the bathroom door. "The walls are closing in on me," he said. "With this shut I can't raise my elbow while I brush my teeth."

I went back to texting Mr. Vargas. *Would request be better coming from you?*

"Don't stand in front of the mirror," I said to Xander. "Spit into the toilet instead of the sink."

The last time I asked her for anything, he texted, *Mimi decided to stay in Los Angeles.*

I couldn't blame Mr. Vargas for sweating me for product. He was back there in New York with winter setting in and the publicity department hovering. While I was here in the land of milk and honey, doing what?

Xander, mostly.

Here's the joke I decided I ought to tell Mr. Vargas: I ask Mimi for pages. She smiles and hands over completed novel. In the acknowledgments, she thanks me for my computer skills and inspiring "Pollyanna" outlook on life.

See, the way a joke works is that it presents you with an impossible situation. Your brain recognizes the situation as impossible so you laugh at the absurdity of it. Here's what really happened when I asked Mimi for pages. She said, "When I am ready to give you something of mine, I will be sure to let you know."

Then just like that it was Christmas.

This isn't to imply things didn't go on in the interim. Things happened. But if you'd like to keep believing in the perfection of Xander Devlin, kind of in the way I kept trying to convince myself Santa was real after I saw the guy in the red suit having a cigarette out back of the Westroads Mall, you'll need to ignore certain events that occurred during this time:

———

To give me a break from my routine and to prove he is a stand-up guy, Xander offers to pick Frank up from school one Friday afternoon. I am moved and grateful, and spend the stolen hour conditioning my hair and giving myself a pedicure. When I emerge the car is in the driveway and I can hear them going at it on the piano. I decide not to interrupt and go to fold laundry and get dinner started.

After I slide the stuffed shells into the oven I smooth back my newly glowing hair and pad barefoot into the living room, where as it happens the piano is playing by itself. So I wander through the glass house and then into the Dream House looking for Frank and Xander, my panic gradually increasing to a crescendo when I find Xander in the yellow bed, napping.

"Where's Frank?" I ask.

"Frank?" he echoes, still stupid from sleep.

I am in the station wagon, barefoot and burning rubber, before Xander can finish speaking the sentence "I must have fallen asleep."

I am grateful that Frank, having decided he'd been forgotten and that he'd better walk home, chooses the route we take in the car. Did I say "walk"? Because after several blocks, Frank decides to hitchhike. I find him on the corner of Bellagio Terrace and Linda Flora Drive, right hand hiking up right trouser leg to expose a tempting expanse of burgundy and navy argyle sock, left thumb awag. A pose, Frank explained once safely ensconced in the backseat, combining the hitchhiking techniques of both Clark Gable and Claudette Colbert from that famous scene in 1934's *It Happened One Night.*

"That was the first film to win all five marquee Oscars, a feat not repeated until 1975's *One Flew Over the Cuckoo's Nest*, a movie I have never watched," Frank says.

"Don't," I say.

"Okay. The Gable/Colbert scene is so famous that it was mimicked in a Laurel and Hardy bit as well as a Looney Tunes short. It inspired generations of hitchhikers to prevail upon the kindness of strangers to help them reach their final destinations."

As mutilated corpses stuffed into drainage ditches, I do not say. What I do say is, "It's illegal to hitchhike before you're twenty-one years old."

"Oh. I didn't know that. I know it's wrong to indulge in criminal activities, but I do like those black-and-white-striped suits and matching caps that convicts wear. They'd make excellent pajamas. Do they let you keep them once your time is served?"

"Convicts wear orange jumpsuits that zip up the front now. The cut is not slimming, and a redhead like you should steer clear of head-to-toe orange," I say.

"I will never hitchhike again."

Miraculously, Frank and I arrive home without being discovered by Mimi, and well before the stuffed shells are ready to come out of the oven. "That looks delicious," Frank says as I pull the pan out of the oven and slump, exhausted and relieved, against the counter. "Why aren't you wearing any shoes?"

———

Xander disappears for days, without explanation. It is none of my business what he does with his free time, which is of course every hour of every day. Still this seems vaguely impolite, particularly when I have prepared a dinner for four centered on a kale-feta casserole that Frank hates but Xander loves.

The upside is that when Xander returns he has new, lunatic photographs to add to Frank's collection in the gallery. When I ask Xander where he snapped a shot of what appears to be a woman's back bearing a shoulder-to-crack tattoo that matches the mural she's standing in front of, he says, "She's just a friend."

———

I come to fetch Frank and Xander from Dream House, where they are curating the collection for just an hour, they promise, until it is time for Frank to come in and do his homework. An hour has passed, then another half. When I let myself in through the side door to the garage, opening it sucks an unidentified flaming cinder out into the driveway. I chase it down and stomp it out, then go back in.

"What was that?" I ask Frank, who is leaning over the railing holding a tissue. He's wearing the seersucker suit with the watch chain across the vest plus his straw boater, and looks for all the world like a passenger using his hankie to wave good-bye as he departs on the *Titanic*.

"I am setting tissues on fire and letting them drift to the floor."

"What? Why?"

"To observe air currents. It's a science project Xander invented to keep me busy."

I am up the ladder before you can say stop, drop, and roll. "No more," I say. "Give me those matches."

"Xander said it's all right. The garage floor is concrete."

"It's not all right. Give me the matches."

Once I make Frank turn out his pockets and take off his hat and shoes and socks so I can be sure he has no matches concealed on his person, I go looking for Xander. He is sitting cross-legged on the bed, wearing headphones and sorting through photographs. At first he laughs at me. When he can see that I find nothing about this situation funny, his response is, "Relax, Alice. Let the kid be a kid for once."

In late October, Frank and Xander plan an elaborate, supposedly surprise birthday party for me. Frank, of course, can't keep his mouth shut about it. So, in secret, I exhaust myself helping Frank make preparations that Xander "plans" but seems unwilling or unable to execute. The big night comes, and no Xander. He is kind enough, however, to leave Frank a note, which Frank eventually finds in his pocket and shows me. "I don't do birthdays. X," the note reads. Which means X does not see the gigantic fluffy white coconut cake he told Frank I would love. Nor the elaborate fake candles Frank insisted we make out of drinking straws fitted with crayon-drawn flames with glued-on sparkle.

To protest Xander's absence, Frank has a gigantic tantrum. I have sparkles in my hair for a week. It is longer than that before we see Xander again.

I am twenty-five years old now. But still not old enough to know better.

I hate coconut cake.

I almost forgot this one. Or I keep trying to forget this one. Xander and Frank are on the piano bench, finishing up a duet. Mimi stands behind them, one hand resting on Frank's head in that proprietary way mothers have that tells the world that this child is hers, she loves this child and this child loves her right back. Her other hand rests on the nape of Xander's neck. It's telling me something, but I'm not sure I want to know what.

15

The sad part about this stretch of the story, after my
birthday and before Christmas, was how much
Frank missed Xander. With Xander gone, Frank refused to touch the piano, and it wasn't worth the struggle to convince him that he should. When he wasn't at
school all the kid wanted to do, ever, was hang out in
the Dream House, sitting on the edge of its world, chin
propped on one of the intermediate slats of the railing and legs dangling over the side, as if he were on a
bridge, fishing.

After a day or two of trying to interest Frank in some
fun activity like running round in the yard brandishing
his plastic machete or giving me yet another tour of his
gallery or watching *Casablanca* for the fifty billionth
time, I gave in and sat on the lip of platform beside

him, legs dangling and chin propped. Frank took my hand and said, "This is the disappointing part I tried to warn you about." After that, we sat there holding hands for I don't know how long.

Something about the two of us sitting there like that reminded me of my mother keeping me company on the stoop the summer after my father left. I hadn't thought about that in years. I can hardly remember what he looked like, which seems wrong, since I wasn't all that little when he abandoned us. My mother had given me a box of photographs of him that I'd misplaced somehow, so there was that. But I think the real reason I lost his face was that I imagined every man who set foot on our block would turn out to be my dad. Over time all those faces that weren't his gradually wiped out the memory of the face that was.

I started drawing pictures to keep busy. But as time went on I found myself taking a pretty big slice of my identity from the fact that I was incredibly awesome at drawing horses and bulldogs, two animals seen on my block about as often as my father. "It's all in the ears," I would explain to my grade-school fan base when they pumped me for my secrets. "They're triangles." Solemn nods all around.

That mediocre knack plus my excellent grades and economic hardship got me a full ride at Nebraska. But

I had no illusions about my artistic talent and more or less gave up painting when I moved to New York. The materials were messy and expensive. Also volatile and smelly, which didn't make me a popular tenant. I switched to doing pencil sketches and charcoal caricatures of tourists in Central Park, thinking maybe I could make some money doing that. But horses and dogs were far easier clients to satisfy and I quit the park after a few months. Art was for trust-funders, the truly talented, and deluded souls who thought they were. I had to make a living. But not as an accountant. I know it would be the sensible thing to do. But please, not just yet.

The last drawing I'd done was of Mr. Vargas's daughter Carolyn. I wanted to give him some kind of thank-you gift for my new job-not-in-accounting. I nabbed a snapshot from his desk, photocopied it, and worked from that. Drawing that way is kind of a cheat, since life's three-dimensional angles and shadows are frozen in time and two dimensions for you. But if he were half as pleased as my mother pretended to be when I gave her yet another drawing of the pony I'd never have, that would be fine with me.

I thought my portrait turned out well so I put it in a little frame. Mr. Vargas thanked me effusively but I couldn't help noticing that it disappeared from his desk right away. The last time I went to visit Mrs. Vargas in the hospital, though, I saw my drawing of Carolyn on her bedside table alongside a photograph of the freshly minted Mr. and Mrs. Vargas on their wedding day twenty years before. I am not the sort of person who cries in hospital rooms but I came very close to doing it then. My art might not be good for much, but I guess it was good for something.

So the next afternoon when Frank and I reported for our Dream House vigil I came armed with a pencil and blank index cards. I sat at the yellow table churning out sketch after sketch of the kid in all his favorite outfits, which pleased him even more than I imagined it would. He got up and went to work in his gallery again, arranging and rearranging my drawings on the wall to form a narrative only he understood well enough to discuss with himself.

After that, it was only a matter of time until Frank had the bright idea of dragging out one of the big blank canvases in the atelier rack so I could cough out a portrait for him to give his mother for Christmas. This was his pitch: "What do you give the woman who has everything but money and living room furniture?"

"A coffee table?"

"My mother doesn't drink coffee. Also, coffee tables are a menace."

"A menace? Says who?"

"Says William Holden. Or he might have if he had survived his deadly encounter with a coffee table on November twelfth, 1981. What my mother needs is a portrait of me to hang over the mantel."

"Except I'm not a very good painter," I said.

"She won't care. My mother is fond of looking at pictures of me no matter how meritless they are. She keeps a box full of particularly embarrassing photographs from my childhood under her bed. Me in diapers or strapped in my high chair with baby food in my hair or asleep in a position which, based on posterior elevation in relation to the angle of neck and the squash of face against pillow, she calls 'ass over teakettle.' I imagine that getting down on her knees to pull that box out must hurt a great deal because more than once I have seen her crying while looking at those pictures. That's why I think it will be such a good idea for her to have a large painting of me up high where she can see it without having to overtax her joints. I am willing to offer you this commission because you are on the payroll already and I have no money to hire anybody else." He turned out his pockets to illustrate their emptiness. "Also you have nothing else to do all day while I am at school so you might as well."

He had me there.

"**What have** you done with Xander?" Mimi asked me not long after that. Frank was at school and I was mopping the kitchen before I headed out to the Dream House to get to work on my commission.

I was still struggling with the fact that Mimi had left her office during daylight hours so I needed a minute to come up with an appropriate answer. Finally I managed, "What?"

"I haven't heard Xander playing the piano. I like to hear Xander playing the piano while I'm working. That's why I bought that piano in the first place."

"I can figure out how to turn the piano on for you if you like."

"If I wanted to listen to the piano playing itself, I think I could manage to flip a switch," Mimi said. "It doesn't say much for your intelligence if you can't hear the difference between a human being and a computer playing a piano." She stormed off.

Everything irritates Mimi, I wrote in my notebook that night before going to sleep. I erased that and replaced it with, *Everything I do irritates Mimi.* That seemed a whole lot closer to the truth.

"**Xander will** be back before Christmas," Frank mused while we were driving home from school the next day. "He doesn't have any family but us."

"Xander has no family?" I asked.

"He has a mother and a father and a sister and a dead sister but other than that no family to speak of, which I have surmised because he never speaks of them."

"A dead sister? What happened to her?"

"I don't know. Just last night my mother was saying how much he reminds her of somebody dear to her. Have you ever heard of Joe DiMaggio?"

"The baseball player? Xander reminds your mother of Joe DiMaggio?" I tried to remember what Joe DiMaggio looked like. Black hair. Big nose maybe? A good-looking guy as I recall, but not particularly molded In-the-Manner-of-Apollo.

"No, Xander reminds my mother of someone else. Are you familiar with screen siren Marilyn Monroe?"

"Xander reminds your mother of Marilyn Monroe?"

"I can only assume you're unfamiliar with Marilyn Monroe as Marilyn Monroe is a woman and Xander is a man."

"I know that, Frank. I'm familiar with Marilyn Monroe. Everybody on the planet is familiar with Marilyn Monroe."

He considered this a moment. "Do you think they know about her on Mars?"

"I don't know about on Mars. As you were saying."

"As I was saying, Joe DiMaggio was married to Marilyn Monroe for two hundred and seventy-four days in 1954. While they were honeymooning in Japan Marilyn took a break to entertain our troops in Korea. 'Joe, you've never heard such cheering,' she told him. Joe said, 'As a matter of fact, I have.' Just before Christmas I am to be student of the week, which calls for me to stand in front of my class and tell the story of my origins and my life until the present day. I would like it if there were cheering but I'm not setting my heart on a big ovation because no one has received one so far, not even the kid whose dad is a firefighter who parked his fire truck on the playground and let us climb all over it. My entourage will be on hand for my presentation, of course. My mother will come, and she'll call Xander and he'll be there, too. Fiona will ask for a pass so she can attend as well."

"So will I."

"No thank you," he said. "Please."

Frank was more restless than usual the night before his presentation. I heard him knocking around at all hours and finally decided to slip out and see if I could coax him back to bed before he woke up his mother and the rest of Los Angeles.

The living room lights were on and Frank was talking loudly enough to reach the top balcony of the biggest theater on Broadway. Then the lights went out and stars splattered the living room walls. They held steady for a moment, then revolved lazily around the room. "Since the dawn of time, mankind has been fascinated with the stars and planets that populate our galaxy," Frank declaimed.

"That's your old night-light," I heard Mimi say. "I put that away when you started kindergarten."

I peeked around the corner to see what was going on in there. Frank had closed the piano and put his night-light on top. It was one of those old-fashioned paper carousels with a lightbulb inside that gradually warmed the air above it and made its pinwheel vents spin the shade with its cutout stars faster and faster.

"I stumbled across it when I was looking for my marbles so that Fiona and I could play a high stakes game of Ringer at recess. I realized the night-light was just the thing I needed for my presentation."

"It belonged to your uncle when he was a baby," Mimi said. "It's older than I am. Please be careful with it."

"You told me all that when you were packing it for storage."

"I did?"

"You said we'd better put it away so we'd still have it to use when my little boy came along. It was a fragile old thing, you said, so we'd better put it in a box on the top shelf to keep it safe. That's where I found it."

"We used to watch it together for hours," Mimi said.

"Every night for half my life. I've missed that fragile old thing, but I understand the necessity of thoughtful preservation. Ninety percent of the films made during the silent era have been lost to history. Their negatives were printed on unstable and highly flammable cellulose nitrate film and were destroyed in vault fires, tossed to make room for newer movies, or stored so carelessly that they crumbled to dust."

"You're almost ten years old, Frank," Mimi said. "I can't believe it."

I had to make myself leave. Otherwise I would have had to admit that I was eavesdropping.

As it turned out, neither Mimi nor Xander made it to Frank's presentation.

Though I wasn't on the guest list, I knew it was slated for Friday at 2:00 P.M. on the last day of school before winter break, to be followed by nondenominational refreshments and lively discussion. According to Frank. Which is why he nixed my idea of baking Christmas cookies. That morning I made brownies for Mimi to take and let it go at that. But I started to worry when Mimi didn't mention the presentation or how she planned to get there. When I delivered her lunch I knocked and waited. She didn't come to the door but I didn't leave her tray like I normally would have. I steeled myself and knocked again.

When she opened the door she didn't look happy. "I'm sorry to disturb you," I said. "But I wanted to tell you that I made brownies for you to take to Frank's presentation. And to ask if you want me to drive you, or if you want to go on your own. His presentation is at two." I could tell she wanted to close the door on me so I edged forward and angled my foot against it.

"Don't come in here," she said.

"I wouldn't dream of it. I just need to know what time you want to leave."

"I'm not going. He gave me the gist of it last night so I don't need to be there."

"But he's expecting you."

"I'm working," she said. "That's what I was doing until you felt like you had to pound on my door and remind me of what you think my responsibilities are. Let me tell you what my responsibilities are. I need to sit at my typewriter until my book is done so that Frank and I don't end up living in a refrigerator box. Now go away."

I went. I didn't want to stop going until I got back to New York. I think the only thing that stopped me was the idea of Frank standing in front of his class, no entourage in attendance, getting an ovation from nobody. So I boxed up the brownies, got in the car, and drove to school.

The visitor's log in the office was turned to a fresh page, so I flipped back to the one before it to see if Xander had signed in. He hadn't, but I was early so he might make it yet.

"I think this pen is out of ink," I said to the student working behind the desk.

"I'm sorry. I'll find another." She started rifling drawers.

"Fiona," the office lady I didn't know said. "Stop making such a racket. Pens, top left drawer."

Fiona. The girl was tall enough to be a third-grader, and skinny. A cute but fairly average-looking kid with blond hair and huge blue eyes that would seem less arresting once her face grew big enough to accommodate them. She wasn't wearing a sling or a kilt or a cardigan or a bow in her hair. But how many Fionas could there be at one school? "You're Fiona?" I said. "Will you be at Frank's presentation?"

She handed me the pen. "I'm Fiona. What presentation?"

"Frank is student of the week. He's giving his presentation this afternoon. He said you might be able to get a pass and come to it."

"Who's Frank?"

"I'm sorry," I said. "There must be another Fiona at this school."

"I don't think so."

I had a sick feeling in the pit of my stomach. "Frank has a friend named Fiona. She's in the third grade."

"I'm in the third grade," she said. "If there is another Fiona, she isn't in the third grade. I would know."

"I must have the details wrong then. This Fiona broke her arm the first day of school."

"I broke my arm the first day of school," she said. "But I don't know anybody named Frank."

Paula brushed past on her way into the principal's office. "She's talking about the fourth grader who dresses up," she said. "My little friend who eats lunch with me every day." She disappeared down the hallway.

Fiona wrinkled her nose. "Oh, that kid. He asked me if he could try my sling on once. He's weird." She drifted away from the counter, which I was glad of, because otherwise I might have lunged across it and grabbed her neck and used my thumb to wipe those contemptuous wrinkles off her nose. And I might have pushed her septum through to the other side of her skull while I was at it. Then we'd talk about the difference between weird and one-in-a-million.

Frank's presentation began with the night-light and the bit about mankind's fascination with the planets and stars. I hadn't thought much about how all that was supposed to tie in with the story of Frank's origins and his life until the present day. Here's how: Frank's story was that his father was a rocket scientist and a pioneer of unmanned travel to Mars.

The kid didn't get any further than that. He said, "I don't belong here," and just stood there while the stars rotated on his axis. Then he lay down on the floor and went stiff. Miss Peppe turned on the lights and unplugged the night-light and thanked him for sharing. A couple of the kids applauded weakly and one raised his hand and asked if Frank's dad was R2-D2 or C-3PO. Miss Peppe shushed him and I hoisted Frank over my shoulder in a fireman's carry, grabbed the night-light, and got out of there.

I left the brownies on the desk where I'd been sitting. I hoped that the kid who raised his hand would eat one and choke on it.

"It wasn't my best performance," Frank said on the drive home. "I'm sorry you came."

"I'm not," I said.

"Why wasn't my mother there?"

"Your mother had to work. She had a deadline." I didn't mention that she'd missed every deadline in the schedule Mr. Vargas drew up before I left New York.

"Ah. Well. She heard the chapter about her last night anyway."

"Yeah, what happened to that part today?"

"I noticed that she wasn't there to hear it, so what was the point? I suppose Xander couldn't make it, either."

"No," I said, and left it at that.

"I understand. My father missed my birth because he was working out a glitch with the Mars Odyssey before liftoff. Xander must have had a deadline, too. The thing that's great about Xander is that sometimes you can count on him to be there when you really need him. For example, when we needed to replace the sliding glass door. Also, the night I was born he drove my mother to the hospital and stayed with her while I made my entrance into this world."

The rearview mirror wasn't big enough to encompass this conversation. I pulled to the side of the road and turned around to look at him. "Wait a minute. Are you saying that Xander was there when you were born?" I asked.

"In the delivery room, holding my mother's hand," he said. "Feeding her ice chips. Encouraging her to push. Apparently it was quite dramatic. There was lots of blood, plus screaming of bad words that anyone with a soul would consider forgivable under the circumstances. Xander tells me that I was a little jaundiced when I emerged, so he sat beside me in a rocking chair in the nursery while they finished baking me under a heat lamp. I often wonder how differently the famously jaundiced Algonquin wits might have turned out if there had been heat lamps in their day to finish baking them at birth. It's too bad Fiona wasn't able to make it to my presentation."

I was so rattled by what he'd just told me that I said without thinking, "I met Fiona in the office."

Frank didn't say anything and I could see that he was folding up inside himself.

"Are you okay, Frank?" I asked.

When he didn't respond I got out of the car and came around to sit with him in the back. "Can I put my arm around you?" I asked.

"No." After a while Frank pressed his face against my shoulder. "I met Fiona once, too," he said. "I heard that her injury came about thanks to a surfeit of imagination and then her name was so lovely and full of promise that I decided I really ought to introduce myself. I was terribly frightened at the thought of doing that but I hoped we might be friends so I was brave. But as it turned out she was just like all the others."

16

Winter break saved Frank from the hell of other children for almost a month.

The rainy season had started, so we didn't go much of anywhere. I was unprepared for the forty-days-and-forty-nights quality of rain in Los Angeles. Insane apocalyptic downpours that went on steadily for hours without interruption, as if some celestial somebody had turned on a tap in the heavens full blast and forgotten about it. Sometimes at night I'd open my curtains just to watch the waterfall outside and listen to its monsoonal roar. You could smell the dampness of the earth inside the house, even with all the windows closed. I thanked god for the stucco wall that would, I hope, save us from sliding down the hillside or at least cushion our fall if we did.

Most mornings Frank and I would suit up in big black oilskin raincoats and wellies and struggle giant mortician's umbrellas through the deluge out to the Dream House to work on our project. The portrait wasn't going so well. The air was wet and heavy, the oil paint refused to dry even with three portable fans pointed at it, and there was no accelerant in the Dream House that I could find. Instead of waiting out the wet paint I pressed on, which meant the portrait gradually took on a queasy muddiness of blurred pigments and smudged lines that reminded me of how hog slop looks on hot days when it smells so bad that even the pigs are put off their feed.

Frank, bless his heart, hovered and offered pointers. But it was hopeless. I should have put the canvas aside and played Clue with the kid until the weather or my head cleared, but I was on a deadline. I hated to disappoint Frank, and now his disappointment seemed inevitable.

"I don't understand why you're having so much trouble," Frank said to me a few mornings before Christmas. "Your sketches are utterly charming."

"Thanks," I said. We were across from each other at the yellow table. I felt so dejected I closed my eyes and put my forehead on the table and left it there. The air was so full of moisture, even that paint felt damp.

I heard the kid get up to rummage around the Dream House. There were no big sharp knives in the joint. If he wandered too close to the edge, the creaky floorboards would give him away in time for me to stop him from going over. I couldn't open my eyes. I needed a break from seeing.

I listened to him open one of the flat files, rustle some paper and bang around this and that. It was sort of like listening to a radio play. Despite myself, I was enjoying trying to figure out what he was up to. After he was done with whatever it was, he came and pressed his cheek against my shoulder blade. "Alice," he said, "wake up."

When I raised my head and looked I saw that Frank had plucked my soggy canvas from the easel and clipped a big piece of watercolor paper in its place. To the upper-right corner he'd pinned a sketch I'd done of him in his Little Prince outfit with binoculars in his hands and scarf billowing behind him. "I've been observing your technique and have come to the conclusion that oils are not your first love," he said. "I thought you might be more comfortable doing something more impressionistic, maybe along the lines of this sketch writ large and brightened with a watercolor wash. There are some Auguste Rodin portraits done that way that I'm very fond of."

I was willing to try anything. "Watercolor drips, so the paper needs to be flat," I said.

"Is that so?" Before I could scrape my chair back Frank had fetched the paper and smoothed it out on the table in front of me. "I don't know much about watercolor other than it's sometimes undervalued in comparison to oils as it is easily damaged, hard to preserve, and pooh-poohed by critics as the province of hobbyists and Victorian ladies, despite being one of the most vital yet difficult mediums to work in. I hadn't considered the dripping, although of course it makes perfect sense. Alice, I learn something from you every day."

I was done with the thing in the hour. It was dry by dinnertime. The hardest part of the whole business was getting the portrait back inside the house without tearing it or crumpling it or getting it soaked in the downpour.

The most outstanding characteristic of my finished piece, I thought, was that it was big enough to cover the unfaded square over the mantel. There wasn't time to frame it, so we didn't. Frank and I stole into the living room as Christmas Eve flipped over into Christmas day and tacked it up there. As we did I saw that his stocking—one of his argyle socks, actually—hung from the lip of the mantel, lank and empty. I hoped Frank hadn't noticed, too. After I herded him back to bed I gathered up whatever I could find to stuff in it. A pair of scissors. A roll of tape. A pack of chewing gum. My hairbrush. A set of fake mustaches I had planned to wrap for him and put under the tree. Anything to fill the void.

Christmas morning, Frank's sock bulged with nothing I'd put in it. I found my contributions tossed in a mixing bowl outside my bedroom door, with a note from Mimi that read: "I believe these things are yours."

Everything except for the mustaches. Those she wrapped very nicely, adding a typed tag that read: "For Frank, With Love, From Alice." Frank was so delighted with the mustaches that he put on three right away. One on his lip and the other two over his eyebrows. After that he said he would like for me to hug him and he stood there without flinching while I did it.

Mimi seemed genuinely surprised when Frank took the T-shirt blindfold off her head and swept up a hand to indicate the watercolor. "Ta-da," he said. "Merry Christmas, Mama."

I have to admit, the watercolor looked pretty good up there. The light was hitting it just right and my tight deadline had kept me from overworking it. You wouldn't be able to pick the kid out of a lineup with it by any means, but you could see Frank in it if you really looked.

Mimi sat on the couch for a long time, really looking. When she finally said something, it was, "Where did you get that?"

"Alice," Frank said.

"Where did she get it?" she asked, as if I weren't standing right there.

"She painted it," Frank said. "I wish you had been there to see her do it. It only took her about an hour, start to finish. Maybe less. It was like magic."

Mimi nodded. I could see her eyes fill with tears.

"What do you think of it?" Frank asked.

"I think it absolutely captures you," she said.

That night after I'd gone to bed somebody knocked at my door. My heart started thumping. Had Mimi come to thank me? More likely it was Frank. "Come in," I said.

It was Mimi. "Do you have to take everything that belongs to me?" she asked. I couldn't believe I'd been foolish enough to think she'd have anything nice to say.

I woke up a few nights after Christmas because of the piano. The thing I noticed about it right away that I don't think I'd ever understood before was that it didn't sound like it was playing itself. I looked at my alarm clock. It was after midnight. I stumbled into the living room and found Xander planted on the piano bench, giving the keys a good going-over with as much uncomplicated joy as ever. Mimi was right. You really could tell the difference.

I stood in the doorway listening for a while before I said, "What's that you're playing?"

He smiled at me angelically, as if he hadn't been MIA for a minute. Then he said, "It's a song by Frank Loesser."

"What's it called?"

" 'What Are You Doing New Year's Eve?' "

"You're pathetic," I said, and went back to bed.

PART V

After the
Rains Came

January 2010

17

The deluges ended suddenly, without sending the glass house sliding off the cliff and onto the 405 freeway; but for those of us inside, things went downhill fast anyway.

Having Xander around didn't improve Mimi's temperament much that I could see. Frank, of course, was delighted to have his itinerant male role model back. For belated Christmas Xander had given Frank a hula dancer you stick to a car's dashboard. He let Frank sit up front while they backed the station wagon down the driveway and drove back up again, over and over, all the while watching the hula girl shimmy. Frank invited me along for the ride, but the last thing I wanted was to be in close quarters with Xander, even if only for a few hundred feet.

With Xander on-site again, I was forced to play the heavy, always prying Frank free to eat or take a shower or brush his teeth and go to bed. Although Xander looked well fed, flossed, and rested, none of us were witness to the effort that went into any of that anymore. Xander didn't eat with us, I didn't sleep with him, and if the walls of the Dream House bathroom were closing in on him while he brushed his teeth, Xander wasn't sharing his pain.

But the real suffering came once Frank started back to school. When I drove him there on the first day he leaned up between the seats to expound on the origins of the national dance of the Dominican Republic, a step whose name for some reason or other was based on the French word *meringue* and whose tight foot-work was informed by the chains that once bound its enslaved creators together. Frank liked to imagine the hula girl loved that particular two-step most of all, even though she supposedly hailed from an unfettered island on the other side of the world. He was still muttering about that to himself when I dropped him off. It was mid-January and just cool enough to make his E. F. Hutton suit a seasonally appropriate choice. He was wearing a pair of gold elephant-head cuff links Mimi had given him for Christmas. The way the tassel on his fez kept time to his step as he merengued across the playground made me feel almost cheerful. I couldn't believe I had been so nervous about blowback from December.

So of course there was an incident. Mimi was called in to the principal's office. But when I, Mimi-by-proxy, turned up to see the principal I was turned away with a stern note saying he wanted to have a word with Frank's mother not one of her employees.

"What happened?" I asked Paula.

"Since you are not his custodial parent, I'm not allowed to release that information to you."

"Since when?"

She leaned across the counter and whispered, "Since we have a new principal. He's big on protocol and accountability. Insists we call him Dr. Matthews because he has a Ph.D. in child development. Doesn't have kids of his own, so he's an authority. In his opinion, anyway."

Frank was in a chair by Paula's desk, clutching his crushed fez to his chest and rocking. She shepherded him out to me without touching him once, a tour de force performance worthy of a theremin virtuoso. Before passing him off, Paula stooped to make herself eyebrow-to-eye level with Frank. "We'll lunch together soon, okay, honey?"

"Pip pip," Frank said.

She straightened up and said to me, "Dr. Matthews says Frank can't come back to school until Frank's mom comes in to meet with him."

"The new principal is a doctor?" Frank asked. "My grandfather was a doctor. He stitched soldiers back together in the trenches during World War I so they could go home and be with their loved ones again."

"Different kind of doctor," Paula said.

In the car, I asked Frank what had happened to the old principal. "Paula told me he went to a better place," he said.

Oh, dear. "What better place?" I asked anyway.

"Istanbul," he said. "Or Constantinople. I forget which."

I decided to let it go. "So, what happened to your fez?" I asked, checking him in the mirror as I did so. He cradled its battered carcass and started making a horrible sound, like the shrieks of a clubbed walrus. I'd never heard Frank cry before so it took me a minute to realize that was what he was doing. I didn't waste time pulling over to comfort him. The kid needed to go home.

Frank had stopped crying by the time we pulled into the driveway, but it was a struggle getting him out of the backseat as he'd gone all statue-of-a-deposed-dictator on me again. Somehow I managed to drag him out and lean him against the car. I was trying to boost him up over my shoulder when Xander appeared. "What's up, pal?" he asked Frank.

Frank broke away from me and stumbled over to Xander, pressed his face against his shoulder, and said, "I don't belong here. I want to go home."

"You are home, my friend," Xander said.

"No, I'm not, no I'm not, no I'M NOT!" The howling started again.

Before I could fill him in, Xander swept Frank up and ran into the house with him. I followed. He lay the kid across his bed and I wrapped Frank up tight in a blanket. Then Xander sat on the edge of the bed and took him across his lap. He rocked and hummed something to him I couldn't quite make out. Frank stopped making the walrus sounds and said, " 'Over the Rainbow.' Louis B. Mayer tried to cut that number from *The Wizard of Oz* because he thought it slowed the story down." Then he fell asleep.

Xander eased Frank onto the mattress and I wedged pillows around him. "Nice touch with the blanket," Xander murmured. "What the heck happened?"

I felt my face flush dangerously. Why was Xander the only one who ever seemed to appreciate me? "There's a new principal at Frank's school," I said.

"Uh-oh."

We backpedaled into the hall and found Mimi just outside Frank's door, pressed against the wall and looking as terrified as a jumper on a ledge working up the nerve to end all the suffering once and for all. "What's going on?" she asked.

"Frank got sent home," I said. "They wouldn't say why and he was too upset to tell me. Paula in the office said to give you this."

Mimi opened the note and read it in front of us. She put the paper back in the envelope when she was done. "My life was so much easier before I had Frank," she said.

We left xander with Frank while Mimi changed into her Audrey Hepburn ensemble and we drove back to the school. It wasn't an outfit I would have chosen, but I think she wore it in solidarity for her son. I was glad to see she left the head wrap and glasses at home this time.

Since I wasn't a custodial parent Paula "showed me to the waiting room," which meant she set me up on boxes filled with Xerox paper in a storage room, pointed to the air vent it shared with Dr. Matthews's office, then held a finger to her lips. I nodded.

The guy had the kind of piercing, self-satisfied voice that carried well. Good for clandestine listening-in, but undoubtedly hellish for anyone trapped in an elevator or an office or an area code with him. Mimi was a lot harder to hear, but I was able to make out enough words here and there to follow the conversation. Seems our darling Fiona had asked Frank if she could try on his fez. I could imagine Frank's face as he handed it over, his sweet, blank expression only those closest to him could read as delight. I could see him thinking maybe Fiona wasn't like the others after all.

Fiona took the fez, threw it down, and stomped it. When Frank snatched it back she incited the mob of bullies she'd gathered to chase Frank around the playground, trying to grab it again.

We talk, and then we join hands and run from our enemies.

I heard Mimi say "Fiona" but I couldn't make out the rest of what she said.

"Fiona's motivations are understandable. New girl, looking to establish her place in the playground hierarchy," Dr. Matthews said. "But my feeling is that Fiona isn't the one at fault here. We need to examine what you as an involved and caring parent can do to forestall incidents like this in the future. If you're honest with yourself, Mrs. Banning, you have to admit that you're allowing Frank to make himself a target."

After hearing that, my feeling was that Dr. Matthews should never have children of his own.

I heard Mimi murmur something, which he countered with, "You must realize that Frank's manner of dress separates him from the other children."

I waited for Mimi's outraged answer, "But Frank isn't like the other children!" She said something, but in a voice so soft I couldn't catch it.

Mimi was silent on the way home. When I couldn't take the suspense any longer, I asked, "How did it go?"

"It's none of your business how it went," Mimi said.

"Mimi, look, I know—"

"You know nothing, Alice. And what makes you think you can call me Mimi?"

"You told me to call you Mimi."

"I never told you to call me Mimi."

"You did," I insisted. "The day Frank asked to stay late after school. I made you eggs. My hair was wet. Remember?"

"Why are you arguing with me? Stop the car. Stop the car right now. I can't bear your face for another minute." Not that she was even looking at me.

I pulled over and put the car in park. Its nose was pointed downhill, so when Mimi flung the door open it scraped and hung on the curb. I've never seen curbs as high as the ones in Los Angeles. Frank explained to me on one of our adventures last summer that they were built tall to keep the sidewalks from flooding during the rainy season. Having weathered that now, I understood.

I imagine Mimi intended for her exit to be fast and dramatic, but what followed was a Chaplinesque struggle of tiny woman vs. world. She had to scale the Kilimanjaro of that curb through an opening hardly wider than a handbag. Her shimmying ascent made her Audrey Hepburn sheath scale her thighs and one of her shoes fall off. Once she summited, Mimi dropped out of sight behind the car door. From what I could see through the crack and from the way she was grunting, I guessed she was lying on the sidewalk, fishing around underneath the car for the lost shoe. Eureka! She stood again, leaned against the car to put the shoe on, yanked her dress down and brushed it free of sidewalk grit before turning to address me. As a courtesy I pushed the button to roll down the passenger-side window so she could say her piece.

"It must be exhausting to be so sure of yourself all the time," Mimi said. "Well, I'll let you in on a little secret, Alice. Being perfect doesn't make people love you." Then she tried her go-to move, slamming the door in my face. Even though it wasn't open very wide, the door of a Mercedes station wagon weighs about a thousand pounds, and I don't think Mimi weighed a hundred, so it took some work for her to unstick the door from the curb to shut it.

"Can I give you a hand with that?" I finally asked.

"I don't need you to give me a hand with anything," she said. "Ever again."

"Have it your way." I rolled the window back up.

Once Mimi struggled the car door shut, she fumbled her phone out of her purse and dropped it on the sidewalk. I was worried she'd broken it and thought about rolling the window down again to ask her to let me drive her home. I still had enough kindness wiggling around inside me though to resist the urge. I know from my time in New York that anger can be an exhilarating tonic that lifts some people over life's rough patches. I was pretty sure Mimi was one of those people. So I sat tight and watched her pick her phone up and dial, talk for a minute or two and check her watch. I waited on the side of the road until a cab pulled up and she got in. She never looked at me once.

Later that afternoon Mimi appeared in the kitchen while I was chopping red peppers for a salad. I knew better than to think she'd come to offer an apology.

"Here's my credit card," she said. "You need to go out and buy Frank some T-shirts and jeans and tennis shoes."

I wiped my hands on a towel. "I'll do it if you really want me to, but he won't wear those things. Not in a million years."

"He has to," she said. "That windbag I had to waste an afternoon talking to said Frank would be safer if he'd learn to disappear."

"Frank will be miserable," I said.

"Frank is a child. He'll get over it. That sanctimonious idiot in charge of his school now says if he can't learn to fit in he has to go somewhere else."

"If Frank has to 'fit in' to go there, maybe Frank should go somewhere else."

"I wouldn't give that man the satisfaction."

I picked up the knife again and really gave those peppers what-for. "This isn't about the principal or you," I said. "This is about Frank."

Instead of blowing up at me, Mimi closed her eyes the way Frank did sometimes when the world was just too much for him. It was the first time I'd ever seen anything of his face in hers. "Frank has already been somewhere else, Alice," she said. "He's been invited not to return to so many somewhere elses that any other somewhere he hasn't been to yet might be even worse than this one."

The next morning I explained to Frank that khakis would probably be okay for him to wear to school with his new T-shirts and tennis shoes, and that we'd work up to wearing jeans in a week or two. Or not. Up to him. I wanted to make it seem he had some control over the situation.

Frank stood there in his underwear and argyles, staring at the clothes I'd laid out. Two fat tears rolled down his cheeks. "I don't know how to wear these," he said.

"It's easy," I said. "The shirt pulls over your head and you don't even have to button it."

"But surely no one can want me to go out in public in a shirt meant to be worn as underwear."

"Lots of kids wear T-shirts out in public and think nothing of it."

"Lots of kids chase me around the playground, too, but that doesn't make it right."

I didn't have a comeback for that.

Frank didn't eat his breakfast. He sat at the table, staring at his waffles and plucking at the place where his collar should have been, stroking his bare forearms, scrabbling at his wrists that would under normal circumstances be cuffed and cuff linked.

Xander had to carry Frank out to the car and ride with us to school. I offered to let him drive Frank on his own, since Frank would probably like that better anyway. "Don't be ridiculous," Xander said. "I'll just sit back here with my buddy. I'll walk him to class, too, to be sure he gets there safe."

When he got back in the car, Xander said, "This is a bad idea. A bad, bad idea."

"I think so, too," I said.

"Mimi is a genius, you know. But sometimes smart people do the stupidest things."

"Mimi doesn't know what else to do," I said, surprising myself now by sticking up for her. "Frank has gotten kicked out of so many places already."

Xander shrugged. "So what? Who hasn't?"

Me, I didn't say.

"It's lucky I could drop everything and come when she called," Xander added. "You know, I have to wonder sometimes what that woman would do without me."

Her book wasn't finished yet, but I was. I told Mimi I was leaving before I told Mr. Vargas. I wanted my bridges burned.

"Nobody's holding you prisoner here," Mimi said. "Go."

"You'll be all right," I said. "As long as Xander's here you don't need me."

"Xander," she said. "Ha."

18

Packing my bags was easy. E-mailing Mr. Vargas to explain why I was deserting my post wasn't. No matter how sane I sounded at the outset of each effort, by the time I was a line or two in, I started to sound as whiny as a jilted lover. How can I help Mimi when she keeps me at arm's length? She doesn't appreciate me. There's someone else, someone blonder, prettier, and more popular. I'm coming home.

I got a call from Frank's school but pressed "ignore" and turned my cell off. If there was a problem, it was Mimi's problem now. Or Mimi's and Xander's. Not mine. I sat there holding the phone, feeling guilty and worried and not typing anything else to Mr. Vargas. Somebody knocked. If Mimi needed me to pick up Frank, I'd do it. Just this one last time.

It was Xander. He hadn't been in my room since last summer when I thought I'd dreamed In-the-Manner-of-Apollo to life. Back when I was a know-it-all teenager, I'd wondered how my sensible mother had gotten hornswoggled into marrying a deadbeat like my dad. Seeing Xander there on my doorstep, I finally got it. Sometimes smart people do the stupid-est things.

"Mimi says you're going back to New York," Xander said. "How long will you be gone?"

"I'm not coming back."

"What?"

"Mimi won't let me do the work Mr. Vargas sent me to do. She doesn't like me. Frank only tolerates me. I don't belong here. I want to go home."

"Mimi likes you as much as she can like anybody. Frank loves you. He'll be devastated."

I felt a twist in my gut. "Not with you around, he won't."

"That's not true."

"Of course it is. I'm sloppy seconds whenever you're here."

"Not in my book." Xander stepped closer. "Don't I count? Maybe I'll be devastated when you go."

"Ha," I said. That syllable reminded me of something, but I couldn't remember exactly what.

"Hey." He touched my cheek so lightly that only the tip of his middle finger brushed against my skin. "Are you leaving because of me?"

"Are you Frank's dad?" I asked.

He stared at me for a minute, then took my forearm and shoved me farther into my room and closed the door. "Why would you ask me that? Do you think I would have gone after you in Mimi's house if Mimi and I had been together once?"

He went after me? I'm ashamed to say how that thrilled me. "I never said you two were romantically involved. You could have done it as a friend. People do that." I imagined then how Mimi would phrase that request. Pardon me, could you spare a thimbleful of sperm? Although of course she would have worded it more carefully. "Thimbleful" isn't a unit of measure you want to link up with a guy's manly parts in any context. Not if you want something from him.

"We're friends," Xander said. "But not like that."

"What kind of friends are you then?" I asked. "Because for the life of me, I can't figure out how you fit into the picture here."

"What do you mean?"

"Frank told me you were in the delivery room with Mimi the night he was born. That's kind of a lot to ask of some guy who's just a friend."

Xander sat down on my bed and collapsed back, his arms splayed wide. "Sweet suffering Jesus," he said. "Mimi has nobody, Alice. Nobody." He lay there for a minute, staring at the ceiling. Then he sat up and said, "Do you know what that's like?"

"So, what are you saying? It's you? Not you? I'm curious."

He gave me one of those long hard looks you give someone on the street when you start wondering if that's somebody from your old neighborhood or an actor you've seen on television or an enemy from another life.

"You're not curious, Alice. You're selfish."

I've been called a few names in my life—boring, mousy, Goody-Two-shoes, suck-up. Not selfish. Never selfish.

Xander pushed past me. His eyes passed over my face this time like he'd never seen me before in his life. Like I was air.

Mimi was right. It had been nice to be so sure of myself. Now that I didn't have that compass anymore, I'd never felt so lost. I dropped onto the red love seat and hated myself for a good long time. Here are some adjectives I aimed at myself: Self-righteous. Judgmental. Perfidious. Smug. The kind of person who's convinced the world would be a better place if everybody else would just shut up and listen.

I was the voice of Dr. Matthews coming through the air vent.

From the rain the hills had sprung a tender, hopeful green that wouldn't last out the week. My stomach started growling but I wasn't hungry. I needed to call a cab but I didn't do it. It wasn't like I was going to miss my plane or anything. My plan was to show up and take the next spot on standby any airline offered up.

When the knock came the second time, I didn't answer. Mimi didn't knock again. She let herself in. "You're still here," she said.

"I was just calling a cab." I didn't turn to look at her.

"I need you," she said.

"Whatever it is, Xander can help you out."

"Xander can't drive."

"What do you mean? Of course he can drive."

"He doesn't have a license."

I turned around when she said that. Even though she was more than old enough to be my mother, I'd never thought of Mimi as old until then.

"He drove the station wagon to pick up lumber to fix the door," I said.

"He can't kill lumber," she said. "I need you to drive me to the hospital. Frank is on his way there in an ambulance."

"It's all my fault," Mimi said.

I was driving as fast as I could without killing us. "It's not your fault. Don't say that."

"It is," she said. "After you got through talking to me, I was sitting at my desk thinking I wouldn't have had to let you in my house if Frank had never been born."

They had called from school to tell Mimi that Frank had had a seizure.

"A seizure?" I said. "That's not so terrible. A seizure can be caused by almost anything. Low blood sugar. Lack of sleep. Heat. An allergic reaction." Brain tumor. I skipped that one.

"Brain tumor," Mimi whispered. "That would explain so much."

The not-Paula office lady had telephoned. "I called your partner Alice," she told Mimi. "But she wasn't answering. You'll probably want to get in touch with her before you leave for the hospital."

Frank had two mommies. Honestly, the kid could have used a dozen.

On the way to the hospital, Mimi told me the whole sad unfictional story of the end of Julian.

It started like this: "I always thought my mother was a fool. Then I had Frank."

Up until Frank, Mimi felt confident she'd be a better mother than Banning had been. Mimi had Julian all figured out. Her brother was astoundingly good at a few things and terrible at everything else. So when their mother told him he needed to come inside and do his homework in some subject Julian had no talent for, like French or physics, Mimi would slip in and do it for him. It was easier to get away with than you might imagine, since Julian's handwriting was so illegible that when he started high school his mother buckled and bought him the portable typewriter Mimi used now. All Julian had to do was scrawl his name at the top of the lessons Mimi typed up while Julian threw balls at the side of the barn until the siding splintered and broke and it got so dark you couldn't make out the white of the ball against the weathered gray of the wood anymore. So what if Julian didn't know the difference between the Treaty of Versailles and the Treaty of Verdun? Her brother was different from other kids. Special. He'd outgrow being an oddball someday; or he'd be so famous for something that no one would care about his awkwardness anymore.

Still, it had been a relief when her brother left for college. She loved him, of course, but sometimes found his strange flatness as off-putting as everybody else did. The house was so much more peaceful without him banging around in it. The rest of them could get some sleep at night. Well, Mimi could, anyway. Her mother had stopped looking like she slept, ever, years ago. Dr. Frank spent most nights at the hospital, sewing up drunks, pronouncing victims of car crashes dead, delivering babies, what have you.

Mimi could see how upset Banning got when she tried to talk to Julian on the phone while he was away at school. He never spoke in sentences. Just "fine," or "okay," or "not really." And when his grades came Banning would hold the envelope in her hand for a long time, then open it, scan the paper inside, crumple it, and toss it in the trash without showing it to anybody else. It was too bad, Mimi thought, that she couldn't be with Julian to do his schoolwork for him.

Then Mimi went off to college, too. Being away from home was a relief she hadn't anticipated, like giving up a pair of shoes you loved but hadn't realized were pinching the life out of your toes until you put on ones that fit. At college, Mimi didn't talk about the

Gillespies. She realized it was a whole lot easier to ask other people questions about themselves. Everybody said she was so easy to talk to, but "talk at" was closer to the truth. Still, Mimi was happy, or pretended to be, which almost made it seem so.

Halfway through the second semester of her freshman year, Julian showed up at her dorm. She was in her room reading. Mimi remembered the sentence passing under her eyes when she heard the crazy pounding on the door to her suite. "nobody, not even the rain, has such small hands" She'd just gotten finished thinking that the line of poetry itself was beautiful but would it kill the guy to capitalize the words at the beginning of each line and use proper punctuation?

Then one of her roommates came to get her.

She sighed, put her book down, and went to the door. "Julian," she said, and gave him a hug even though he never wanted to be hugged. She knew her roommates would think it was weird if she didn't do it.

"He's really your brother?" one of them asked. Mimi couldn't for the life of her remember the girl's name. "You never told us you had a brother."

Julian took all this in but didn't say anything. He did look kind of upset, for Julian anyway.

Mimi led him into her room and sat on the chair at her desk and he sat on the chair by her roommate's desk.

Mimi was glad her roommate was out. She was always out with that boyfriend she talked about every waking minute. Conrad. Funny, Mimi couldn't remember that roommate's name, either. "What's up, Julian?" she asked.

"I've been scouted by the Atlanta Braves. The scout said he wasn't leaving until he had Julian Gillespie's signature on an Atlanta Braves contract."

"Oh, Julian! That's so exciting! That's what you've always wanted. What happened after that?"

"What happened after that was he left without my signature, because my signature is worthless without parental approval because I'm still a minor. The signature he needed was from Dr. Frank Banning. Or Mrs. Frank Banning. Either one, or both."

"Well, that won't be a problem, right?"

"It will be a problem. It is a problem. Mother won't sign and she won't let Father do it, either."

"Why not?"

"Because I've flunked out of school."

"Oh, no."

"Mother says I have to finish college first. Mimi, I'm no good at school. I hate it there."

"Did you tell her that?"

"Yes."

"What did she say?"

"She said if I applied myself I could make good

grades like I did in high school when you were doing my homework."

"She doesn't know I was doing your homework."

"No, but I do. It's hopeless, Mimi. Mother said we aren't the kind of people who have sons who grow up to play sports and marry movie stars. We're the kind of people who have sons who make good grades and grow up to be doctors."

Mimi couldn't help noticing that no mention was made of what kind of daughters their kind of people had. But in fairness this story wasn't about her.

"Did she say anything else?"

"She said if she was going to have a son who was going to grow up to be Joe DiMaggio, she might as well have married Elvis."

Mimi could never quite figure out that line of reasoning. But she couldn't help wondering if marrying Elvis had ever been an option for Banning. Every time her mother mentioned the splash she'd made with Elvis, which was often, it made Mimi remember overhearing Banning on the telephone, saying to one of her friends what a shame it was that Julian was beautiful and could have his pick of the girls if he'd just show any interest, but Mimi, bless her heart, was such a homely, frowny-faced runt that nobody would ever want her. She'd have to get a job. Banning said "job" like it was "leprosy."

"You have to help me, Mimi," Julian said.

"I don't know," Mimi said. "Sounds like you may have to figure this one out for yourself. I have a paper to write. Nobody is going to write it for me."

"I've figured this one out already. I want to play baseball. I'll die if I can't play."

Julian was staring at her. Mimi knew that numb look, that posture, that set of the jaw. When he got like that he couldn't be reasoned with. At least he was still on the chair. Sometimes when he got especially mulish, Julian would lie on the floor and refuse to budge. Mimi was only about half his size now, so that was the last thing she wanted to let happen.

"You'll be fine. Daddy survived the Marne. You'll make it through this."

Julian didn't say anything for a while. When he did, it seemed like a non sequitur. "Those girls out there didn't believe I was your brother," he said. "They said if you had a brother, they would know about it."

"So? I don't have to tell everybody everything."

When Julian didn't say anything else she picked up her book again and went back to reading. She hoped he'd get bored and leave. If he didn't, well, he could spend the night on her roommate's bed and she'd worry about him in the morning.

As it turned out, that wasn't necessary. After a few minutes of sitting there while Mimi studiously ignored him, Julian got up and left. She didn't realize he hadn't left by the door but had chosen instead to step out a window in her suite that looked over a quadrangle six stories below until she heard a tangle of voices far away, and then a siren.

"I never told those girls I had a brother," Mimi told me. "And then I didn't have one."

When Mimi and I got to the emergency room admissions desk, she tried to tell them why she was there. "My son—" she said, and the rest of the sentence stuck in her throat. It happened over and over. "My son—" she'd say, and choke.

Finally I put my hand on her arm and said, "Our son Frank Banning came here in an ambulance. We just got a call from his school."

I said that without thinking. I suppose the office lady we didn't know planted that idea in my head. The way it flowered turned out to be a thing of beauty. At the hospital, of course, they wouldn't let anybody beyond the swinging doors who wasn't a member of the immediate family.

The clerk at the admissions desk checked her roster. "You got here fast," she said. "His ambulance hasn't arrived yet. You should think about driving ambulances yourself."

19

Until he was stabilized, the clerk told us, only one
parent could go behind the swinging doors to
meet Frank as they wheeled him from the ambulance
to the emergency room.

"You go." Mimi's lips barely moved when she said
it. She was pale and still and had her fists clenched in
her lap and her eyes closed.

When they rolled him in, it took me a minute to realize it was Frank because he was dressed in the T-shirt
and khakis and tennis shoes he'd cried over wearing
that morning. Then I saw how slowly the gurney was
moving and put my palm against the wall to keep from
collapsing. There's no need to rush, I thought, because
he's already dead. The T-shirt did it, on the playground, with a knife to his heart.

But the paramedics looked neither crushed nor sympathetic. They looked pissed. Frank's body wasn't covered by a sheet, either, as it would have been in a hospital drama. Why waste budget on hiring an actor to play a corpse, I could hear Frank's explaining voice say, when nonunion pillows under a sheet work equally well? Frank's eyes were squeezed shut in a way that didn't suggest death. Also, he was moving, his limbs jerking ever so slightly, arrhythmically, like a horse twitching off flies on a hot summer afternoon.

He was faking.

Once, standing on a street corner in New York waiting for the light to change, I saw a bicyclist get hit by a taxi. He'd zipped through a red light the way bicyclists do sometimes, and the greenlit taxi was going fast, as taxis will. The bike crunched under the tires and the bicyclist got tossed onto the hood. His body shattered the windshield before he rolled up and over the roof. I don't know if the bicyclist lived or died, because that was when I did an about-face and walked as quickly as I could in the opposite direction. A good person would have stuck around to help, would have called 911 and made a statement to the police. I couldn't do it. I couldn't stick around to bear witness to an act of such shattering foolishness, something that would ever after alter the life of the bicyclist, the taxi driver, his passenger, and the innocent onlookers like me who couldn't unsee the guy rolling over that taxi roof. I didn't want to know how it actually ended. I needed to believe that everything turned out okay.

Seeing Frank lying on the gurney like that, I fought the urge to pull another about-face. I willed myself to go to him, and almost but not quite put my hand on his forehead.

"Frank," I said. "Are you okay? What happened?"

"I was being pursued by a pack of coyotes on the playground and ended up flat on my back. I assumed I'd been brought low by some type of seizure. The principal saw me lying there and told me to get up. I explained my situation and he said, 'If you're having a seizure, we need to call an ambulance.' Miss Peppe told him that wouldn't be necessary. But he said if I claimed I was having a seizure, then by gum, I was going to the hospital."

"He said that?" I asked.

"Not exactly. He didn't use the phrase 'by gum.' But that seemed appropriate to the situation. Did you know ancient man chewed a gum derived from birch tar during the Neolithic period more than five thousand years ago? Also, I'm guessing, ancient woman."

I felt a little bit like having a seizure myself. "So Dr. Matthews called an ambulance to come and get you instead of calling me?"

"In his shoes, I would have opted for giving you a jingle, but I would rather not be in the principal's shoes because they were right by my head while I was convulsing and I would rather drop dead than wear horrible shoes like that. I suppose the principal called the ambulance because he is a doctor and so he might assume I required hospitalization." While he spoke, Frank forgot to twitch.

I had to put the hand I'd had hovering over his brow on the gurney to steady myself. "He's not that kind of doctor, you know," I said.

"I know," Frank said.

"Can't you see he's faking?"

I'd pulled one of the paramedics aside while the other carted Frank into the emergency room.

"You his mother?" he asked.

"Yes," I said. It was easier than explaining.

"Can I see he's faking? Hmm. What do you think?"

"Then why did you pick him up?"

"When the school called, we had to go. Once we got there, we had to take him. We're legally bound to. As the principal told me more than once, in case I'd forgotten."

"But I don't understand. Frank's done this before. The school never used to call an ambulance to come for him. They called us."

The paramedic shook his head. He looked disgusted. "That guy's a tool. Stood over the kid, saying, 'You have a seizure, we call an ambulance and you go to the hospital. That's how things work in the real world, my friend.' Like that's any way to teach a kid a lesson. Give an eight-year-old boy a chance to cut class, run red lights, and blast a siren? What kid says no to that?"

"He's almost ten," I said.

He shrugged. "Still."

"The school told us Frank was having a seizure," I said. "They didn't say 'faking a seizure.' I've never been so scared."

"Maybe you're the one the principal wanted to teach a lesson. He seemed like that kind of guy."

In the waiting room, I explained what had happened. "Mimi," I said. "Frank's all right."

She opened her eyes but her face didn't register any emotion. "He'll never be all right," she said. "He's like my brother." She picked up her purse and headed for the door.

"Where are you going?"

"Back to work."

"What about Frank?"

"You stay with him. I'll take a cab home."

"You're going to leave without seeing him?"

"I'll see him when he gets home."

"Mimi," I said. "He needs to see you."

"I understand that you're trying to help, Alice," she said. "But I don't need to see Frank as a patient in an emergency room setting if I don't have to. I don't want that image stuck in my head. Not right now. I'm very near the end."

I touched her forearm. "Of course," I said. "I get that. Go. Don't worry. I'll take care of everything."

"How gratifying for you," she said. "Now take your hands off me."

I did. She left.

I pushed through the swinging doors again in time to hear Frank saying to a nurse, "Tinkerbell gave my mother a gown when she had to come to the emergency room, so I wondered if you might loan me a waistcoat. Or, failing that, a doctor's white lab coat. Size small."

The nurse exchanged a look with the intern examining Frank. "Are you cold, sweetheart?" she asked. "I can get you a blanket."

"I'm not cold," he said. "I'm embarrassed."

"There you are, Mom," the intern said when he saw me. "Our friend Frank is in good shape now, so if you'll follow me and sign some papers, we'll be done here."

He showed me to a chair in an empty room and sat down next to me in the narrow space alongside the examination table, underneath a staggering array of monitoring equipment. Without a patient on the slab, the machines were quiet and the lines of colored light stretched flat across the screens. The intern fitted his palms together and stared at them, like some guy who had some very serious praying to do and didn't know quite how to start. Even to me he looked young. I had to figure he might not have come across a whole lot of kids like Frank in his training yet.

After he got through studying his hands he looked up at me from under his brows. He had such a kind face. I felt for him.

"About Tinkerbell," I said. "I can explain."

"I think Tinkerbell is the least of your problems," he said. "I'm worried about your son."

"So am I," I said.

By the time we got done with the talking and the paperwork it was almost dark outside. I tried to hold Frank's hand on the way to the car but he snatched it away. I decided he'd been through too much already for me to bust him for that this time. Frank got in the backseat and strapped himself in. I got in on the other side, next to him. "You can't drive the car from back here," he said.

"I know. What's going on with you, Frank? Is there anything you want to talk about?"

"As a matter of fact, there is. Where is my mother? I can't help noticing that she keeps missing pivotal moments in my day-to-day life."

"She had to go back to work."

"On her book?"

"Yes. She's very near the end."

"How do you know? Have you seen it?"

"I haven't. She said."

"I don't understand the delay," Frank said. "I wrote my book in an afternoon. I certainly hope this project of hers ends up being worth all the Sturm und Drang."

"I hope so, too," I said. "I know your mother wants to finish as soon as she can so she can get back to spending more time with you."

"I have had about enough of this for one day," Frank said. "It's time for you to stop talking."

Neither of us wanted to go home yet. There was a marathon Keaton festival at the silent movie house, so we went there instead. We came in partway through the one on a steamboat where Buster, a poor boy in love with a rich girl who's the daughter of his father's steamship archrival, sneaks off his father's broken-down paddle wheeler in the night to be with his love. To throw his dad off the scent, Buster mounds pillows under the covers of his bunk so his father would think he was asleep there. When his dad ripped the blankets back and uncovered Buster's ruse, I started laughing and couldn't stop.

"Shhhhhhhhh!" Frank hissed when it became clear I wasn't going to be able to put a sock in it. "I understand that it's a humorous situation, Alice, but we'll be ejected for disruptive behavior. The management does that. You will not like it. I know."

"I'm sorry," I whispered. "Stay here. Don't move. I'll be right back."

Out in the lobby, I drank from the water fountain and took some deep breaths to calm myself. Then I called Frank's psychiatrist and left a message. I hoped Mimi had done that already, but I had my doubts. After that I called Mr. Vargas. He sounded so glad to hear my voice I almost wept.

"Alice!" he said. "What's the good news?"

When I didn't answer for several beats, he said, "Alice?"

"I'm sorry," I said. "What? You're breaking up."

"I said, how are things there?"

"It's Mimi," I said. "She's very near the end."

"Great!" he said. "See? Patience. Patience and kid gloves. Works every time."

I couldn't help picturing those kid gloves. Red ones. Elbow length. Italian. Beautiful gloves. Not gloves I would have dreamed of before knowing Frank.

"Alice?" Mr. Vargas said. "Alice? Are you there?"

"Yes," I said. "I'm here."

Frank and I watched that Buster Keaton movie to the end. And the one that came after it. By the time we got back to the house Frank was asleep. I managed to get him out of the car without waking him and half-dragged, half-carried him into the house and tucked him into bed, tennis shoes and all. I could hear Mimi typing so I didn't bother to tell her we were back. She could figure it out for herself.

I don't know how long I stood there looking at Frank's face illuminated by a shaft of light falling through the bedroom door. When he was asleep he looked so harmless. He was a beautiful child, really. Just handsome enough to catch a few extra breaks in life, but not handsome enough to be hamstrung by it. It was the way Frank packaged himself that pushed him over into the spectacular. That nobody could take from him, no matter how many small-minded men in horrible shoes might try.

I lay what I thought of as his Ragged Frank outfit—the blown-out morning pants and tattered tailcoat that were as close to owning sweats as he got—on top of his bedclothes so he'd see that instead of the T-shirt and khakis he'd gone to sleep in. I left his top hat on his bedside table. By that time I was practically asleep on my feet—horses sleep standing up, did you know that?—and put myself to bed, too. I didn't turn on the light, just tottered over and pulled the covers back.

Underneath the covers, I found Xander.

"What are you doing in my bed?" I asked.

He opened his eyes and blinked sleepily. "Hold on, Goldilocks. This is my bed, remember? I thought you blew town so I moved back in. What's going on?"

"I didn't go," I said. "Scoot over. Keep your mouth shut and your hands to yourself."

I talked, though. Boy, did I ever. I ended up telling Xander all the stuff about the day that I'd wanted to spill to Mr. Vargas. "So then Frank says, 'Do you know that ancient man was chewing a gum derived from birch tar during the Neolithic period more than five thousand years ago?' He just scared the liver out of all of us, and he's talking about the history of chewing gum?"

Xander raised his hand.

"What?"

"Can I say one thing?" he asked.

"Okay."

"Frank couldn't wear his armor today," Xander said. "Facts were all the protection he had. Facts were his force field."

20

When I woke up it was light out and Frank was howling. I was in the hall outside his room without any memory of running there. He was with Mimi, wearing the Ragged Frank ensemble, his arms wrapped around his mother's calves. Mimi was wearing the typical cardigan ensemble, plus Frank's top hat.

"I don't belong there!" he shouted.

"I'm very near the end," she answered. There was something flat and dead about her voice that frightened me.

"I don't belong there!"

"I'm very near the end," she insisted. I realized then that her tone of voice reminded me of Frank.

"Stop it, both of you!" I yelled.

"Alice, wake up," Xander said. He was shaking me by the shoulders.

I opened my eyes. It wasn't still black night outside, but it wasn't light yet, either. "Okay," I said. "Okay, okay. What time is it?"

"It's just before six."

"You have to get out of here, now," I said. "This never happened."

I wish I could tell you that what actually happened that morning made a whole lot more sense, but it didn't. Mimi told me to take Frank to school. Dressed in a T-shirt and tennis shoes. Also jeans.

"Did you talk to his psychiatrist?" I asked.

"When? I had to spend half the day at the hospital, and after I came home I had to go right back to work. I don't need to talk to anybody's psychiatrist. Frank will be fine. He has to be. This is not a negotiation. Stop wasting my time."

Xander stood in front of the garage watching us back down the driveway. He was barefoot and in boxers, something he couldn't do in mid-January in Alabama or Nebraska. He had his arms crossed over his chest, cradling each elbow in the opposite palm. Every line of his body said: "This is a very bad idea."

"You want to take Xander with us?" I asked Frank, looking over my shoulder.

"He isn't dressed," he said.

I stayed like that, twisted backward, using my eyes instead of the rearview mirror to guide myself down the driveway. I imagine Xander waved at Frank as we left because Frank gave a sad little salute that didn't seem directed at me. I didn't want to look. I didn't want to see.

Instead of dropping Frank off at school I parked and got out of the car with him.

"Where are you going?" Frank asked.

"I'm walking you to class," I said.

"That won't be necessary," he said. "This time I'm prepared for the worst."

"You're really brave, Frank," I said. "I'm proud of you."

"Thank you," he said. "It's easier to be brave when you're carrying a knife."

"Get back in the car," I said.

I pulled over at a park. "Oh," he said. "Are we going to the playground? I love it in the early morning, when the sand is freshly raked."

"Give me the knife," I said. I was expecting one of the big sharp knives from the kitchen or maybe the plastic machete, but what he had tucked into his argyle sock was an old-fashioned letter opener shaped like a sword in a battered green leather sheath embossed with gold. "Where did you get this?" I asked.

"From my mother's desk. It belonged to my grandfather."

"You were in your mother's office? Doing what?"

"Looking for my mother."

"Wasn't she in there?"

"She was. Asleep on the floor."

"I understand why you're upset, Alice," Dr. Abrams said. "But let's look on the positive side of this. You have to admit it's a feat of imagination for a nine-year-old to get himself rescued from a threatening situation by an ambulance. Really, it's a kind of genius."

"I'm not sure the ambulance was his idea," I said. "Anyway, I'd prefer less genius and more judgment."

"You say that now," she said. "But you'll be glad of it someday."

"But I'm here now," I said. "I won't be around for someday."

I had called Frank's psychiatrist after I frisked him at the park. "I think it's a good idea for you to talk to Dr. Abrams today," I told him.

"I don't think it's a good idea at all. I don't want to talk to anyone else," Frank said. "I just want to talk to myself in the voice of a 1940s radio announcer. We are at the playground already, so I don't see why you won't let me do it."

"You can do that all you want," I said. "In the car." I stuffed him inside the wagon and dialed the shrink. She picked up my call right away and I stood with my back to Frank while I outlined the situation. "I had a cancellation," she said. "Bring him now."

When I got there Dr. Abrams explained that I couldn't come into the room with them since I wasn't Frank's parent. I'd already lied and said Mimi had asked me to bring Frank in, so I didn't push it. They had a muffled, intense conversation that I couldn't quite make out despite pressing my ear to the door. When they stopped talking I hopped into a chair and picked up a magazine. When Frank emerged I looked up at them both with a radiant, guilty smile.

"I have a couple of quick questions," I said to Dr. Abrams. "Can I duck into your office for a minute while Frank waits out here?" That's when we had our talk about genius vs. judgment. Also I asked if she thought Frank should go back to that school.

"I really can't discuss Frank any further with you until I've talked to his mother. You understand," she said.

"Of course," I said.

I took frank back to that playground and left a message for Paula in the office, asking her to call my cell when she could talk freely. I'd loaned Frank my sweater because I could see he was jonesing for a piece of clothing to cover his bare arms. He'd found a paper grocery bag somewhere and had turned it wrong side out and twisted and crumpled it into the shape of a top hat. To make it hold the shape he'd taken the lace out of one of his sneakers to use as a hatband. I had to give the kid props. He had a gift. But I also had to admit that this particular ensemble didn't make him look 100 percent sane.

I was watching Frank pacing, one shoe flapping, giving 1940s radio announcer Walter Winchell a run for his money, when my phone howled. "I can keep an eye out for him, but I can only do so much," Paula said. "I will tell you Dr. Matthews thinks Frank's a nuisance and that he can't possibly be that smart. He likes children who make high scores on standardized tests and smile a lot. He doesn't like Frank."

"He doesn't understand Frank," I said. "Frank's light-years beyond smart."

"I know, honey. But Dr. Matthews isn't."

"Mimi wants to know what do you think we should do."

"Frank got off on the wrong foot with Dr. Matthews and Mimi didn't kiss up to him in their conference. I don't think you can get on his good side now," Paula said. "If he doesn't find an excuse for expelling Frank, he'll drive him out some other way. He's done it to a second-grader already, and let me tell you, Alice, it wasn't pretty. It breaks my heart to say this because I'll miss my little friend, but if Frank were my son I wouldn't send him back here as long as that man is in charge. To be honest, I may not stick it out here much longer myself."

I had to do something.

I wanted to tell Mimi everything Paula had said but I knew she'd get mad at me in a shoot-the-messenger way that wouldn't help a bit. Frank's shrink had shut me out and I couldn't bring myself to tell Mr. Vargas how badly I was failing him. I was running out of people to go to for advice.

Sometimes just explaining your predicament—to a bartender, a priest, the old woman in a shift and flip-flops cleaning the lint traps in the Laundromat dryers—is all it takes to see a way out of it. Trust me, I didn't turn to Xander because I thought of him as a child-rearing sage; honestly, who is? It was just that Xander knew all the characters in our sad little drama and could lend a sympathetic ear. When he suggested a few weeks of therapeutic hooky for Frank until Mimi was done with her novel and could start living in the world outside her head again, I was able to convince myself that it was a spectacular idea.

"How do you propose we do that?" I asked. "Mimi expects me to take Frank to school every morning."

"You leave with him dressed for school, park around the corner, and I meet you there. Frank changes into Frank clothes in the backseat. The three of us hang out until it's time to 'come home from school.' Frank changes clothes, you drive up the driveway, I show up later. We'll get through this, Alice. You can count on me."

I was desperate. I was in.

Except I didn't see how we would get Frank to understand he couldn't breathe a word of our plan to his mother. "I'll handle that," Xander said.

They had a conference on a park bench. Frank was wearing a loud plaid zoot suit I'd never seen before, with taxi-yellow suspenders, yellow pocket handkerchief, dice cuff links, and two-toned shoes. Xander, in ancient jeans and a T-shirt, looked like he was having a session with his new bookie, Little Frankie, whom he'd met while working as a grip on the set of a remake of *Guys and Dolls.*

"So when I change my clothes, do I do it in a phone booth?" Frank asked.

"Nope. Backseat of the station wagon. We won't look."

"Good. Phone booths are hard to find these days. Can I ask you something?"

"Of course."

"Did I get kicked out of school?"

"No way, pal. You're on hiatus. Once your mother and her book are squared away, we'll find you a new school you'll like much better. Until then, let's not tell your mom any of this. She has enough to worry about already."

"I'll miss my friends," Frank said. "Paula. Miss Peppe."

"And they'll miss you. But that's how it is for academic staff. Students come and go like waves on the beach. I guarantee you, Frank, of all the generations of kids that Paula and Miss Peppe have known and will know, you're the one they'll remember best. You're the one they'll miss the most."

Frank nodded. "You're probably right."

I had to hand it to Frank. He took it like a champ. And he had been right about Xander all along. There were times when you really could count on him.

Do we believe Mimi's almost done with her book?" I asked Xander that night after Frank had gone to bed and we had, too.

"No idea," he said. "How does that joke about the deer go? The one that ends with 'no idea'?"

"What do you call a deer with no eyes," I said. "No idear. I hate that joke. I picture the deer stumbling around in the woods, bumping into trees."

"I wouldn't worry about that. The coyotes will get the deer before the trees do." He tried to kiss me but I pulled away.

"She types all day," I said.

"Alice, she's been typing as long as I've known her. Less since Frank was born, but still. She could have written a dozen books by now. Six, maybe. Four, at least."

"All that typing and she's never finished anything?" This was very bad news.

"How should I know? The woman is a sphinx."

"Are you kidding? She tells you everything, Xander. You're the sphinx."

Xander rolled to his side and narrowed his eyes at me. "What's that supposed to mean?"

"You never tell me anything about yourself."

"Are you kidding? I'm an open book. What do you want to know?"

"Why don't you have a driver's license?" I asked. "Does it have anything to do with your sister who died?"

He propped himself up on an elbow. "Mimi told you about that?"

"Some," I said, fishing. "Nothing" would have been closer to the truth.

Xander lay back and stared at the ceiling for a while before he said, "I'm going to go play the piano for a little while." He pulled on a pair of pants and his T-shirt. "There's this piece I've been trying to get under my belt forever."

"Xander," I said. "What happened to your sister?"

"Which one?"

"The dead one."

"She died," he said. "A long time ago. I don't want to talk about it."

After he left I lay there listening for I don't know how long to Xander play something that I finally realized was the theme from *Chariots of Fire*. Had Frank asked him to learn that one? I'd never watched that movie with the kid but I imagined he must like the Jazz Age English menswear in it very much.

You could count on Xander sometimes as long as you remembered not to make a habit of it. After our first day of The Three Musketeers Cut Class, he disappeared again. No notes, no postcards, nothing. It didn't seem to worry Frank this time, or even bother him much. I think he was so relieved to be free of school that nothing else mattered. As for me, if I believed Xander wouldn't vanish again, I was kidding myself.

Those abbreviated Southern California winter days Frank and I spent wandering through Los Angeles were a recap of our halcyon time last summer before Xander was in the picture. I chased Frank through museum galleries. We went to the little municipal airport and looked for the yellow biplane. We kicked through the freshly raked sand at the playground. We even went to the beach, where Frank rolled up his Tony Curtis yachting chinos and waded into the gray surf. He stood there for a long time with the waves lapping at his ankles and a look of powerful concentration on his face.

"Let's go, Frank," I said finally. "It gets dark by rush hour now and I don't want to get stuck in that."

"Not yet," he said. "I'm busy."

"Doing what?"

"An experiment."

"Are you trying to see how long you can stand barefoot in cold ocean water before your toes fall off?"

"No. I am thinking very hard about Paula. I want to find out if the power of my thoughts, boosted by the naturally occurring electricity found in salt water and the intrinsic energy of the tides, will enable my brain to connect with hers."

"Huh. Interesting. Could work I guess. How will you know if it does?"

Frank looked at me like I wasn't the sharpest blade in the drawer. "I'll hear her voice in my brain, answering my question."

"I'm sure she misses you a lot, Frank," I said.

"I know that. That wasn't my question. I asked Paula to name her favorite Warner Brothers musical from the 1950s. All those lunches together, and we never talked about that."

I discovered that walking around with a school-aged child on a school day outside of school is a nerve-wracking adventure. Particularly if you don't have a flair for truancy and the kid you're with is as high visibility as Frank. People asked questions. I had to have my excuses lined up.

"Parent-teacher conferences," I used when people were paying attention to my answer. Also "doctor's appointment." "Religious holiday" required checking a calendar before we left in the morning. When I could see people were more interested in staring at Frank than in listening to what I said, I trotted out "Power outage." "Measles outbreak." "Fire in the canyon." "Coyotes on the playground."

I also fielded a lot of the questions like the ones I used to ask. "Is he from another country?" "Is he on his way to a film set?" And of course, "Does he always dress like that?" Now that I knew more of the answers I found myself falling back on Mimi's "Some version of it." I didn't know how else to explain Frank in twenty-five words or less.

One afternoon a week or so after Frank went AWOL, we were parked around the corner from the house while he changed into his I'm-just-a-regular-California-school-kid mufti in the backseat. I stood on the curb with my back to him to give Frank his privacy. A blond woman carrying a cardboard box and leading a little boy by the hand walked past us. I know this is the kind of thing that happens in neighborhoods across America every millisecond, but seeing a pedestrian in the hills of Bel Air in the middle of the afternoon is an event worth noting. Nobody walks anywhere in that neighborhood, particularly at that time of day.

"Hi," I said when she passed. I was so busy trying to study her discreetly that I hardly saw the kid. She was very pretty, but that wasn't why I was staring. Something was so familiar about her.

"Hi," she said, smiled and kept walking. I inspected my cuticles until she was halfway up the block, then looked again. She had a choppy haircut, either expensive or self-inflicted over the kitchen sink, and a tattoo on her neck. Something jarred loose in my head. Was she the "friend" from Xander's photograph? I kicked myself for not getting a better look at her face.

After Frank finished changing, we rounded the corner and drove up to the gate. I could see somebody waiting in the driveway. As we got closer I saw it was the same girl, facing the entry keypad as if she expected to be buzzed in any minute. Her little boy was on the sidewalk, cuddled up against the wall in a piece of shade.

I pulled into the drive and rolled down the window. She turned around and gave me a dazzling smile. "Can I help you?" I asked.

"Oh, you live here," she said. "I saw you around the corner. If I had known, I could have given you this box back there."

"What's in the box?" I asked.

"Something for Frank. From Xander. Not to be opened before Frank's birthday. Xander didn't want to send it through the mail."

Frank was leaning out the window now with his arms outstretched.

"Sit down, Frank," I said. I told the girl, "You'd better give that to me."

"Sure thing." She handed it over, then turned and held her hand out to the little boy. "Come on, Alec," she said. "We don't want to miss our bus."

I had never seen a picture of Xander as a child, but after seeing that kid's face, I didn't need to.

21

I made sure Frank was asleep before I crept out to the Dream House with Xander's box under my arm. Mimi still set the burglar alarm every night at dusk even though Xander had never gotten around to reconnecting it after he replaced the sliding glass door. Once I started opening my bathroom window before I went to bed I stopped reminding him to do it because the night air smelled like heaven. It was the one thing I'd imagined about California that was actually true. If I ever create my own fragrance, I will call that fragrance "Nuit de Bel Air."

I knew by then the main house was no place to hide anything from Frank. I found that out when I asked him where the zoot suit came from. "From a box under my mother's bed," he said. "Given the antic paper the box was wrapped in, I suspect she got it for my birthday. But I'm growing so fast now that I decided I should wear it while the wearing was good. I was very careful loosening the tape so I can slip the suit box back inside the wrapping. As long as she doesn't see me in it, my mother will be none the wiser."

Inside his antic wrapping, sometimes Frank could be like any other kid. "What were you doing looking under your mother's bed?" I asked.

"Trying to ascertain where she's sleeping these days," he said. "When she forgot to lock her office door, I found her asleep in there. As you know."

"That's when you took your grandfather's letter opener."

"Indeedy."

Did I mention what Xander thought was an appropriate birthday present for a ten-year-old boy? Roman candles. As in fireworks. Small handheld ones named "Silent but Deadly." How thoughtful! Xander had taken into consideration Frank's aversion to loud noises when he picked a bouquet of explosives for the birthday boy.

Xander was also kind enough to include a package of non-Roman birthday candles, the joke kind with magnesium-laced wicks you can't blow out.

I thought about putting the box straight in the trash, but given the incendiary nature of the package and inquisitive raccoons and the grocery-cart-pushing deposit reapers who dug through the cans in the wee hours I thought that might not end well, either. Instead, I hid Xander's gift in the Dream House fridge. I figured the only person who would find it there was Xander. If he ever came back.

While I was there I dropped in at Frank's gallery to check out the photo of the girl in front of the mural. Bingo. Tattoo Girl. Using the magnifying glass to examine the photo, I noticed now in the corner of the frame a small foot that at first seemed to belong to an abandoned doll. But with my new information plus a shadow cast by a childish head full of ringlets, I guessed that foot belonged to Alec.

"What do you want for your birthday, Frank?" I asked the next morning. I was folding one of his detested T-shirts into a cardboard box we kept on the backseat of the wagon for his quick-change cache. Frank had just wriggled into his Teddy Roosevelt trousers and puttees, which he wore today with a plain white shirt and his pith helmet. The look was more safari than San Juan Hill.

"Dr. Livingstone, I presume?" I said when I saw what he was wearing.

"Dr. Livingstone died without realizing his dream of locating the source of the Nile," Frank said as he climbed into the backseat and strapped himself in. "When the British government asked for his body to be sent home, the tribe he had been living with cut his heart out and buried it under a tree because they believed his heart belonged in Africa. For my birthday I would like to have a bow and arrows."

"No way," I said.

"It's true," Frank said. "Dr. Livingstone was born in Scotland but had been living in Africa for a very long time."

"I believe that," I said. "But I'm not getting you a bow and arrows. You could put somebody's eye out with an arrow."

"I want the arrows fitted with suction cups in place of arrowheads."

"Oh. Those. Okay then."

"I would also like an outfit like the one Robin Hood wore, circa Errol Flynn."

"Let's go find one," I said.

"Dr. Livingstone might not have found the source of the Nile," Frank mused as we pulled away from the curb, "but he did find Victoria Falls. Which he named after the queen of England at the time. Obviously."

"Obviously," I echoed.

"The indigenous people of the area knew about the falls already, of course. They called it 'The Smoke That Thunders.' I wonder whether you could pull out somebody's eyeball with a suction-cup arrow."

See? Just like any other kid.

The costume store Frank decided we should go to turned out to be in one of the seedier parts of Los Angeles. The store windows on Hollywood Boulevard were filled with flashing lights and mannequins wearing the barest suggestions of clothing, costumes for more unsavory adventures than Frank had in mind. "This neighborhood was once the epicenter of all things glamorous," he said. "Grauman's Chinese Theatre. The Egyptian. Cocktails at Musso and Frank's. Strobe lights for premieres and limos lined up around the block. Now look at it. I can't." He wasn't speaking metaphorically. Frank's eyes were shut tight and he walked with a hand on my shoulder so he wouldn't fall off the curb. No idear.

He relaxed a little when we reached our destination, though I did have to stand between Frank and the rack of rubber zombie masks. As it turned out, the store didn't carry Robin Hood circa Errol Flynn or circa anybody else. "But," the woman working the counter said, "we do have Peter Pan."

Frank tried it on and assessed himself in the mirror. "This will do nicely," he said. "And should we ever return to the hospital, I can wear this to take my friend Tinkerbell out to lunch."

On the way home, Frank asked, "By the way, what happened to that box from Xander?"

To distract frank from the question of Xander's box I decided to let him use his birthday bow and arrow set as soon as we got home. As it turns out, there is no- where more fun to live when you have a high-quality suction-cup bow and arrow set than a house made of glass.

Most afternoons when Frank "came home from school" he'd rush in, change into the Robin Hood/ Peter Pan ensemble, and run out hoisting his quiver to his shoulder. He figured out pretty quickly that height improved trajectory, so he created an imaginary par- apet by opening the moon roof of the station wagon and standing on the backseat. After opening and clos- ing it a few thousand times, the roof got stuck open. I didn't want to bother Mimi with matters that weren't life-and-death, so we took it to a mechanic without mentioning it to her. The mechanic told us the repair would cost more money than I had to front for it, so I told him we'd have to wait. "You sure?" he asked. "I don't want to be the voice of doom, but February is square in the middle of the rainy season."

"We have a garage," I said. Even if we never put the car inside it.

Aside from his imaginary parapet, Frank also favored a perch among the branches of the shade tree just outside his mother's office window. He'd discovered that he almost always hit his target if he drew a bead on the window through the Hula-Hoop hanging there. I decided not to stop him after I helped gather up his arrows and noticed that he'd used a red Sharpie to draw a heart inside all the suction cups.

I'd been so sure I'd put those Sharpies where he'd never find them, in a Ziploc taped inside the toilet tank above water level. The kid couldn't be trusted with permanent markers. He drew on everything, including the soles of his mother's socks. Also hearts. I discovered that sorting laundry. Mimi had taken to leaving hers in a bag outside her door every few days with a note attached. *Wash.* The only way we knew she was still alive in there were the bags of laundry and remains of meals on trays she left outside her door. And the typing. Typing, typing, typing.

"**When is** your birthday, anyway, Frank?" I asked at breakfast one day.

He stared a full minute before asking me, "Are you going to say 'knock knock'?"

"What do you mean?"

"You must be joking. You know when my birthday is."

"How would I know?" I said. "Nobody ever told me."

"You know my birthday. You know it by heart."

"No I don't," I insisted.

"Yes you do," he said. "You just don't know that you know it."

"If you don't tell me when your birthday is, how will I make arrangements?" I asked.

"My mother will take care of everything."

My mother would have taken care of everything. She might not have been able to give us a glass mansion on a hilltop, but every year on my birthday, without fail, she made me a beautiful cake. Some kind of chocolate. I can close my eyes and smell it right now. Forget "Nuit de Bel Air." Make my fragrance "Toujours Chocolat."

What if Mimi forgot Frank's birthday? A kid needs cake on his birthday. "What kind of cake will she make?" I asked.

"Chocolate, of course," Frank said. "Coconut is not the most delicious cake in the world."

Now I guess I should tell you what happened to that box from Xander.

In many ways I blame myself.

PART VI

The Fire

22

"Alice, wake up."

I opened my eyes and turned on my lamp. Frank. Wearing the zoot suit. In the house. I sat up. "What are you doing wearing that? I thought you didn't want your mother to know you'd found it."

"It's okay. It's my birthday."

"It is? Happy birthday! What's today?"

"February twelfth."

"Abe Lincoln's birthday," I said, rubbing my eyes.

"Also Charles Darwin's. Also mine."

"What time is it?" I asked.

"Three A.M."

"And you woke me up at three A.M. to tell me it's your birthday?"

"I woke you up because I need your help."

That got my attention. "What's going on?"

"It was raining a little bit," he said. "And you'll recall that the moon roof of the station wagon is stuck open."

I swung my legs out of the bed and felt around with my feet for my tennis shoes. "I'll go put it in the garage."

"I did already."

"You drove the car?"

"Xander showed me how. Up and down the driveway, remember? I don't need a license to do that."

"Okay," I said. "Good, I guess."

"Not entirely good."

Oh, no. "Did you wreck it?"

"I think I may have. But not in the way you'd imagine."

That's when the explosions started. They sounded more like gunshots, really. Four gunshots. One, two. Threefour. I smelled something that wasn't Nuit de Bel Air wafting through my bathroom window. Smoke. The Smoke That Thunders.

"What did you do, Frank?" When he didn't answer right away I took him by the shoulders and gave him a shake. "What did you do?"

"I seem to have set the station wagon on fire."

I ran down the hall. The sliding glass doors were wide open and I could see the station wagon in flames. Also on fire? The Dream House.

Frank bumped into me when I stopped running. "Oh," he said. "It's all burning now. I tried so hard to blow out all those birthday candles. I kept trying and trying but they wouldn't go out and then I got scared because flames were coming out of the moon roof. I decided it wouldn't hurt if I left a few birthday candles burning and I ran."

"You found Xander's box," I said.

To get technical, unless you open the gas tank and start a fire in that, cars don't actually blow up like they do in the movies. Gas tanks are designed not to explode. Fire needs air to flourish, which it doesn't get in a sealed-off gas tank. If, however, you aim a Roman candle at a cardboard box of clothing you've sighted through the open moon roof, the incendiary material in the candle will set those clothes on fire. The cardboard will catch, then the upholstery, next the foam inside the seat. Once all that gets going, the heat will shatter the windshield and expand the air in the tires until they blow. When tires explode, those explosions sound like gunshots. One, two, threefour.

A very gentlemanly fire captain explained all this to me after the worst of it was over. That was after Mimi had been taken to the hospital in an ambulance and Xander was handcuffed and shoved in the back of a patrol car. I was on the couch holding Frank wrapped tight in a blanket. The captain had carried him inside and laid him, still asleep, across my lap. He spoke quietly so he wouldn't wake Frank up, but when Frank was out like that, it was more like a coma than sleep.

"You got lucky," the captain said. "We're still in the rainy season, and that big wall around the property kept the fire contained. Otherwise it might have run down the hillside and spread through the canyon. During fire season, we have to evacuate whole neighborhoods."

"Lucky," I said. "Yes." The sun had been up for a couple of hours by then. Happy birthday, Frank.

"Do you have anyplace to go?" the captain asked.

"Can't we stay here?"

"Most people want to leave after a fire, but you'll be okay if you want to stay. The tree took down your exterior power lines but we extinguished the fire before it got in the walls. Your interior wiring should be okay. Have your electrician check it ASAP though, okay?"

"Okay." Although the last time I saw our electrician, he was being shoved into a squad car. "I know this place is a wreck, but it's his wreck," I said, nodding at Frank. "He doesn't like change."

"Got it. Anybody you want to call to come and stay with you?" the captain asked.

"I did that already," I said. "I told him to bring flashlights."

"The DWP should have power up before the day is out. Let me know if they don't." He gave me his card. "Call if you need anything. I'll close the gate behind me when I go to keep you safe."

Honestly, it seemed a little late for that.

I woke up hours later still holding the fire captain's card in my hand and Frank in my lap. The speaker hooked up to the gate buzzed so insistently I decided that was probably what woke me. At least the power was back on.

I looked at my watch. Two-thirty. Frank should be getting out of school soon. If he were still going to school.

I slid out from under Frank without waking him and went to answer the buzzer. "Who is it?"

"Delivery," the voice on the other end said. "I have a birthday cake here for Frank. Is this Mimi?"

I slumped against the wall. Mimi had taken care of everything. "Can you bring it up to the house?" I asked.

"Sure. What's the code for the gate?"

"Two-one-two-two-zero-zero-zero."

"So let me guess. Frank is ten years old today?"

"Yes. How did you know? Did you count the candles?"

"Nope. No candles, just like you ordered. The gate code. Two. One-two. Two zero zero zero. A kid's birthday is one of those number combinations a mother can't forget, right? But you know it's kind of dangerous to use a birthday for a security code like that. Birth dates are the first things hackers try after 'one-two-three-four.'"

So I did know Frank's birthday by heart. I just didn't know that I knew it.

I buzzed the delivery guy in without answering. When I went outside to take the cake from him he was standing in the driveway holding the box, surveying the carnage with a stunned look on his face.

"Is everybody okay?" he asked.

I know. I skipped some parts. The ones I don't like remembering.

After we saw the Dream House on fire, I grabbed Frank's hand and ran to the kitchen, dialed 911, babbled the nature of our emergency, then raced to Mimi's office to pound on the door. "Alice," Frank said after a minute of this. "You know, this door's not locked any-more."

I yanked it open and burst into her sanctum. There was her typewriter that had once been Julian's type-writer. A desk, a chair, a bookcase. No Mimi anywhere, but paper everywhere. Stacks and stacks of it, covered with words. On the desk, the bookcase, the carpet. I don't care what Frank said about Mimi chucking stuff. It didn't look like she threw away any piece of paper, ever.

I tried to sound calm. "Where's your mother?"

"Not here," Frank said. "Maybe in her bedroom. I tried there earlier tonight but it was locked."

We bolted down the hall and laid siege to Mimi's door. We heard fumbling with the lock and then the door swung open. Mimi was in one of her lacy white nightgowns, looking half-asleep and completely an-noyed. Frank threw himself on her. "Did we wake you?" he asked.

"Yes," she said. "Look at you. You're wearing your birthday suit."

"I'm sorry," he said. "I'm sorry I'm sorry I'm sorry."

"It's okay," she said. "It's your birthday. I was going to give it to you today anyway."

"Why weren't you in your office? I looked for you everywhere. Except here, because you locked the door."

"I know, baby. But I really needed sleep. I almost killed myself finishing that book in time for your birthday. I've been an awful, neglectful mother these last few months and I feel terrible about it. But now it's done and I'm all yours again."

"I hate that book." She put her arms around him and he buried his face in her shoulder.

"It's okay, Monkey. The bad part is over now."

Not quite. "The Dream House is on fire," I said.

"The Dream House?" she asked.

Then we were in the backyard together, Mimi and I watching a wall of the guesthouse buckle and send sparks twirling up into the sky. The eucalyptus next to it exploded in flames and burned oily-bright and hot against the night sky. In the distance we heard the wails of fire trucks converging on us fast.

"Sirens," I said.

Frank still had his head burrowed into his mother's shoulder. She looked at me, glassy-eyed, and said, "This isn't my fault."

"Of course it isn't your fault. Come on. We need to move. Let me take Frank. I'm bigger than you."

"Don't you touch him," she said. "Don't you dare." She picked the kid up and clutched him even more tightly.

"Fine. Anything. Let's go. Now. Fast."

Even weighed down with Frank, Mimi reached the front yard before I did. We heard a terrific crash then and all the lights in the house went out. "The gate," I said to Mimi, and ran down the driveway to open it manually so the firefighters could get in. While I waited for the fire trucks I looked up toward the house. The side angled toward the Dream House reflected the conflagration, making it seem twice as big and the yard out front twice as dark. There was just enough moonlight for me to pick out Mimi's wraithlike nightgown, a paper cutout against the black background of grass at night. The chunk of darkness where her shoulder should be must have been Frank. I was amazed that she still held him. My arms would have given out long since.

Up where the driveway ended, part of the eucalyptus that stood alongside the Dream House had fallen across the yard and into the shade tree outside Mimi's office. Now Frank's favorite perch and repository for random artifacts was burning, too. The Hula-Hoop's circle and the lollipop shape of the tennis racket were dark against the flames for the moment it took them to catch. Where was the machete?

Then firefighters were streaming up the driveway, dragging hoses. "Is everybody out?" one of them asked me. He turned out to be the captain.

"Yes," I said.

"Everybody everybody?" he asked.

"Yes. Everybody."

"Where are they?"

"Front yard."

"Good. Stay there with them."

I reached the two of them just as a flaming branch of the shade tree fell away from the trunk and crashed through Mimi's office window. The curtains went up in a flash and we could see fiery bits of paper spin upward in hot drafts. Mimi dropped Frank and lit out for the house. I started after her, but then Frank flashed past me on his mother's heels. I grabbed him around the waist and left it to the firefighters to catch Mimi.

When Frank and I caught up to them, Mimi and a fireman were arguing. "Lady, I don't care if you left your book in there," the fireman was saying. "Buy yourself another book. I can't let you go back inside."

"You don't understand!" Mimi tried to twist free of him.

"Mom. Mother. Mama. Mimi. Ma. Mommie dearest." Frank was yelling every variation he could think of to get her attention. Recognizing that the fireman would make the perfect lectern, Frank had shaken me off somehow, scrambled up his back, and put an arm around the guy's neck for balance. "We're all in this together, Mama!" Frank shouted. "You and me and Alice. If your book burns, my book will burn and Alice's book will burn. Are you listening to me? What did I just say?"

The fireman was so distracted by Frank's chokehold that Mimi was able to duck his grip. "Alice's book will burn? Frank, what are you talking about?" She plucked her son from his perch and stood him on the grass in front of her. "What book?"

"The book she keeps under her mattress. She writes down everything that happens. I'm always eager for the newest installment. It's like I'm living in nineteenth-century New York, waiting on the docks for the latest chapter of Dickens to arrive."

Even a person as tiny as Mimi can look terrifying against a backdrop of swirling flame. "You're writing a book, Alice?"

"It's not a book," I insisted. "Just some notes for Mr. Vargas."

"Isaac asked you to spy on me?" She pressed the heels of her palms into her eye sockets, then started pounding her forehead with her fists.

"Mother, you stop that right now," Frank said. "How many times do I have to tell you that hitting your head is bad for your brain?"

Mimi picked him up, stamped his forehead with a kiss, then handed him off to me. "Take him. Whatever you do, don't let him go," she said, and bolted for the burning house.

She put up quite a fight when the fireman caught her the second time. It took him plus a couple of paramedics to subdue her. Two of them held her arms and legs while one gave Mimi a shot to calm her down enough to get her in the ambulance. Once she was strapped in, the fireman dashed back to us. "Are you two Alice and Julian?"

"Alice and Frank," I said.

"Is Julian still inside the house?"

"Julian is my uncle," Frank said. "He's dead."

The fireman's eyes widened. "In there?" But Frank had turned into about four and a half feet of board lumber and lay unresponsive on the grass.

I touched the fireman's shoulder to turn him away from Frank. "Suicide," I said, speaking softly so Frank couldn't hear me. "Long ago. She was with him when it happened."

"Got it. I'll pass that along to the paramedics."

When we turned back to Frank the kid was shivering. Because California is a desert climate, when the sun isn't shining directly on you it can get pretty chilly. The fireman brought us one of those shiny aluminum astronaut blankets they hand out to disaster victims. I wrapped Frank up tight and sat on the grass with him in my lap until he stopped shaking and loosened up again enough to talk.

"Alice," Frank said after the firefighters started rolling up their hoses. "She's finished her book. Things will be better now, right?"

"Right," I said. "Go to sleep."

The craziest part of the whole night, in my opinion, was that he did.

Or maybe the craziest thing was this: There was a melee at the gate. I saw Xander plow into the gawker-control barricades the police had set up across the driveway. He ran right over them as if he were a steeplechaser who'd forgotten the hurdles were meant to be jumped. One of the police officers took off after him, shouting. When Xander wouldn't stop, the officer caught him by the back of his shirt. I saw Xander punch the guy and break free. Another officer joined in the pursuit and put Xander in handcuffs.

"But I live here," Xander shouted.

I decided not to get involved.

"Let's see your driver's license then, sir." I had to admire the cop's restraint. It was interesting sitting there on the grass listening to them. Their voices carried across the flat of the lawn the way voices skim across the surface of a swimming pool sometimes, letting you in on the conversation of two people lying on blankets on the other side of the water, whispering to each other.

"You'll have to uncuff me so I can get to it," Xander said in a calmer voice. The officer did and Xander massaged his wrists. "Can you tell me how the fire started?" he asked.

"Kid playing with fireworks," the officer said.

"Was anybody hurt?" Xander asked as he pulled out his wallet.

"Somebody left in an ambulance," the officer said. "That's all I know."

Xander threw his wallet in the officer's face and took off running. They caught and cuffed him again. "I can't show you something I don't have," he wailed. "I don't have a driver's license."

They'd stopped listening by then. They hustled him none too gently down the driveway and shoved him into the backseat of a squad car.

After they left, I picked up Xander's wallet. There wasn't much in it. No driver's license, of course. Three crumpled one-dollar bills. A monthly bus pass. A piece of paper with a phone number written on it, and the words *Sara's new cell.*

Or maybe the craziest was this: a fragment, half paper, half cinder, floated down and landed on my head while I sat there with Frank sleeping in my lap. Bits of paper had swirled everywhere before the firefighters were able to get the blaze in Mimi's office under control and for some time after that. The dew had fallen so the grass was damp enough now that the arsonous bits sizzled and died without starting any new small fires.

I wasn't trusting dew to save my hair. I grabbed that fragment and crushed it out against the grass. When it was completely extinguished I could see the part of sentence it held: *and then Alice*

And then Alice put Frank's birthday cake in the fridge in the kitchen and went into what was left of Mimi's office to see if she could find any part of that finished novel.

Everything was gone. Everything but sodden, scorched carpet and lacy remnants of incinerated drapes and splinters of wood and a sad lump of metal that must have been her typewriter and muddy gray piles of ash. Here and there, scraps of burnt-edged paper with a word or phrase on it. Maddening bits of what must have been her novel the day before, reduced to word puzzles and haiku.

23

After the fire Mimi was put on a seventy-two-hour psychiatric hold at the hospital. The admitting doctor informed me of this over the telephone after I made it clear I couldn't leave my distraught younger brother, aka Frank, to come in for a chat. I had no intention of taking Frank to the hospital while his mother was in lockdown. I knew he'd insist on seeing her and I also knew that Mimi wouldn't want him to see her and in the end all three of us might end up being put away. I told the kid his mother was so tired they'd tucked her in bed in a very private room so she could sleep there uninterrupted for three days straight. "She's on hiatus," I said. "All of us could use a little rest, right?"

"We're keeping your mother under observation as a precaution," the doctor explained when we talked.

"I don't want to cause you unnecessary alarm, but the paramedics told me about the situation with your late uncle. Also I see from her hospital record that your mom is unusually accident-prone, and that she was brought to the hospital this time after becoming hysterical because her house had burned down. Hmm. That might make me a little hysterical, too."

I wanted to tell him that Frank, code name Jeopardy, was the disaster magnet and that Mimi was collateral damage. I just couldn't frame it in a way that wouldn't make Frank sound like a criminal or a maniac. "Only part of it burned," I said. "The guesthouse. Her office. It was an accident. Could have happened to anybody."

The doctor paused so long that I wondered if he was writing down what I'd said or considering what to make of it. "What I'm trying to say is that events like these are red flags. The kind of self-destructive urge that took your uncle can run in families. Things that get written off as accidents—car wrecks, drownings, 'accidental' fires—aren't always accidents. Have any other relatives died under questionable circumstances?"

Banning. "My mother's mother," I said. "She drove her car into a fence."

I'd gone outdoors with the phone so Frank wouldn't hear me but kept an eye on him through the glass. He was wrapped in a comforter and rolling around on the living room floor. It didn't make me feel great about my "parenting" that Frank turned to a comforter for comfort instead of me.

When would this kid's real mother come home? My own mother said she'd often thought that when she walked the floor with my infant self in the middle of the night. Was it easier to be a parent when you could carry the kid around without breaking a sweat, or did that lightness make it too tempting to throw it out a window when it wouldn't stop shrieking?

A horrible thought occurred to me then. Had Mimi picked a guardian for Frank? She must have done that, right? But who? According to Xander, Mimi had nobody but him. Xander, and her few billion fans outside the stucco wall. I hoped she hadn't chosen Xander. For all his charms and handyman skills, I wouldn't ask Xander to housesit a cat.

The day Mimi went into the hospital, the second massive blizzard in a week hit New York City, a climatic double whammy that media wags alternately tagged "Snowmageddon" or "Snowpocalypse." Mr. Vargas managed to get a flight out somehow anyway, and called from the Los Angeles airport to say he was picking up his bags and rental car. He'd be in Bel Air within the hour. I told Frank we'd wait for Mimi's old friend and mine outside the gate so he could find the house. The truth of it was that I didn't want Mr. Vargas to meet Frank for the first time in front of a pile of smoking rubble. That's the kind of first impression that's hard to shake.

Besides, it was so lovely outside the wall that it seemed a shame nobody was out there enjoying it. A soft, warm breeze was already shaking loose petals from the ornamental pear trees on Mimi's block that had erupted into blossoms overnight. I was tempted to try to catch a petal on my tongue as it drifted to the sidewalk, but held my right hand out palm up until one settled there instead. So this was February in Southern California. No wonder the silent movie guys threw over New Jersey to come out here, where most days were warm and the desert and ocean and snow-capped mountains and the gardens of Shangri-la were all within easy reach. But how was a normal person, me for example, who'd grown up with the usual up-and-down cycle of seasons supposed to keep track of the passage of time? Who learned to handle adversity when every day was more intoxicatingly gorgeous than the one before it? What mind could grasp that anything could go wrong in a place like this? I could see why so many people who came out here expecting easy fame ended up losing their grip.

"Alice. There." With the petals wafting down around him, Frank looked like a child inside a snow globe, one wearing a glen-plaid Clarence Darrow suit, leather aviator's cap and goggles, looking for a yellow biplane come to scoop him up. "In the Lamborghini." He pointed. "That must be your friend."

"No pointing, Frank. That isn't him. Hold my hand please. I don't want to lose you."

Frank clutched my fingers so tightly that I winced. After that I didn't correct him when he pointed at every Italian sports car or English luxury sedan that tooled down the street because I was grateful for the chance to flex every time he dropped my hand.

Finally a nondescript sedan with Arizona plates that screamed "rental car" turned onto our block. I knew right away that it was Mr. Vargas. I let go of Frank, waved and shouted. As soon as the car nosed into the driveway, I ran to open the driver's side door.

While Mr. Vargas fumbled with his seat belt, I looked over my shoulder to summon Frank to meet him. No Frank. Wait. Yes Frank. Flat on his back on the sidewalk, eyes squeezed shut and hands balled in fists.

I abandoned Mr. Vargas and knelt alongside the kid. "What's wrong, Frank?" I asked.

"You rushed that car like one of my mother's fanatics, Alice. The man inside must be terrified."

"Look at me, Frank," I said. The kid cracked one wary, begoggled eyelid open. "The man in that car knows me, remember? We're friends, so it's okay for me to be excited to see him." I don't think I'd been more excited to see anybody in my life.

Mr. Vargas came and knelt beside us. "You must be Frank," he said. "I've been looking forward to meeting you."

Frank pushed the goggles up on his forehead to get a better look at him. I guess he was on the fence about Mr. Vargas because he shut his eyes again after he checked him out but didn't put the goggles back on.

"Look, I brought you a present, Frank. Is it all right for me to call you Frank?" Mr. Vargas stood, pulled a cylindrical something from his pocket, and gave it a long, rattling shake. "Alice said to bring flashlights. So I brought you this special one that's powered by shaking. No batteries required."

He had Frank's attention then. The kid sat up and took the flashlight, shook it hard, turned it on, and nodded. "Well done," he said. "Now that you've delivered it, please leave."

On day three of Mimi's sequestration, Frank and I set off by city bus to fetch her home. Mr. Vargas offered to take us in his rental car, but Frank refused to set foot in it or even have him along on the bus ride. "Fine," Mr. Vargas said. "I have important things to do here. I need to buy a few groceries. Rug shampoo. A new mop."

"I'll have a beer and a mop," Frank said. "That's what the skeleton said when he walked into the bar." Whether the joke was meant for Mr. Vargas or me was impossible to say. Up until then Frank had insisted I stand between the two of them whenever we were together, as if the man were a rubber zombie mask that had sprouted arms and legs.

I'd been so paralyzed by our disaster that I hadn't cleaned up the ashy footprints the firefighters had tracked through the house. "Oh, Mr. Vargas, don't," I said. "I'll call a cleaning service. Or I'll do it myself when we get home."

"Nonsense," he said. "It will keep me busy until you get back."

So Frank and I set out by bus, stopping at every street corner in Los Angeles along the way. Frank insisted we visit the mall across the street to buy Mimi Valentine's Day candy before the hospital. I gave in without a fight. There wasn't any point in saying she'd been waiting too long for us already.

On the upside, one day post-Valentine's the hearts were half-price. Frank chose the biggest ones still available, three of solid chocolate that cost twenty-five bucks apiece even on special. "Why three?" I asked, being careful not to sound confrontational.

"One for me, one for my mother, one for you," he said. Just when you wanted to strangle the kid for being impossible, he'd come up with something like that to cut your anger off at the knees.

Mimi had checked herself out of the hospital and was long gone by the time we finally got there. I wasn't surprised, but Frank was stunned. Before he launched into a seismic fit I managed to convince him that Mimi had called home, talked to Mr. Vargas, and was so excited to see him after so many years that she'd taken a cab back to Bel Air before we'd crawled through half of Los Angeles on the bus. "We could take a cab ourselves, you know, and get home much faster," I added. We were talking on the bench at the hospital bus stop.

"I only ride in taxis with my mother, Alice," Frank said. "If what you suggest is true, why didn't she call to alert us of her departure?"

Because she hates me. "Because she never learned my number, I bet," I said. "It was programmed into her cell."

"I doubt that," Frank said. "My mother has no problem with numbers in a series. She'd be the first to tell you that she's good with numbers but terrible with money. I know because she's told me that more times than I can count on my fingers and toes. Maybe your cell was turned off. Or you forgot to bring it."

I rooted through my purse and all my pockets. "You're right, Frank. I forgot my phone. I'm the stupidest person alive."

"That's not true. In every classroom I've ever been in there have been at least a couple of kids less intelligent than you are. Also one teacher. Who had me transferred to another class."

We went inside in search of a pay phone. Hard to find these days, as noted earlier by Frank. Once we located one, I realized I'd never learned the number to the glass house because it was programmed into my cell. Mr. Vargas would be so disappointed in me. The man hated speed dial. He believed that memorized phone numbers were the sign of a civilized mind.

Frank didn't know his home number, either, though he had memorized the girlhood phone number of his Alabama grandmother who'd died before he was born. Easily. It was "7."

Night had fallen by the time we got back. Mr. Vargas had opened all the curtains and had the lights on in every room except Mimi's office, where we'd covered the broken-in glass wall with a tarp. We could see him in the display case that was the living room, wearing an apron over his suit and watching for us. He couldn't see us hiking up the driveway in the dark because the light inside had turned all the windows into one-way mirrors.

When we unlocked the front door Frank brushed past me, calling "Mama" in that weird monotone of his, repeating it like a squeeze-me talking baby doll left under a rocking chair. I waited in the foyer, not wanting to get in the way of any reunions. The hall carpet looked good as new and the mirrors all around me were free of fingerprints and delicious smells came from the kitchen. I had made none of this happen. I can't tell you what a relief that was. Until now I'd prided myself on being so responsible, but a life without responsibilities was starting to sound pretty great to me. I was starting to think Xander wasn't a deadbeat. He was a genius.

Mr. Vargas came to meet us, pulling the apron over his head, smoothing his hair and straightening his tie. Came to meet me, really, since I was the only one there. "You surprised me, Alice," he said. "I called to find out where on earth you were and heard your phone ringing in the kitchen. Howling, actually. Is the coyote ringtone a West Coast thing? Where's Mimi?"

Once Frank had searched every room and under every bed and inside every drawer and closet and felt inside a pair of Mimi's shoes and even peered into the vacuum cleaner hose and bag, he went out in the yard and returned with his yellow plastic bat. He took the cake box out of the refrigerator and removed his gorgeous, forlorn, untouched birthday cake. He put the cake on the counter and proceeded to beat it to chocolate smithereens. Then he pushed its remains through the kitchen colander and pawed through the crumbs before proclaiming, "Well, that's that. Not here, either."

After Mr. Vargas regained his capacity for speech, he wondered aloud if Mimi had been home at all, since he'd only been at the store for an hour at most. Frank said Mimi had absolutely been there, probably while Mr. Vargas was at the grocery or when he'd been vacuuming in one of the bedrooms. "What makes you think that?" Mr. Vargas asked.

Young Sherlock Holmes pointed out the clues: The vacuum cleaner bag filled with the powdery residue of carpet shampoo, evidence of the recent cleanup of the firefighters' muddy footprints that might have made sufficient racket to allow Mimi to slip in and out undetected by anybody who might ask awkward questions like, "Say, Mimi, where's that manuscript you promised me?" The shoes I'd sent to Mimi in the hospital, still damp inside from being worn home sockless. A suitcase gone from under her bed, her blue and black and gray cardigans missing, plus seven T-shirts and two pairs of jeans, one an embroidered pair she'd inherited from Julian that she only wore on special occasions. Also the watercolor portrait of Frank over the mantelpiece that I couldn't believe I hadn't missed. A nightgown was MIA, and a pair of slippers. Two pairs of shoes I gathered Mimi preferred to the ones I'd picked for her. Seven pairs of socks, something I'd forgotten to include in her care package. Her toothbrush. "Her hairbrush is here," Frank mused, "but her hair is still short enough to do without it." Her purse was gone and her glasses, but not her cell phone. "Either she doesn't want to talk to anybody," he said, "or she knows her computer could pinpoint its location and, by extension, hers." My money was on "doesn't want to talk to anybody."

He ended by showing us an ancient copy of *The Little Prince*, now resting on his pillow. "I know I wasn't reading it last night because I don't understand much French. Although sometimes my mother and I like to pretend we speak it."

That was the difference between Frank and me. I'd recognized the cover art but hadn't gotten past it to the letters spelling out *Le Petit Prince*. "Why do you have it in French, then?" I asked.

"My mother's very fond of this book because it belonged to my Uncle Julian in high school. She had to translate it for him for his French class the way she has to translate it for me." He turned to the flyleaf and showed us "Julian Gillespie" there, printed awkwardly enough to embarrass a second-grader. Seeing Julian's lousy handwriting gave me gooseflesh. *Frank's psychiatrist says it runs in families.*

"If she liked it so much, why didn't she get you a copy in English?" Mr. Vargas asked.

"She's fond of it because it belonged to Uncle Julian. She says the illustrations are the best thing about it anyway. Her capsule review of the story is '*Waiting for Godot, le Junior Edition.* Snore.' She says the word *snore* because sometimes loud noises like actual snores can startle me."

"I'll try to remember that when I go to sleep tonight," Mr. Vargas said.

"After I've canvassed the property thoroughly I may note other tipoffs to her recent presence here," Frank said. "I can start an in-depth investigation now if you like."

I told him that wouldn't be necessary and hustled him into his pajamas. I'd put Mr. Vargas in Frank's monastery cell and made up the red love seat in my bedroom with sheets so the kid could stay with me.

I worried he would have a harder time sleeping that night than ever, but when I tucked him in on the couch he said, "All of us could use a little rest, right, Alice?" and his eyelids fluttered shut. Once I was sure he was sleeping I went looking for Mr. Vargas. He was on the white couch, holding a plastic martini glass.

"What are you drinking?" I asked.

"I didn't get that far," he said. "I ran out of steam after I found the glass. There's something funny about it. The weight's off."

"It's plastic," I said.

"Ah. That explains it."

"Glass and Frank are a bad combination. I'm worried about Mimi, Mr. Vargas. Should we call the police?"

"Call the police? Why?"

"Because she's missing. Something terrible may have happened to her." Sirens.

"Mimi's not missing, Alice. She packed a bag and left."

He had a point. Not one that I liked, though. "What if she doesn't come back?"

"I suppose that's a possibility, but I doubt it. She's done this kind of thing before."

"What kind of thing?"

"Bolted. When Mimi gets overwhelmed, she takes off."

Like mother, like son. Also like Xander.

"But she didn't have a kid before. She wouldn't abandon Frank, would she?"

"Frank isn't abandoned. You're here." Mr. Vargas held the glass to the light and twisted it between his fingers. "Plastic, huh? It does look different when the light shines through it."

I dropped onto the couch alongside him and covered my face with my hands.

"Try not to worry so much, Alice. I don't know where Mimi is, but I imagine she's off someplace trying to piece her novel back together. She knows that you'll take care of Frank while she's gone. She wouldn't have kept you around if she didn't think you could handle the job."

"But I haven't handled the job," I wailed. "You sent me here to transcribe Mimi's book and I never saw a page of it. If I'd done it right, we'd be back in New York having cocktails in real cocktail glasses at the Algonquin now. There might not have even been a fire."

"What I love about you, Alice," Mr. Vargas said, "is the way you simultaneously give yourself too much credit for everything that happens and not enough. Listening to you makes me feel young again."

"This isn't funny, Mr. Vargas."

"Who said it was? Listen to me, Genius. I sent you out here to help Mimi in whatever way Mimi needed help. You did that."

But I hardly heard what he was saying because I'd suddenly thought of something. "Hang on a minute," I said, and ran into my bedroom.

When I came back I thrust my ridiculous-looking unicorn notebook into his hands.

"What's this?" he asked.

"The notes you asked me to keep. Before I went to sleep at night I wrote down everything that happened every day. I really ought to type them out for you. Some of the entries are pretty cryptic and my handwriting isn't the best. But then neither was Einstein's."

"Notes?" Mr. Vargas asked. "What are you talking about, Alice?"

I woke up in the night pretty sure I'd heard somebody knock on my bedroom door. As much as I wanted to stay asleep, I skidded out of bed and went to check.

It was Mr. Vargas, clutching a flashlight and looking embarrassed. I stepped out into the hall and closed my door behind me so we wouldn't wake Frank. "I'm sorry to disturb you," Mr. Vargas said. "But is it conceivable that a raccoon found its way into my bedroom closet? Something's moving in there, but I don't think it's a burglar, as the sound is more shuffling than ransacking."

"I suppose one could have found a way under the tarp over the hole in Mimi's office wall," I said. "But

I imagine a raccoon would go for the kitchen instead of Frank's closet. Although knowing Frank he might have snacks wrapped inside some of his pocket squares. Did you close your bedroom door before you went to sleep?"

"I did. And it was closed when I woke up."

"Let's have a look," I said, sounding braver than I felt. Where was that plastic machete when we really needed it?

When we got to the bedroom I noticed a line of light under Frank's closet door. "Was the closet light on before?" I whispered.

"I didn't notice."

"Follow me," I said.

We went back to my room and I turned on the light. Frank wasn't sleeping on the love seat anymore and the sheets I'd made it up with were strewn across the floor. We found the Nocturnal Rambler asleep on the rug in his closet, the light on, the cashmere overcoat it was never cold enough for him to wear rolled up under his head, an oversized pink cardigan I'd never seen before as his blanket. Frank might be okay with pink but he preferred a more tailored fit so I guessed the cardigan was Mimi's even though I couldn't imagine her in such a cheerful color. The kid had a shoe tucked in the crook of each elbow, as if he worried someone might steal them while he slept. His hands were folded across the copy of *Le Petit Prince*.

We backed out of the closet and reconvened in the hallway. "Frank's protective of his things," I said. "We'd better trade bedrooms."

Before we turned in for the night again, Mr. Vargas and I decided to do a little nocturnal rambling of our own. Outside, a crescent moon tipped our way, spilling silvery Southern California magic all over the sad ruins of the Dream House. The two of us stood in the driveway pondering the heap. Mr. Vargas took a deep breath and said, "Smell that?"

"The smoke? The fire captain said it would smell like burned-down-house around here for a few days, a week tops. He didn't want me to worry about it."

"Not the smoke," he said. "The night-blooming jasmine."

"Oh," I said. "Yes. That."

"Alice, did I ever tell you about the time I set my mother's closet on fire?"

"You did? How?"

"Well, my mother never let me play with matches. So when I managed to nab a big box from the kitchen, I went and hid behind the dresses in her closet to play with them. I figured she'd never think to look for me there."

"Did she?"

"She didn't. I don't think she missed me. Or the matches. After I lit the fortieth or fiftieth one, a dress caught. I might not have been smart enough to see that coming, but I was smart enough to run like heck when it did. My mother was mopping the kitchen when I found her, and she came running with the bucket. That fire didn't have a chance against my mother."

"That doesn't exactly make me feel better about myself, Mr. Vargas, but it gives me hope for Frank."

"You'll like this, too, then," he said. "I didn't have friends growing up. Who'd have thought a sensitive fat kid who wore glasses and read all the time wouldn't get voted Most Popular?"

When we turned back to the house we saw a shaft of light beaming heavenward from Frank's closet skylight. "I guess we should have turned that light off," Mr. Vargas said.

"I bet Frank left it on because he's afraid to sleep in the dark with Mimi gone," I said. "That, or he's signaling the mother ship to come pick him up."

"Frank will be okay, Alice," Mr. Vargas said. "He's an odd duck, but brilliant children often are. It may take him a while, but someday he'll figure out how to live in the world of ordinary mortals." As we climbed the driveway he added, "Frank's not the one I'm worried about."

"So you are worried about Mimi."

He drilled his hands into his pockets and grimaced. "I suppose I'm not as calm about this as I make myself out to be," he said. "I'm worried, yes. But I'd worry more if she didn't have Frank. She's all he's got, and she knows it."

"What about a guardian? Do you think Mimi has chosen one for him?"

"I wondered that myself. So I asked our lawyers to check into it."

"And?"

"Mimi designated a guardian, yes," he said. "Pretty soon after Frank was born. But it seems she didn't get around to discussing it with the guy she picked. And now he doesn't know what to think. Legally, he's not bound to do it, since she didn't ask his permission first."

"Who? Frank's father?" I asked. "Do we find out now who he is?"

"No," he said. "Not Frank's father. Unequivocally not Frank's father."

"Xander?" I asked. "Don't hold out on me, Mr. Vargas."

"Not Xander," he said. "I'm not holding out. I just can't get my head around it." He tapped his sternum with his forefinger. "Isaac Vargas," he said. "Me. She appointed me Frank's guardian."

BETRAYAL AT THE 383

24

I was asleep, dreaming I was shaking a cardboard box next to my ear to figure out what was inside it when I heard Frank say, "Alice, wake up." Since the Dream House was on fire the last time he spoke those words, that sentence catapulted me out of bed. I wasn't fully awake and was so completely wrapped in bed-clothes that I ended up on the floor of my new boudoir, formerly Frank's bedroom. The kid stood over me in his Sherlock Holmes cape and deerstalker, rattling the shake flashlight Mr. Vargas had given him. He grabbed me by an eyelid and focused it on my eyeball.

"Frank!" I said. "Cut that out. What do you think you're doing?"

"I'm checking you for brain damage. In case you struck your head when you fell."

"I'm fine," I said. I sat up and rubbed my hand across my face. "Is anything on fire?"

"What's your name, Alice?" Frank asked me.

"Frank, for Pete's sake."

"Oh dear. Not good. I'm Frank. Your name is Alice." He blinded me with the flashlight again. "Your pupils are responsive to light, but your possible head injury may have rendered you unable to remember the paramedics saying that not knowing your own name may signify brain damage. Also, nothing is burning and olfactory hallucinations can indicate compromised brain tissue. George Gershwin imagined he smelled burning rubber for weeks before he died of a brain tumor on July eleven, 1937. We should call an ambulance."

"We do not need to call an ambulance, Frank. My name is Alice Whitley, okay? I asked if something was on fire because the last time you woke me in the middle of the night, something was. What do you need?"

"I need to look for Xander."

"Why?"

"Because he's lost."

"I wouldn't waste my energy thinking about Xander. I'd worry about my mother," I said as I kicked myself free of the sheets and stood up. Xander needed to get lost, if you asked me. He was as guilty of setting the Dream House fire as Frank was. More. What's worse, every mention of Xander's name forced me to consider that I might be somewhere on that continuum of guilt. I should have soaked those Roman candles in a bucket of water, cut off the fuses, and driven them halfway to Vegas to bury them in the desert.

"But, Alice, your mother is dead. No amount of thinking on my part will bring her back."

"Not my mother, Frank. Your mother."

"Why should I worry about my mother? She's not lost. Mr. Vargas knows where she is."

Mr. Vargas knew where Mimi was? That was news to me. By then I was awake enough to realize I'd better zip it about worrying about Mimi if I didn't want Frank to go rigid on the floor. "I'm going back to sleep, Frank," I said. "So should you." I picked up the sheet and coverlet, rearranged the bed, and got in. Once I was back under the covers Frank perched on its edge. "Do you want me to tuck you in, Frank?" I asked.

"That's all right. I'm not tired. I'll sit here until you've rested enough to talk."

I sighed. "What do you want to talk about, Frank?"

"Looking for Xander."

"What makes you think we need to look for Xander?"

"I told you. He's lost."

"Xander's not lost, Frank. He's probably outside Salt Lake City right now, blowing a wad of cash." I thought of the three sad, crumpled singles in his wallet that he didn't even have.

I guess Frank was thinking about that, too, because he said, "Xander doesn't have a wad of cash to blow. All the money he has is in his wallet, which you're keeping in your purse. Also his monthly bus pass. He wouldn't have invested in a monthly bus pass if he meant to leave town before the month was halfway done. He's not crazy, you know."

I was so beyond getting mad at the kid for going through my purse again that I stifled a massive yawn. "Can't this wait until morning, Frank?"

"It could. But then I wouldn't have an excuse to use this excellent flashlight." He gave the flashlight the kind of two-fisted, elbow-intensive shake that bartenders at the Algonquin probably used when mixing martinis for Robert Benchley and his crew of jaundiced wits. Then Frank put the flashlight in my hand, pulled his bubble pipe from the pocket of his cape, and extracted a small rolled-up piece of paper from its bowl. He smoothed it on the bedside table, grabbed my hand and directed the flashlight's beam onto it.

"So," he asked. "How early is too early to telephone this 'Sara'?"

At breakfast the next morning I sent Frank to the yard to pick a rose for Mr. Vargas to use as a pocket square. While the kid was outdoors I asked Mr. Vargas if he knew where Mimi was.

"Of course not," Mr. Vargas answered. He put down his knife and fork and wiped his hands on his napkin. "What makes you ask?"

"Because Frank thinks you do," I said.

"Why would he think that?"

Before I could let him in on what Frank told me the night before, the kid burst in with the rose and thrust it at Mr. Vargas to smell. I put my hand on the back of the chair to keep Mr. Vargas from tipping over when Frank came at him.

"Lovely," Mr. Vargas said. "I think I've smelled it enough now, thank you, Frank."

Frank crammed the blossom into Mr. Vargas's breast pocket and then arranged its tips with a neurosurgeon's care.

"So Frank," Mr. Vargas said, "tell me, what's your favorite thing about school these days?"

"Not going," Frank said. "I'm on hiatus. Like my mother."

"I see," Mr. Vargas said. "Just as well. School isn't for everybody, you know."

"I know," Frank said matter-of-factly, then launched into his spiel about Winston Churchill, Ansel Adams, Noël Coward, and their fellow dropout luminaries. He offered to show Mr. Vargas the list with all the names on it that Mimi kept in her bedside table drawer.

"After Mimi comes back I'd love to see it," Mr. Vargas said. "A gentleman doesn't go through a lady's drawers without permission."

"Ah." Frank nodded. "Now I'm wondering if you're the gentleman Alice always references."

"He is, Frank," I said. "Mr. Vargas is the gentleman."

I saw no point in involving Mr. Vargas in our search for Xander since we were only doing it to occupy Frank's mind and, okay, mine until Mimi was back from her mysterious hiatus. So I was glad when he shut himself away with my notebook after breakfast.

I made the kid wait until 10:00 A.M. to call Sara's number. Which gave him plenty of time to decide what ensemble would be most appropriate for this type of investigative work, as he lacked the requisite gumshoe trench coat and fedora. The E. F. Hutton suit, or the Clarence Darrow? Overcoat with top hat, or without? His good white tie and tails? I'd started out the morning exhausted and exasperated with Frank, but if trying on clothes kept him calm and happy while his mother was out of pocket, I was willing to play along.

"The Thin Man, I presume," I said once he settled on a smoking jacket over pajamas, a pencil-thin fake mustache from the set I'd given him for Christmas, and a plastic martini glass. The martini glass was the clincher.

"The 'thin man' is the skeleton in the movie *The Thin Man,* so if I were portraying that character I'd be holding a beer and mop. This," Frank said, waggling the fingers of his free hand in front of his smoking jacket, "is an homage to Nick Charles, society detective, as portrayed by William Powell, brother of Eleanor Powell."

"I don't think they're actually siblings," I said.

"Maybe not," Frank said. "But I like to imagine they are."

When the time came to phone Sara-whoever-she-was, I brought the portable handset into Frank's bedroom. While we sat on the bed together, Frank declaimed the numbers while I tapped them in. When I entered the last one and put the receiver to my ear, Frank put an arm around my shoulders and pressed his left ear to my right one.

I hung up. "Frank," I said. "What are you doing?"

"Listening in."

"Really? Do you think I have nothing in between my ears but air and a piece of string?"

"That's right. Your brain is fairly dense. Maybe I should listen in on the other handset."

"Fine." I handed the receiver to Frank, put the paper with Sara's number in my pocket, and went into the kitchen to get the other handset. When I came in he had the phone to his ear and was saying into it, "My name is Frank Banning. I'm investigating the disappearance of Xander Devlin. Where were you on the night of February eleventh and the subsequent morning of February twelfth? Uh-huh. Uh-huh."

I sat on the bed beside him, took the paper with Sara's number from my pocket, and punched the numbers into the kitchen handset. When I held it to my ear a woman's voice said, "Frank, please tell whoever that is that you're already using the phone."

I grabbed Frank's receiver and pressed "end call" on both his and mine. "You memorized Sara's number, didn't you?" I asked.

"What a ridiculous question, Alice. Next I imagine you'll ask me to recite the multiplication tables for you. Please. Pressing 'redial' works much faster than inputting all those digits. You should try that when you call her back."

It didn't take us long to establish that Sara was Tattoo Girl, the young woman who'd delivered Xander's box to Frank.

"Did Xander tell you what was inside the box before you delivered it?" Frank asked.

"Your birthday present," Sara said. "That's all I know. What was in it?"

"Roman candles."

"That sounds about like Xander," Sara said. "Please tell me he had enough sense to come and set those fireworks off for you, Frank."

"He came," Frank said. "But I'd set them off already and the Dream House was well on its way to burning to the ground by the time he arrived. Before I could explain what had happened the police hauled him away in handcuffs. We haven't heard from him since, so we're worried he feels responsible for destroying his home away from home."

"He ought to feel responsible," I said. "Who gives fireworks to a child?"

"Wait a minute," Sara said. "February twelfth? Did all this happen last week? If you're thinking of suing Xander for giving Frank fireworks or me for delivering them, you're wasting your time. He has nothing and neither do I. We don't even own a car."

Before I could assure her we had no such intentions, Frank muscled in with, "That's not true. You have Alec. I don't know him personally but he looks like a keeper."

"I have Alec. Yes. He is a keeper. You're right." She sounded less hostile after Frank said that.

"Tell me," Frank said, "was Xander in jail long enough to be fitted for an orange jumpsuit?"

"I pawned my wedding ring as soon as he called so I could bail him out as fast as possible. Xander hates being in jail. Listen, everything you're saying is news to me. All Xander told me was that he'd punched a cop."

I was still grappling with *wedding ring* and so had fallen a couple of paces behind. "Wait," I said. "Xander's been in jail before?"

After a longish pause, Sara asked, "Exactly how well do you know Xander?"

"Well enough to know he doesn't have a driver's license, doesn't do birthdays, and that he never graduated from Julliard because he broke his arm in two places during his last year there."

"He never graduated because he broke his arm? Did he tell you how he broke his arm?"

"No," I said.

"I didn't think so."

"How did he break his arm?" I asked.

"He needs to be the one to tell you that," she said.

Before we left the next day for the fancy department store where Sara told us Xander had a gig playing piano, I stopped by my former bedroom to let Mr. Vargas know we were leaving. I didn't invite him along because I knew Frank would be absolutely against that.

When Mr. Vargas opened the door to my knock he was wearing a rumpled dress shirt with the tail untucked, a pair of suit pants, and socks. The guy's hair was a mess. I'd never seen him look untidy before. "Did you sleep in your clothes, Mr. Vargas?" I asked.

"I forgot to pack pajamas," he said. I saw that he had my notebook in his hand and that he'd flagged a number of pages with yellow Post-it notes.

Frank elbowed me aside and said to Mr. Vargas, "I like what you've done with your hair."

Mr. Vargas was enough of a student of Frank already to know the kid was incapable of sarcasm. "Thank you, Frank," he said. "I call this style 'the Albert Einstein.'"

Frank's eyes lit up. "If you borrowed one of my mother's cardigan sweaters and a fake mustache from my collection you could star in a biopic of Albert

Einstein," he said. "May I loan you one of my mother's cardigan sweaters and one of my fake mustaches?"

"Sure," Mr. Vargas said.

"You'll need shoes," Frank said. "But no socks. Einstein didn't wear socks." He skedaddled off.

When Mr. Vargas sat on the red love seat to pull off his socks, I noticed the imprint of his body on top of my fluffy white comforter. He hadn't even bothered to get under the covers last night. From the looks of him, I wasn't sure he'd been to sleep at all.

Mr. Vargas asked, "How does Frank know about Einstein's socks?"

"His lack of socks, you mean?" I asked. "How does Frank know anything?"

Mr. Vargas rolled his socks into a ball and tucked them into the corner of the suitcase he hadn't unpacked. He put my notebook away in the desk drawer.

Once Mr. Frank of Bel Air was done with Mr. Vargas, he did kind of look like Albert Einstein. Frank was so pleased by the results that he said, "I think he should come with us on our adventure today, Alice, don't you?"

"I think that's a great idea," I said. "But you need to invite him yourself. Be polite. Use his proper name when you ask him. That's the way gentlemen like Mr. Vargas do it."

"But I don't know his name!" Frank screeched, so unexpectedly that both Mr. Vargas and I jumped. He drummed his forehead with the heels of his fists.

"Whoa. Frank. It's okay. Calm down. I just said his name. It's Mr. Vargas."

Just like that, the jovial Mr. Frank of Bel Air was back. "He can use Xander's bus pass," he said. "I happen to have it right here in my wallet." Frank pulled his wallet out to show us. The wallet was oxblood leather, looked older than I was, and had been embossed with the letters *JG* in gold, which made me suspect it had been Julian's once. "The difference between Xander's bus pass and my bus pass is that his is blue and mine is orange because the orange bus pass is for a child and adults are blue. Shall we three go now?"

I wasn't about to argue about taking the bus or ask how Xander's bus pass had jumped from my purse into his wallet.

"You there, sir," Frank said to Mr. Vargas. "Allow me to hold on to this bus pass for you. I don't want you to lose it as it represents much of Xander's current net worth."

Before we left I wrote "Mr. Vargas" in Sharpie on Frank's hand.

Frank sat with Mr. Vargas and talked to him all the way to the department store. Nobody bothered staring at Frank and his seatmate, Nobel Prize winner Albert Einstein, because Fake Marilyn Monroe and Artificial Charlie Chaplin, en route to Mann's Chinese Theatre to pose for photographs with tourists, were in the back of the bus sharing a newspaper. As they left, I nudged Mr. Vargas to make sure he noticed. We watched the two of them walk away from their stop together, holding hands. I couldn't help thinking things might have worked out differently for real Marilyn if she'd gone for a guy with a sense of humor while she was alive.

At the mall, though, locals you'd think would be jaded were thrilled to see Half-Pint E. F. Hutton, monocle screwed into his eye socket and holding his Grandpa Einstein's hand. They parted in front of us and spun in our wake in sync, like choreography for a 1950s Warner Brothers musical.

Once we were inside the store, Frank stopped abruptly. "Hey. Wait a minute," he said. "Is this the kind of place where a fellow could buy a trench coat, or is it all handbags and lipstick?"

"There must be a men's department," Mr. Vargas said, "where I could also buy pajamas."

"I thought you wanted to find Xander, Frank," I said.

"I do, but I thought we could squeeze in a little shopping, after, since we're here. My mother hates department stores. I don't know why. Agreed, a Los Angeles department store is not as exciting as a souk in Casablanca, but it does have indoor plumbing." Then Frank Banning, Private Eye, held up his finger and got a look of intense concentration on his face. "Shhh," he said even though he'd been the one doing all the talking. "Do you hear it? Xander's here."

"I hear it," I said. I did. The joyful abandon, like a golden retriever fetching an old tennis ball.

"By the escalators," Frank said. "Over there." He aimed his elbow to direct our gaze. It wasn't that much better than pointing with his finger, but still, I can't tell you how gratifying that concession to good manners was to me. There might be hope yet that Frank would remember to chew with his mouth closed someday, too.

He was right. Xander was over there. In a tux, at a baby grand. A lot of the shoppers brushed past without a second look. The armchairs around the piano, however, were filled with old ladies who'd lost interest in fashion around Mamie Eisenhower's time but who still had it in them to appreciate a handsome man at a piano. Alec sat on the piano bench next to Xander looking unbearably adorable in a tiny tux of his own. Things were looking up for Xander's net worth. I had a feeling he'd earn a wad of cash big enough to carry him at least as far as Akron before this performance was over.

He finished the piece with a flourish and acknowledged the spatters of applause. "I'm Xander Devlin," he said, then swept his palm to Sara, standing in the curve of the piano. "My darling sister Sara, who puts up with all my nonsense." Then he put the hand on Alec's curls. "And, of course, the star of any show, my nephew Alec."

Frank, who'd been watching the whole performance through his monocle, lowered it and said to me, "Aha! Brother and sister. Like William and Eleanor Powell."

Xander locked eyes with me across the piano. He bolted, abandoning his nephew on the piano bench. He beat it out of there so fast that the two adoring old ladies he dove between checked to see if he'd made off with their handbags. Sure, he was handsome, but those ladies weren't born yesterday.

"Xander!" Frank yelled. "No running!" Then the kid took off after him.

"I have to—" I said to Mr. Vargas.

"—go after him," he said. "Yes. I know. Run."

25

If you asked me why a chicken would want to cross the road in Los Angeles, I would have to say it was because that chicken loved pancakes so much he wanted to be one.

Frank chased Xander out of the mall and down the diagonal slash of the glass-encased escalators splitting its facade. Many double-wide shoppers-with-bags placidly taking in the palm trees and Hollywood Hills got their zen in a wad when I elbowed past, hot on his trail. I burst out onto the street to a symphony of screaming brakes and horns honking. Xander was across the way already. Frank was frozen in the middle of the road, a bus lurched to a stop so close to him that the kid could have reached out and rung the handlebar bell on the bike in the rack on its front.

I heard someone screaming Frank's name before I realized I was the one doing it. Without thinking, I lunged into the street to grab him before he lay down on the pavement. I got Frank back on the curb somehow without remembering the particulars. Once I had him safe there, I crouched to shove my face into his line of sight. "Frank, what were you thinking? You could've been killed. You could've caused an accident. Don't ever do anything like that again. Do you hear me?"

Frank grabbed the light pole alongside us in both hands then and slammed his forehead against it, saying, "stupid, stupid, stupid," in between blows.

"No, no, no, no, Frank," I said. "Shhhhh. Stop." I pried his hands free and put myself between him and the lamppost.

Xander, bless his deadbeat heart, had waded through the traffic and knelt, tux be damned, next to Frank. When he began singing quietly, Frank stopped. "Frank Loesser!" he shouted. " 'What Are You Doing New Year's Eve.' My grandparents danced to that at their wedding!"

It was like magic, the way that calmed Frank down. And how much it made me squirm. I realized that was the song Xander had played when he came back to the glass house post-Christmas. Yes, the very number I'd egotistically assumed he'd trotted out for me. Now I had to think it had been Xander's way of telegraphing Frank that his itinerant male role model was back in residence. Mr. Vargas was so right about me. I really did give myself too much credit sometimes. I felt so embarrassed that pounding my head against a lamppost almost seemed like a good idea.

"Hey, pal," Xander said. "Come here. Can I see your head?"

"Don't tell my mother," Frank pleaded.

"Your secret's safe with me." Xander brushed the kid's hair back with two fingertips. His forehead looked surprisingly okay. Just a little red. "Now let me see your thumbs." Frank held them out for Xander to inspect. They looked even redder. "Good thing your thumbs took the hit for your brain case," Xander said. "You got off easy this time. Next time you might not be so lucky. What's up with you, little man?"

"I needed to find you. I have had about enough of people disappearing on me."

"I hear you," Xander said. "But you know what's the best thing about me? As long as there's breath in my body I'll come back sooner or later. I'm not so easy to shake." Xander fingertipped Frank's hair forward to cover the red spot. "There you go. Good as new. No one will be the wiser."

Then Xander vanished into the crowd.

Before I had time to get into a lather about it, a cab pulled up and Xander bounded out of the backseat. "Sorry to duck out on you like that," he said. "You can't flag cabs in most of Los Angeles the way you do in New York. About the only upside of not driving is that you know where all the cabstands are. Alice. Frank, your chariot awaits. Get in."

"But Frank only rides in taxis with his mother," I protested.

"Until today," Xander said. "Today our boy becomes a man. You first, Alice. Then Frank."

"Since you're coming back to live with us, Xander, Alice will give you your wallet back," Frank said. "You'll have to sleep on the living room couch though because your home away from home burned down in the fire."

We got in with Frank sandwiched between us. Before the cab pulled from the curb, the kid started throwing himself around in the backseat and chanting, "Stop stop stop stop stop."

"Everything's okay, Frank," Xander said. "Calm down. Alice and I are right here with you."

"Everything is not okay. We're leaving Our Good Friend Him behind." Frank leaned across Xander and rolled down the window. He was the only one who'd

noticed Mr. Vargas had materialized on the curb, holding his side and panting.

I caught Frank by his knees before he was able to
fling his entire body out the taxi window. "Dr. Einstein, I presume!" he bellowed, semaphoring wildly.
Mr. Vargas looked up, smiled and waved. Frank must
have noticed the name I'd written out on his hand then
because he tacked on, "Mr. Vargas! I say old man. Your
chariot awaits!"

Mr. Vargas got in front with the driver and we set off
for Bel Air. Frank hooked his fingers over the back of
the front seat and replayed our adventure for the two of
them, leaving no incident unturned. I locked the door
on my side and collapsed against it, closed my eyes, and
let myself be lulled by the drone for a while. When I
opened my eyes again I looked across at Xander, who
was staring out the window on his side, frowning.

It was late afternoon by the time we got home, although it felt like it should have been midnight. Frank
insisted the cab drop us off at the gate and made us
wait until it had rounded the corner before he entered
in the code. Then he grabbed Mr. Vargas by the hand
and started up the drive with him, swinging his arm
so vigorously that I worried he'd dislocate Our Good
Friend Him's shoulder.

I started up the hill behind them but Xander stopped just inside the gate. "Are you coming, or aren't you?" I asked.

Xander was taking in the pile that had once been the Dream House. The blackened skeleton of the Mercedes. The empty eye socket of Mimi's office under its tarpaulin eye patch. I'd forgotten that he hadn't seen the carnage in daylight yet.

"It isn't pretty, is it?" I asked.

"Sara told me the manuscript burned in the fire. I can't go in there, Alice. I can't face Mimi."

"Well, you're in luck," I said. "Mimi's gone."

"Gone where?"

I shrugged. "Nobody knows."

"Is that why Frank was so eager to find me?"

"I guess."

"The way Frank ran out into the street after me today," he said. "He could have been killed."

"It's a wonder he wasn't," I said. "You know Frank would follow you anywhere. How could you run from him like that?"

"It wasn't my fault the kid followed me."

"Nothing's ever your fault, is it, Xander?" I said. "You know what? You're the one we should call Jeopardy. You're dangerous for Frank to be around. That kid needs a role model, not a partner in crime. You need to grow up, or get lost for good."

I started up the driveway without him. "Alice, wait," he said. "Listen. For just a minute, okay?" He grabbed my elbow. "You're right. I'm too old to be this stupid. I'm going to change. I promise."

"Prove it," I said.

"Prove it? How?"

"Tell me what happened to your sister."

Be inside *in a few,* I texted Mr. Vargas. *Are you okay with Frank?*

More than okay, he replied. *Take your time.*

"We're good," I said, and put my phone away. "Why don't we sit down someplace?"

Xander marched up the driveway in front of me, eyes averted from the rubble, every line of his body crying out for cigarettes and a blindfold. We sat on the front stoop with our backs against the blue slate entranceway. It was warm from the afternoon slant of sun and we could see all the way to the ocean over the top of the stucco wall.

Xander didn't linger on details. "My sister and I were in a car accident together," he said. "I lived. She died. That's all you need to know."

"No it isn't. What was your sister's name?

"Lisa."

"Who was driving?"

"I was."

"How old were you?"

"Twenty. Lisa was fifteen. That day."

Ah. That would explain *I don't do birthdays.* "So how did it happen?"

"I wasn't drunk," he said.

"I didn't say you were."

"Everybody thought I must have been until I tested clean. My problem wasn't something you can just sleep off." Xander put his hands on his thighs and rubbed them back and forth against his jeans, as if he meant to warm them up or wipe them clean of something. "I hate talking about this," he said.

"Too bad," I said. "Go on."

"Okay. Well. We were on the way to the store to buy soda for her birthday party. I thought that would be as good a time as any to give Lisa her present. It was something I'd been practicing all summer in empty parking lots. There's not a lot to do for fun in a small town in Vermont if you don't drink or do drugs. I couldn't play the piano all day, although now I wish I had learned that ridiculous Vangelis piece she was crazy about for her birthday instead."

"What ridiculous Vangelis piece?" I asked. "Who's Vangelis?"

"I forget how young you are sometimes," he said. "You probably weren't born yet. You couldn't get away from that song that summer. The one from *Chariots of Fire*."

Oh. The piece he'd been trying to get under his belt since forever. "Forget Vangelis," I said. "I want to know what happened to Lisa."

"I showed her how to send a car into a three-hundred-sixty-degree skid is what happened. Lisa and I were big fans of trashy action movies with insane car chases. She loved that spin just as much as I thought she would right up to the point where I lost control of the car and it slammed into a tree."

Xander's parents never forgave him. The State of Vermont did, after eighteen months of a three-year sentence for criminally negligent homicide. So did Sara, after she was grown. She'd even demonstrated his absolution in her eyes by naming her son Alexander, after him. "But Sara was just a kid when it happened," he said. "I think she forgave me because she thought I was all the family she'd have left someday. Now that she has a family of her own, I'm sure there are days she wishes I'd never been born. I know her husband feels that way. So I try never to stick around long enough to let her down."

He'll only disappoint you.

"If you think you'll always let people down, that's all you'll ever do," I said.

"You sound like my mother," he said.

"You're old enough to be my dad."

There are worse places for a relationship to die, I guess, than on the front stoop of a glass mansion with a view of the ocean at sunset above its stucco wall. As these things go, it wasn't even all that painful. Xander and I sat there together for a while, watching the sky go pink. "We used to eat our lunches here," he said at last. "This was the only place you could still see the water after the wall went up out front."

"We?"

"The crew who built that wall. Also, Mimi couldn't watch us here."

" 'Mimi couldn't watch us.' What's that supposed to mean?"

"When we worked around the back she used to stand at the glass and stare at us. I guess she thought we couldn't see her. The other guys thought she was weird, but she just seemed lonely to me. So I decided somebody ought to talk to her. Her mind must have been a million miles away the day I did because she didn't seem to notice me until I rapped on the glass. She almost jumped out of her skin. It was like she'd seen a ghost or something. I guess she decided I was harmless though because she came out every day from then on to chat with me. As it turned out, we had things in common. We talked about missing the seasons. The East Coast. New York. I helped her pick out the piano. She asked me to fix things. The rest you know."

Xander left without coming inside. He said his sister was expecting him.

"What about Frank?" I asked. "He's expecting you, too."

"I need to sleep," he said. "Tell him I'll be back first thing tomorrow to patch things up with him."

"Tell him yourself."

"No thanks. There's too much going on in there. I'll be here half the night if I come in. I need to sleep. Frank will understand."

"Go," I said. Frank was right. This was the disappointing part. Frank might understand why Xander didn't show up as promised—or he might not. Then who would have to pick up the pieces? Not Xander. But in the end it wasn't up to me to talk him into staying. No point in trying to explain to Xander that nobody likes being let down, particularly not kids. With children in the house, you're on call around the clock whether you like it or not. You don't get the luxury of enough sleep when that was what you needed most to keep yourself from going over the edge. You'd think somebody Xander's age would've figured that one out already. Maybe if he started sticking around more he'd get it. Alec would teach him. Or Frank, who'd taught me. Frank was the master.

Mr. Vargas was out cold on the white couch, like a man who'd trained himself eons ago to grab shut-eye in whatever foxhole he stumbled into. Frank had changed into his Robin Hood attire. He was standing over Mr. Vargas with a suction cup arrow notched into his bow, carefully fitting it over one of his Good Friend Him's eyelids.

"Frank," I hissed. "Personal space."

Mr. Vargas startled all of us then with a snore so loud and sudden that he woke himself up. Frank and I escorted him to bed, Mr. Vargas insisting that he really wasn't tired.

I made Frank some dinner and let him eat it on the couch in the family room for the first time ever while we watched *Double Indemnity* together. I didn't want to put him to bed until I was sure he was spent. Otherwise I figured he'd sneak in on Mr. Vargas to complete his research on the utility of suction cup arrows for extracting eyeballs. When he finally fell asleep on the couch I picked him up and carried him into his closet. I was pretty impressed with myself for being able to carry him so far without breaking a sweat. I guess I'd gotten a lot stronger than I'd been when I first came to live with them. I guarantee you Frank hadn't gotten any smaller.

After that I went and sat on the piano bench and looked out the windows. Since Mr. Vargas's arrival, we'd taken to leaving the curtains open at night so we could enjoy the twinkling lights outlining the higher hills in the distance. It was the only time you could really imagine what the views from the house must have been like once.

I was about to put myself to bed when I heard the rustling that meant Frank had started to roam. I switched the piano light on. He was drawn to it like Gloria Swanson looking for her close-up.

"What are you doing?" Frank asked. "Why aren't you in bed?"

"I could ask the same of you." I scooted over on the bench. "Sit. Hey, I remember these pajamas."

"Yes. I wore them the day we met."

"Do you remember what we were listening to that day?"

"Of course. *Rhapsody in Blue*. We discussed Gershwin and Charles Foster Kane and Fred Astaire."

"Can you play that song, but quietly so we don't wake up Mr. Vargas? I still don't know how to turn this thing on."

While he was fiddling with the player mechanism, Frank said, "In *Casablanca,* nobody asks Dooley Wilson to play 'As Time Goes By' using the words 'Play it again, Sam.' People always get that wrong. Ingrid Bergman comes the closest. She says, 'Play it, Sam.'"

Once the piano got going he sat down beside me again. "I miss my mother," he said.

"I know you do, Frank."

"It's stressful for me to be without her for so long."

"You're being really brave, Frank."

"She'll be home soon."

"I hope so."

"Oh, I know so," Frank said. "I don't suppose you and I will have much time together after she comes back. I expect you and Mr. Vargas will go back to New York."

I made my hands into such tight fists my nails cut into my palms. "That's the plan." I hesitated, then said, "You know that I love you, Frank. No matter what happens. No matter where I am."

"I love you, too," Frank said. "We'll always have Paris." He pressed his face to my shoulder and we sat there listening for what seemed like a hundred years. "Can I ask you something, Alice?" he said at last.

"Sure thing, Frank."

"My mother hasn't known you long and yet she named the only female character in her book Alice. There are a number of male characters and though she has known me for a decade, not one of them is named Frank. Why?"

26

Frank rolled back the Oriental runner in his closet—
the only nice rug in the whole house really—to
show me the trapdoor underneath. It had hinges sunk
flush with the floorboards and was fitted with a brass
ring in a square brass housing like they use building
yachts and Frank's closet and maybe even the *Titanic*.
Here's where I confess that I never once rolled that rug
back to vacuum underneath it.

"This is my place for special treasures," Frank said.
"I think it was built as a bomb shelter or somewhere to
store sweaters or the family jewels or a place to hide out
from the Nazis." He opened the trapdoor and locked
the hinges so the door wouldn't come crashing down
on our heads.

The cedar-lined cavity had a five-step ladder lead-ing down to it and deep shelves full of boxes and bun-dles and things, all laid out with a curator's zeal. "Can I borrow your flashlight?" I asked. Frank shook his head and flipped a switch under the lip of the space. A system of bright spotlights and footlights came on inside. I recognized it as the beacon from Frank's closet that Mr. Vargas and I saw that night in the yard.

Frank and I peered into the cavity, our craniums almost touching in the middle. There was a low wooden stool at one end with a lidded cardboard manuscript box resting on it. I couldn't quite make out what was scrawled across its top.

"That's her book," Frank said. "There, on the stool I stand on to reach things on the top shelves. Some-times I sit on it, too, while contemplating the relics of my ancestors' pasts and my own."

"I'm not sure I believe it," I said. "How did it end up down there?"

"You may remember that the night of the fire I'd been looking all over for my mother. That's how I hap-pened to find Xander's box."

"Yes."

"Well, before that I tried my mother's office door and it was unlocked. While searching for her I stumbled onto that box. I tucked it under my arm to investigate later and planned to return it the next day, but by the next day there was no desk to return it to. So I put it in here for safekeeping." He hopped down into the space and I climbed down the ladder after him. During our six-step journey from one end of the cavity to the other Frank gestured to its laden shelves. "This is the top-secret repository of my childhood," he explained. "As you are a student of all things Frank Banning, I give you carte blanche to examine whatever interests you." He handed me the box Mimi had labeled *Draft 2/11/10*. "I'm tired. I'm going to bed now."

"Going to bed? Where?" We were, after all, standing shoulder-deep beneath his closet floor, which was serving as Frank's current bedroom while I slept in his bed.

"In your bed. Which is actually my bed. With your permission. Feel free to come to me with any questions."

"I will," I said. "Thanks."

In less than a minute he was asleep and I was on that stool with the box in my lap. I took the lid off and saw the real title of *Draft 2/11/10* typed on its cover sheet. *Alice and Julian.*

I turned the page over and read the paragraph: "My IQ is higher than 99.7% of the American public, but you'd have no way to know that since I fell against the curb. I'm a smart kid made dumb in the classic sense of the word: speechless, not thoughtless. Alice is a lovely person who isn't much to look at, so my accident has made us perfect companions. I never had a friend before Alice."

There I stopped. I took the box to Mr. Vargas.

Mr. Vargas raced through the first few pages on the love seat in his room that used to be my room, then put the manuscript down and went to the bathroom. He came back with his eyebrows dripping.

"Are you okay?" I asked.

"I'm fine. I was splashing water on my face. I needed to know I wasn't dreaming."

I made Mr. Vargas a pot of coffee and went to check on Frank. He was out cold. The cavity was open with the lights still on. I was surprised to see I'd left it open. I guess I wasn't the careful person I'd always imagined myself to be. I was someone who forgot her phone on the kitchen counter on the way to pick up a patient from the psych ward. One who left Roman candles where kids could find them and trapdoors open for anybody to tumble into. Maybe I wasn't the one people should be calling Jeopardy, but I might be imperfect enough for somebody to love me someday.

Somebody aside from Frank, or Mr. Vargas, or my mother, I mean.

Before I shut the hatch I knelt for one last look into the abyss.

Frank did give me carte blanche.

I hopped down into what I'd started to think of as the Dream Bunker. I wandered its miniature aisle, examining the bounty of little hats and shoes that Frank must have outgrown ages ago. The clothes I'd purged from his closet, stuffed under my bed and forgotten, were now folded neatly. The plastic machete was there, Frank's skateboard, the paper bag top hat he had made at the playground. The pink plaid ice pack and the burgundy Hermès scarf that had once belonged to Banning. The three chocolate hearts he'd bought the day his mother disappeared. A beagle pull toy with a big smile and sad eyes and a tail made out of a spring finished with a green bead that looked like it had been made about the time that guy in *The Graduate* put his arm around Dustin Hoffman's shoulder and murmured to him, "Plastics."

The beagle's flat plastic ears were screwed to its head so they could swing when it moved and its plastic wheels were uneven on purpose so the thing would wobble from side to side, swinging those ears as it dogged a toddler's footsteps. I picked it up and turned it over. On its belly someone had written "Mimi" in marker in a girly hand definitely not Mimi's. Banning's maybe? It was hard to imagine Mimi stuffing the beagle into her suitcase along with Julian's typewriter when she ran away to New York and literary fame and misfortune. But here it was.

There were envelopes of drugstore-developed photos spilling over with snapshots and negatives. A frame made of Popsicle sticks with a photo of a much younger Frank inside it, just as dressed up then as now and as unsmiling as a Civil War soldier setting out for the front. The big, heavy photo album Frank had shown me way back when. I sat down on the stool and flipped through its pages again. The photographs looked very different now that I knew more about the cast of players. Especially the ones of Julian. With his long hair cut off in a golden halo I couldn't help noticing that he looked an awful lot like a young Xander, the Mr. Fix-it I hadn't met when I saw those pictures the first time around. No wonder Mimi had stood at the glass staring at the crew building her wall. When Xander rapped on the glass she looked like she'd just seen a ghost because she kind of had.

I put the album back where I'd found it alongside Ziplocs of newspaper articles, big bundles of typing paper tied up with string, bulging manila envelopes and file folders neatly lined up in a rack. I ran a fingertip along Mimi's file-folder labels and froze on one that read DONORS.

As hard as it is to imagine picking a person with whom you'd like to spend an evening based on some stats and personal essays, now I know it has to be lots harder to choose a man to sire the child who will be with you forever.

There were four packets, three with résumés of guys who seemed virtually identical. Those three were over six feet tall and noted in staff interviews to be "devastatingly handsome," "a real James Bond type," and "easygoing, with charm and movie-star good looks." All claimed high IQs and were either college students or graduates or graduate students. Who'd written essays that said things like "I love animals and sports and building cool stuff with my hands." "I would like to travel to some European countries or other foreign places because that is where you can find lots of history and culture and other things like that." "With each new day I derive joy from the knowledge that everything I do makes the world a better place for myself."

Then there was Guy Four. What got to me was his answer to the essay question, "Why do you want to be a sperm donor?"

First, let me say that I don't need the money. I am an aerospace engineer—what wags might call a "rocket scientist—"

My hands started shaking.

—with an exciting career working at a prestigious lab known for sending unmanned probes to Mars and beyond. I work long hours and when I get home I like to sit in my favorite armchair and watch my favorite movies over and over. I don't think of myself as a "loner" because I enjoy the camaraderie of my coworkers at the lunch table and get as much of a kick out of swapping interesting facts I find in the scientific publications we read at our meals as the next guy does. But I confess I'm not a fan of unfamiliar "gourmet" foods and for that matter I don't much like change or needless disruptions in my schedule. Although I had a college girlfriend in college, I don't meet a lot of women in my line of work. I will be forty years old on my next birthday, which I understand to be the cutoff age for sperm donation. Having recently learned that bit of trivia from an acquaintance, I've begun to wonder whether I'll meet a woman I would like to have a family with while my sperm is still at its most viable. Moreover, a single mother raised me so I grew up without a male—

At this point he'd turned the paper over and finished his answer on the back.

—role model and while I think that worked out fine for me, I am not convinced I would be an exemplary father in all the ways a father should be. I am hopeless at sports and other "manly pursuits." I can be impatient and short-tempered. *Living with a child would invite chaos into my life at a time when I'm not sure I'm equipped to deal with chaos. But my mother always wanted grandchildren and I like the idea of creating a child for her sake, even if I never get to see that child, ever. My mother isn't alive anymore, so she would never get to see a child of mine ever, either. But to put a child or children out there, for my mother— that would be wonderful. She was the best. I miss her every single day.*

Somebody—probably Mimi—had drawn a red arrow to that first line on the flip side. Clipped to a new sheet with CHILDHOOD PHOTOGRAPHS typed across the top—a page not included in the other packets— was a photograph of a little boy with smooth red hair and huge brown eyes magnified to lemur size by Buddy Holly glasses. He wore a round-necked striped T-shirt and shorts and sat on a lawn chair holding a birthday cake on his knees that was decorated with five candles and a rocket ship. "May ★ 1965" appeared in tiny type along one fluted white edge of the photograph.

I read his form again from the top. He was five foot eight, nearsighted in one eye and farsighted in the other, allergic to shellfish and cats. The other donors had their own issues: one was colorblind, the second a smoker and prone to keloids, and bachelor number three had some moderate acne scarring and had once struggled with alcohol addiction. There were hypertensive grandparents, a father dead at forty in a car accident, a mother with early-onset diabetes, an aunt who committed suicide, siblings with scoliosis or arrhythmias or hearing impairments. At the end of the stats section I found a line that read, "Donors who provide consent will be open to having their contact information released to any resulting progeny when a child or children reach the age of eighteen. Donors who do not agree to release that information prefer to remain anonymous."

That line of type was followed by two boxes. The first three donors had checked "Consent to Contact." The rocket scientist had checked the second one, the one that said "Anonymous Donor." Alongside that, in Mimi's handwriting, one word. *Him.*

I looked at that snapshot of the little boy with the rocket cake for a long time before I put it away.

Frank's sleeping bag was on a shelf nearby, and I rolled it out on the bunker floor, turned off the lights, and crawled in. At that moment the skylight perfectly framed the moon on its voyage across the night sky. When it traveled out of sight over some European countries or other foreign places with lots of history and culture and other things like that, it was way darker in the bunker than I had thought it would be. I got worried the hinges of the bunker's hatch would fatigue and allow the trapdoor to do its worst. I would die an awful, solitary death down there and it would only occur to somebody to check the Dream Bunker for all that was left of Alice after they smelled a horrible odor coming from under the floorboards in Frank's closet.

So I crawled out of the sleeping bag and wedged a couple of Frank's outgrown wool trousers in where the hinge hinged so the hatch couldn't close all the way no matter what. While I was looking for something that would survive the wedgie undamaged I found a couple of nice little cashmere argyle sweaters and took those back to the floor with me to use as a pillow.

27

The next morning Frank wanted to give his new best friend a tour of the Dream Bunker. Even though Mr. Vargas was also my favorite person in the world, the two of them were so tight already that I'll admit I was a little jealous.

"I'll be eager to discuss what you find in there when I get back," I said to Mr. Vargas. I'd volunteered to drive the manuscript to a copy shop to have it scanned and sent to New York before it could disappear on us again. I could see Frank ricocheting down the hall toward us, so I left it at that. "Don't have any fun without me," I said to Mr. Vargas as he handed over the keys to his rental car

It was pretty clear my boys had been having at least a little fun when I came home because I found the two of them wearing tweedy jackets with bow ties and pocket squares, watching Frank Sinatra, Gene Kelly, and that other guy whose name nobody ever remembers trying to see all of New York in a day in *On the Town*.

"So, in New York City you just raise your hand and a cab appears?" Frank asked Mr. Vargas as I walked in.

"That's right."

"New York sounds like a magical place."

"It can be sometimes," Mr. Vargas said.

"I miss it," I said. "Is that a new jacket, Frank?"

"Oh, this? I'd forgotten about this old thing until I saw what he was wearing." Frank elbowed Mr. Vargas, making me suspect I should re-Sharpie his new best friend's name on Frank's hand. "Then I remembered my mother bought a similar one for me long ago. It was such a delicious shade of loden that we couldn't pass it up. It was always too big for me before now."

It hit me then that all the outfits I'd come to love would end up folded on shelves in the repository of his childhood before very long. Frank would outgrow them, and then what? Would he continue on in his natty path or take to baseball jerseys and tennis shoes like a regular teenager? Assume a uniform of T-shirts and jeans worn into butter-soft tatters, like Xander? His life might be easier for it, but Frank would be so much less Frank then. It broke my heart to think of it.

I handed Mr. Vargas his car keys and said to Frank, "Scoot over." Frank moved himself and the three bundles of yellowing typing paper tied up with string he'd been using as a footstool over, and plastered himself against Mr. Vargas the way the kid used to cuddle up to me. I dropped onto the couch beside him and touched the bundles with my toe. "What have we here?" I asked.

Mr. Vargas used the remote to snap off the movie and blinked at me a couple of times. "Aren't these the things you wanted to discuss with me?"

"No," I said. "What are they?"

"These," he said, "are other manuscripts Mimi wrote over the years and then decided to throw away."

"What?" I asked. And here I thought I'd found the biggest bombshell in that bunker.

"In my role as family archivist, I fished those out of the trash," Frank said. "My mother had spent so much time with them that I knew they had to be worth something. There may have been other manuscripts before I was tall enough to see into her office wastebasket. We won't know the answer to that question until I crack the code of time travel. It never ceases to amaze me what treasures Mama throws away. My gravel collection, for example. I still miss it."

A trove of unpublished manuscripts. So there was one, after all, though Mimi hadn't exactly tucked them away for publication after her death. Xander had said he'd heard her typing ever since he'd known her, and here was the proof. "Have you looked through them, Mr. Vargas?" I asked.

"That would be an invasion of her privacy," he said. "Mimi may not have intended for anyone to read these, ever. We'll have to ask her permission first. The one you sent today she'd written under contract, though, so that's a different matter."

"I can't believe it."

"You know what I can't believe?" Frank asked. "How much time my mother has left in her hiatus. I really want to talk to her right now. I'm sick of being brave about not seeing her. And there are questions I really need to ask her. Questions that have been keeping me up at night."

"Nothing would make me happier than talking to Mimi, but I don't know how to reach her," Mr. Vargas said. "I'm worried she's holed up somewhere trying to write the book she promised me all over again."

"Is that what she's doing?" Frank asked. "When she said she needed a month of alone time, I assumed she needed to finish catching up on her sleep. The three days of rest the hospital prescribed for her weren't nearly enough to make up for all the years I've kept her up past her bedtime."

"Frank," I said. "Have you been talking to your mother?"

"Outside of my head? No."

"So how did she tell you she needed a month of alone time?"

"It was in her note."

I swung my knees around so I was facing him, my nose within an inch of his. "What note?"

"The note I knew she must have left when she couldn't stick around long enough to see me before she went on hiatus. It was in the back of *Le Petit Prince*. Which was a much better place to hide it in than inside my birthday cake or one of her shoes, though it took me longer to find it there than it should have. I must be getting old."

"Frank," I said. "We need to see that note."

"Why? Didn't she leave a note for you?"

I considered several possible responses and settled on, "I guess she was in a hurry." I tried to keep my voice even. "She must have assumed you'd fill me in."

The note said, *I need a month of alone time, Monkey. Can you be brave for me just that much longer? If there's an emergency, Isaac will know where to find me.*

"Is Dr. Einstein Isaac?" Frank asked.

"I'm Isaac, yes," Mr. Vargas said.

"I thought so," Frank said. "But Alice insists on calling you Mr. Vargas. I was confused."

"Isaac Vargas, Frank," I said. "His name is Isaac Vargas."

"So Isaac Vargas," Frank said. "Tell us. Where is my mother?"

28

As it turned out, Mr. Vargas did know where to find Mimi. He just didn't know he knew it.

"Well," Mr. Vargas said, after Frank had turned the note over for us several times and held it up to the light to prove there was nothing else written on it, not even with invisible ink. "There was a place we met the last time I came out here. I thought that if I saw her in person I could talk her out of marrying that preening nitwit and into coming back with me to New York."

"What kind of place?" I asked. "A restaurant?"

"Not a restaurant."

"Was it a museum?" Frank asked.

"No. Not a museum."

All Mr. Vargas could remember was that it was in the Valley somewhere, close to the studio where Hanes

Fuller was shooting interiors for the ill-starred art-house western that would put a bullet in his career. The place Mimi suggested they meet was a bungalow motel, a series of small blue stucco casitas grouped in a crescent around a gravel courtyard. Each had its own little door-less garage attached, he said, so people could drive in and enter their rooms without being seen from the street. The neon sign over the parking lot had a palm tree on it, he knew that. He just couldn't come up with its name.

Frank was so hot to find his mother that he didn't bother changing his wardrobe before we left. He clamped his deerstalker hat on his head, grabbed his bubble pipe, and lit out for the rental car. "*Allons-y!*" he shouted over his shoulder. He dropped the bubble pipe then, skidded to a stop, and picked it up. He took that opportunity to explain to us, "*Allons-y* is what the French Foreign Legion say when what they really mean is 'Let's blow this Popsicle stand, my friends!'" He whooped and took off again.

Mr. Vargas grinned at me. "I love that kid," he said.

"Get in line," I said.

The three of us headed east on Sunset Boulevard and then swung left up Laurel Canyon Boulevard, while tour-guide Frank explained to Mr. Vargas that

Schwab's Drugstore had once stood on the corner to our right before it was bulldozed to make way for the minimall there now. You know, *Schwab's*, where a sultry young Lana Turner may or may not have been "discovered"—in the rearview mirror I saw Frank making finger quotes—at the soda fountain. Where, in *Sunset Boulevard* the movie, Joe Gillis hangs out with his cronies, though director Billy Wilder had a replica of Schwab's built at the Paramount Studios lot so the movie hadn't actually been shot where the minimall stood now. Did Mr. Vargas also happen to know that Sunset Boulevard, the boulevard we'd just left behind, not the movie, originated as an eighteenth-century cattle path that followed the rim of the Los Angeles Basin and ran from the original Spanish settlement in downtown Los Angeles all the way to the ocean?

"I didn't know that, Frank," Mr. Vargas said. "Thanks for telling me."

"Here's something else you may not know," Frank said. I tuned out his monologue as we left the Los Angeles Basin and drove up Lookout Mountain. I needed to focus on the job at hand. Laurel Canyon Boulevard is another of those impossibly narrow, precipitously curvy and overly trafficked two-laners cut through the Santa Monica Mountains. The things you have to go through, driving in Los Angeles. Mountains. Traffic.

Flash floods. Mudslides. Wildfires. Coyotes. I'd miss the kid for sure and probably the weather come next February, but I wouldn't miss the driving. No wonder Mimi didn't do it anymore.

We made it to Mulholland Drive without plunging over the edge and coasted down the other side into the San Fernando Valley. Frank directed us to the studio in question, which, he informed us, was once home turf for slapstick silent movie king Mack Sennett before his business went belly-up in 1928 and he sold out. Using the studio as our pivot point, we worked our way through the neighborhood in ever-expanding circles. I'll say this for the Valley. Proprietors of charming and expensive-looking restaurants close to the studios don't seem to care if there's a muffler repair shop next door on one side, a head shop on the other, and an end-of-days-looking convalescent home across the street with ambulances hogging all the good spots out front. I guess they figure the parking valets will keep all the grim reality of drugs and engine failure and eminent death from bursting everybody's expense-account bubble.

Frank saw it first, of course. "Neon palm tree! There! Over there!" he shouted, pointing urgently with his elbow. I pulled over in front of a pink motel named "The Sunset." Other than its color, it fit Mr. Vargas's description exactly.

We all got out of the car and stood on the sidewalk, looking. "I don't remember it being called 'The Sunset,'" Mr. Vargas said. "I think it used to be called 'The Blue Hawaiian,' come to think of it. Mimi's reason for picking this place had something to do with Elvis, though as I remember Elvis was dead by then already." He leaned through the arch over the driveway entrance and looked around. "Put some money in the parking meter. I think this may be it."

While Frank took care of the meter, I put my cell on speakerphone, called the front desk, and asked for Mimi Banning. The desk clerk said there wasn't anybody registered there under that name. "How about Mimi Gillespie?" I asked. Nada. "M. M. Banning?" I tried after that.

"We have no one registered here under that name, either," the clerk said. She sounded young, maybe too young to have heard of M. M. Banning. Don't the kids read *The Pitcher* in junior high school anymore?

"Do you have a very small woman who's been staying with you about a week? Middle-aged, pixie haircut, wears cardigan sweaters?" I asked.

The desk clerk wasn't too young to think something fishy might be going on when somebody calls and offers up as many aliases as I had. "I'm afraid I can't share any information about our guests with you," she said. Then she hung up.

I said, "I think Mimi's in there."

"Why?" Frank asked. "That woman just said she wasn't."

"That's just it," I said. "She didn't say she wasn't there. What she said was that she couldn't share information about their guests."

"The unsaid said!" Frank shouted. "Now I get what Dr. Abrams means when she's trying to explain 'subtext.' What would I do without you, Alice? You're the best Dr. Watson I will ever have."

We huddled in the shadows just outside the arch, trying to be inconspicuous while we worked out our next move.

"We can't knock on every door. The desk clerk will notice us," I said. "We need to narrow the possibilities a little."

"My mother didn't come in a car, so don't try a room with one in the garage," Frank said.

"Smart," I said.

"I know," Frank said. "My IQ is higher than 99.7 percent of the American public's."

About half of the carports were empty. "Would it be better to wait until after dinner, when all the guests are parked for the night?" I asked.

"My mother would never open her door for an un-expected guest after dark," Frank said.

Mimi wouldn't open the door for an unexpected guest, ever. "Good point," I said. "So let's do it now. Where should we start?"

"Room Twelve," Mr. Vargas said. "I can still see those numbers on the door. When I knocked, I knocked once, then twice. One, two. Twelve. For luck. Fat lot of good that did me."

Frank took off across the parking lot. I started to go after him, but Mr. Vargas grabbed my arm. "She's his mother. Let him find her, if she's in there. If she's not, well, we're close enough to rescue him if he needs it."

We watched the kid knock on the door, once then twice like Mr. Vargas had. When it didn't open he stepped into the scruffy plantings under the window and bobbed up and down, trying to see in through the shutters. Then he went back to the door and took out his wallet.

"He must be looking for something to write on so he can slip a note under the door," I said. "I wonder if he has a pen? I may have one." I scrabbled through my Mary Poppins satchel, looking.

Mr. Vargas started patting down his pockets but didn't find one either. "Uh-oh," he said. "What's he up to now?"

I looked up from my purse and saw Frank had his orange bus pass in one hand and the handle to Room Twelve in the other. He slid the card into the crack between the door and the jamb and popped it open. For someone who claimed to know it was wrong to indulge in criminal activities, Frank sure seemed to have a knack for it.

When we nabbed him at the scene of the crime, Frank was spinning with joy. "She's here!" he said. "But she isn't here. I've already looked under all the furniture."

It was obvious Mimi had taken up residence in Room Twelve. There was an open box of her favorite pencils on the desk alongside two stacks of yellow legal pads, one tall and pristine, one shorter and rumpled. We could see that the top page of the short stack was covered with her handwriting. A cardigan hung from the back of the chair at the desk, and the watercolor of Frank I'd painted her for Christmas was stuck in the mirror frame over the dresser.

"I have a great idea," Frank said. "We'll all hide in the closet, and when she comes back in we'll jump out and yell, 'Surprise!'"

"That's a horrible idea, Frank. She'll have a heart attack," I said.

Honestly, Mr. Vargas looked like he was the one having a heart attack. He stood behind the desk chair.

"This sweater," he said, touching the cardigan. "This was mine." He sat heavily on the bed.

"Where's my mother?" Frank asked. "I'm going out to look for her." Before I could stop him, he had flung himself out the door. So I flung myself out after him.

I didn't notice one of my sneakers had come untied until I tripped over its lace and tumbled down the two concrete steps outside the door. It was a real Mack Sennett pratfall that I'm sorry Frank missed, since it would have made him laugh the way I'd always dreamed of making him laugh. When I stood up again I saw Mimi halfway across the courtyard. I didn't recognize her at first. She was wearing a baseball hat she couldn't possibly have stolen from Frank because he wouldn't be caught dead in one. What I guessed were Julian's embroidered jeans because they were way too big for her. A white T-shirt, no cardigan, since it's always so hot in the Valley. It was absolutely Mimi though because she had dropped the plastic laundry basket and gathered Frank up in her arms.

"Oh, Frank," Mimi said. "I love you, Monkey. I've missed you so much. What are you doing here? Is everything all right?"

"Everything is all right now, Mama," Frank said. "You're here, and so am I. Guess who else is? You'll never guess so I'll show you. But first, let's talk about that hat. Did it belong to Uncle Julian?"

"No," Mimi said. "I bought it in a drugstore across the street."

"Good," Frank said. "That means I don't have to feel bad about demanding you remove it before I surprise you with who's here."

"Is it Alice?" Mimi asked when she pried her eyes off Frank's face and spotted me.

Frank took the hat off her head and threw it in her laundry basket. "Of course it isn't Alice," he said. "I said you'd never guess."

"Alice, your knees are bleeding," Mimi said. She noticed that before I did. For a second there I thought she might hug me.

"My knees will be fine," I said.

But Mimi had forgotten me. She was staring at Mr. Vargas standing in the doorway of Room Twelve. "Isaac," Mimi said. "It's you. Oh, Isaac, I'm sorry. There's no book. I've disappointed you. Again."

"You don't have to worry about that," Mr. Vargas said. "Your manuscript didn't burn in the fire. Frank had it all along. He saved it for you. You're going to love this story, Mimi. Why don't you tell her, Frank?"

"Because I'm very busy now," Frank said. "You tell her." It was his big moment of victory, but Frank didn't seem to care. He'd let go of his mother, pulled out his pocket square, and had come to doctor my injuries. Like grandfather, like grandson. "Ooh, there's a piece of gravel with a sparkly vein of quartz stuck in your knee," he said. "Where are my doctor's bag and forceps when I really need them?"

"Frank," I said. "Let's go inside and wash my knees out in the tub."

I pulled the kid inside with me so Mr. Vargas and Mimi could talk in private. The funny thing was, they weren't saying anything yet. The two of them were just standing there, staring at each other. Just as I turned to sneak a look, Mr. Vargas said, "You could never disappoint me, Mimi. Look at you. You're just the same as ever. Except for this." He touched her one white eyebrow with a fingertip. Instead of answering, she reached up, closed her hand over his, and held it against her cheek. I shoved the kid in the room and closed the door behind us.

"I'll get the Band-Aids from your purse," Frank said. By then the kid was as familiar with the contents of it as I was. Then he instructed me to sit on the toilet while he took off my shoes and socks. He held my hand while I stepped into the tub and sat down on its edge. "For once, it's a good thing you were wearing shorts, Alice," he said. "Because if you'd had on long pants, they'd be torn all to pieces. That would have been bad. Pants don't heal the way skin does."

When Frank, my bandaged knees, and I emerged from the bathroom, Mr. Vargas and Mimi were gathering up her things. All business. I took Frank with me and went out to recover Mimi's forgotten laundry basket. It had been upended in all the excitement, so I had to shake things out and refold them before I handed them to Frank to put in the basket again.

While we were busy with that, Mimi came out with her suitcase, which Mr. Vargas was trying to wrestle from her. "Let me," he said. "You go check out."

"I wish I'd known you were coming," she said. "They made me pay for my room a week in advance."

Well, I thought. Whose fault is that? Take your cell phone with you next time. Don't make tracking you down into a scavenger hunt.

Frank carried the laundry to his mother. "Look what a nice job I did putting these back in the basket," he said. "You know what else I did? I rescued your novel. I saved the old ones, too. Did our good friend Mr. Vargas tell you that?" I guess I wouldn't need to write that name on Frank's hand in Sharpie anymore.

Mimi let go of her suitcase and hugged him. "What would I do without you, Frank?" she said.

"I ask myself that all the time," Frank said.

I hung back, watching. Now that I knew him, it really was amazing how much that kid could convey while hardly moving his face. Too bad he and Buster Keaton had never met. They had so much in common. I bet they would have been friends, even if the guy were as old or older than Frank's dead grandfather, Dr. Frank.

Mimi shook me out of my reverie, snapping, "Why are you just standing there, Alice?" She added, "Make yourself useful. Come look under the beds and make sure we're not leaving anything behind."

Frank sat up front with me on the trip home. "Xander says I'm a man now, remember? So I get to sit up front."

I was too frazzled to argue. Mimi and Mr. Vargas had to tough it out in the backseat. I suspected that was fine by them.

We were climbing out of Studio City through Laurel Canyon when Frank said to Mimi, "There's something I need to ask you, Mommie. Something that has been bothering me ever since I read your book. Why is Alice half the title and Alice, Alice, Alice all the way through it when Frank's not in it anywhere? You've known me ten times as long as you've known her."

"You read my book, Frank?" she asked.

"Of course I read it." Frank unbuckled his seat belt and turned around on his knees to get a better look at Mimi. "I missed you, Mama. I wanted to hear your voice."

I checked Mimi in the rearview mirror to see if she was going to bust the kid for being a dangerous passenger, but she was staring out the window. We were almost all the way up the long hill, close to the red light where Laurel Canyon crosses over Mulholland Drive.

"Frank," I said when it was clear Mimi wasn't going to reprimand him. "Sit facing forward. Put your seat belt back on. Right now."

He sat down and rebuckled. "Mother," he persisted. "I'd like that explanation now please."

Mimi sighed. "Well, Frank," she said, "when I said I'd finished my book, that didn't mean I was a hundred percent done. I wasn't ready for anybody else to read it. When I was trying to get started I got so caught up in inventing names for my characters that I wasn't writing a word. So one day I decided I'd use the first names that popped into my head. That was the day you and Alice drove to the beach. Do you remember that?"

"I remember that," I said.

"I wasn't talking to you," Mimi said. "Anyway, Frank, I always intended to change the names. You know, before anybody else saw what names I was using."

Mr. Vargas and I exchanged looks in the rearview mirror. I could see he was thinking the same thing I was. That maybe Mimi hadn't been so much crazy as embarrassed when she refused to hand over her pages. Embarrassed, and a little crazy to let something so ridiculous get in the way of her progress. Particularly when changing that name she'd chosen so impulsively was something you could fix throughout a manuscript with just a couple of keystrokes on a computer. Oh, but wait. Mimi didn't work on computers. I did. Alice. A name I'd crowbarred into her manuscript by saying "Alice" every time she called me "Penny." To Mimi, everything that had gone wrong since I'd arrived must have seemed like all my fault. Me and my stupid name.

That, or Mimi never really liked me. That was also possible.

"I would think my name would pop into your head before anybody else's," Frank said.

"How could your name pop into my head when it's always in there already?" Mimi asked. "I never stop thinking about you, Frank. Not even when I'm sleeping."

"That makes perfect sense, now that you've explained it. I have one more question. What happens to the little boy in your book after the story is over? What happens to him in the end?"

We'd made it through the light at last and left the Valley for the downhill slope of the Schwab's side of Lookout Mountain. Mimi watched Los Angeles rushing up to meet us for about a mile before she said to Frank, "I wish I knew."

29

I'd promised i would leave as soon as Mimi's book was done, so I booked a seat on a 6:00 A.M. flight out of Los Angeles and packed my bags as soon as we got back to the glass house. Mr. Vargas would follow in a couple of days. At least that's what he told me.

I said good-bye and good night early and hustled off to bed. For probably the first time in my life I was glad to set my alarm for 3:30 A.M. A predawn departure, I decided, would cut down on the chances of a tearful farewell. As if either Frank or Mimi were ones for that. There's something to be said for being an emotional flatliner. I can appreciate that now.

I woke up before my alarm went off, but only because Half-Pint E. F. Hutton had put a hand on my shoulder and said, "Alice, wake up."

I bolted upright and switched on the light. "What's wrong, Frank?"

"I just performed an inventory of your suitcases."

"Of course you did." I'd left them packed and ready by the front door. I might as well have attached a note to them that read, "Search me."

Search you? Why? Do you have the answer on a piece of paper tucked in your pocket? Is that the sort of thing you're writing when you're scribbling in that notebook?

Oh, Frank. I cleared my throat. "Did I forget anything?"

"Just this." Frank plunked a leather bag I'd never seen before on my lap. It looked about a hundred years old, like something a doctor might have carried on his horse-drawn buggy to make house calls.

"Did that bag belong to your grandfather, Frank?" I asked.

"This bag? Yes. Don't tell my mother. She doesn't know I know where she keeps it." He opened and extracted the chocolate heart he'd bought me on our way to pick Mimi up at the psych ward. That seemed a lifetime ago but it hadn't even been a week.

"Okay," I managed to choke out.

"This heart was on the shelf in the repository of my childhood, so it's not surprising you overlooked it. The bad news is I'm not sure it will fit inside either of your bags. Trust me, I tried."

I closed my eyes and took a steadying breath or two. "Alice," Frank said. "Are you asleep again?"

I opened my eyes again and checked my watch. The alarm wouldn't go off for forty-five minutes yet. "Nope," I said. "Get your flashlight and meet me in the kitchen."

After we gathered up our tools, we eased out into the yard. The moon was still up and close to full, so we didn't need the flashlight. I'd changed out of my pajamas and into the clothes I'd laid out to wear on the plane, so Frank did the digging for us. He used a big silver serving spoon from the kitchen to shovel a grave for my chocolate heart, under what was left of the tree outside Mimi's office.

"I may not have stayed here as long as Dr. Livingstone lived in Africa," I said to Frank as he pushed the dirt back in the hole with a triangular pie server and used that to pat it smooth, "but this heart of mine still belongs here with you. Since, you know, I'm still using the real one."

Frank sat back on his heels and stared at the ground so long that I worried he was tuning up to cry. Until he said, "We need to put something heavy over this so the raccoons don't dig that heart up."

He could have used my real heart to cover the hole, since it weighed about a ton after he said that. While I was wallowing in how much I'd miss him, Frank was thinking about raccoons. Of course.

We ended up manhandling the blue slate paver from under the closest downspout, where it had been placed to keep the cataracts of guttered rain from washing away the hillside. "You have to put this stone back before it rains again, Frank," I said once we flopped the thing in place. "Tell Xander the next time you see him. He'll help you do it."

"I'll help Frank do what?" Xander asked. Forget raising your hand to make a taxi appear. The way the guy showed up at exactly the right time was pretty close to magic.

"What are you doing here?" I asked.

"Frank told me you were clearing out at four A.M. You didn't think I'd let you get away without saying good-bye, did you?" He reached for my cheek but I leaned away. I didn't want Frank to see. Not that he was looking at us. He'd remembered his flashlight and was using it to signal his close personal friends in outer space.

"Frank told you?" I asked. "How?"

Xander looked puzzled. "How? He called me on the telephone."

"But Frank's terrible at memorizing phone numbers. He told me so himself."

"Who said anything about Frank knowing my number? When he needs to talk to me he hijacks Mimi's cell and calls me. When he calls, I come running. If I can."

Frank was going to be okay.

Or not.

I sighed and told myself to let it go. Energy spent on worrying about a future you can't control is energy wasted. It doesn't do anybody one bit of good.

I knew then I'd lived in California too long. I'd gone native.

"Of course," I said to Xander. "Mimi has you in her cell phone. I hadn't thought of that."

As for Xander's number, of course by then I sort of had it, too. I knew that you could count on him sometimes, just not always. He would never pick up the check because he couldn't cover it. Xander wouldn't fail spectacularly at anything because he didn't have it in him anymore to try hard enough for that to happen. But we all have our strengths and weaknesses. Xander had a good heart and a knack for being happy. He assumed everybody he met would like him because everybody usually did. At first, anyway, before he decided he'd only be a disappointment if he stuck around.

Xander, to his credit, had found his people, ones who understood and loved him the only way he could be understood and loved. Mimi and Frank gave him broken things to fix so he could feel like he was taking care of them. He had them to circle back to when his life felt like it didn't add up to all that much. Mimi and Frank would keep Xander from disappearing, and he'd do the same for them.

The alarm on my watch sounded. "I have to get myself together," I said. "I don't want to miss my plane."

"We'll take you to the airport," Xander said.

"You will, huh? Who's driving? You or Frank?"

"What I meant was we could go with you in the cab."

"What about Mimi?" I asked.

"I don't need my mother with me anymore to take a cab," Frank said. "As long as Xander's around."

"I'll always be here, pal," Xander said. "Sooner or later."

"Well, I can take a cab all by myself, so that's what I'm going to do. And you, Frank, have to put your grandfather's doctor bag away before your mother realizes it's missing."

Frank ran for the house as if coyotes were at his heels. By the time Xander and I got back inside, the bag had been dealt with and Frank had called a cab for me.

"You called a cab for me already?" I asked. "Gee, Frank, thanks. Is that your way of saying, 'Don't let the screen door hit you on the way out'?"

"What screen door?"

"Knock knock," I said.

I let each of the boys carry one of my bags out the gate for me.

"We'll wait with you until the cab comes," Xander said.

"No," I said. I'd had enough of a struggle already, getting myself together. "Absolutely not. It's cold out here. Go back inside. This is not a negotiation."

"You're starting to sound like Mimi," Xander said. "I guess it really is time for you to go."

That made me laugh. Which was good, since it could have gone either way for me about then.

"Here," Frank said then, and handed me his pocket square. "It looks like you may need this soon."

"You noticed, Frank," I said. "Thank you. I'm so proud of you. You know that, right?"

"I know," he said. "You should be."

Acknowledgments

I want to thank my friend Sara Kenney, who read every single chapter as soon as I wrote it, even the ones that should never see the light of day. Thanks to her intervention, they never will. I'm grateful to my favorite teacher in the world, Leslie Epstein, who took me under his wing when I wasn't old enough to know better, and always believed I had a novel in me even if it did take a few decades to work its way out. Somehow my agent Lisa Bankoff saw in my first draft what this book could be someday and nudged me in the right direction. Charlotte Simms stumbled onto the scene just when I needed somebody to laugh at all my jokes. My genius editor Kate Nintzel thought the same things were hilarious and heartbreaking that I did, and made everything she touched so much better that I count myself insanely lucky to have landed with her. Most of all I'm thankful for my mother and my children, who taught me how very little I knew about raising children right, but loved and indulged me anyway and gave me extra credit for trying hard. Also my husband, the funniest man alive, who's patient and handsome and smarter than anybody I've ever met. He also has just one dimple, which is absolutely killer.

About the Author

Julia Claiborne Johnson worked at *Mademoiselle* and *Glamour* magazines before marrying and moving to Los Angeles, where she lives with her comedy-writer husband and their two children.